"He said, 'Tell John Hamilton to let Alex's girl know. The ones that killed him are loose up here.'"

"My God, John!" Jessie stared at Hamilton and took a deep breath. "Are you *sure* that's what Jeb said? Jebediah knew about the cartel, then," Jessie said thoughtfully. "My father must have told him long ago. Jeb knew enough about the Prussians to know they were responsible for his death—the message is clear about that. But how would he know they were up to something in Montana Territory?"

Hamilton shook his head. "I can't answer that. Doubt if anyone can now. Mountain men see a lot of things other folks don't..."

WESLEY ELLIS

LONE STAR

AND THE
MOUNTAIN MAN

A JOVE BOOK

LONE STAR AND THE MOUNTAIN MAN

A Jove Book/published by arrangement with
the author

PRINTING HISTORY
Jove edition/September 1984

ISBN: 0-515-07880-8

Jove books are published by The Berkley Publishing Group,
200 Madison Avenue, New York, N.Y. 10016.
The words "A JOVE BOOK" and the "J" with sunburst
are trademarks belonging to Jove Publications, Inc.

Chapter 1

Jessica Starbuck thrust her hands deeper into the pockets of her sheepskin jacket and blew a puff of frosty air. It was still early fall, but the season already showed signs of a hard winter.

"Montana Territory sure isn't Texas," she sighed. "I'll bet it's ninety-somethin' in the shade in San Antone."

"Unless it's a hundred and four," Ki said soberly.

She shot him an easy grin, thinking about the long, lazy Texas summers that often trailed into November and beyond. There was no mistaking the seasons up here. When autumn hit the far Northwest, folks knew for sure it wasn't August.

She had always had a fondness for this far-off corner of the country. It was big, sprawling, and wide open, a magnificent sight to behold. Looking west of the railhead's collection of tents and shacks, she saw the land rise up to the Beaverhead Range. Past that was the Continental Divide, and the peaks of the Bitterroot Mountains. Northwest was Virginia City, and due north the dark and ugly mining town of Butte. There, men had opened raw and terrible wounds in the blood-red earth.

Jessie frowned and turned away from the mountains. A sudden chill touched her flesh, a cold that had nothing to do with the morning. She was remembering why she was here. Somewhere past the Big Hole Basin was the town of Mule, where they'd taken Jebediah Baker out and hanged him . . .

Jeb was past sixty when he'd come to the Starbuck ranch in Sarah, Texas. Jessie had been barely ten, and she'd never seen anything like Jebediah. He was a big bear of a man, covered from head to foot in buckskin leather faded and worn to greasy black. His beard was bushy white, and a mane of silver hair hung to his shoulders. He'd bellowed out a greeting, hugged Jessie's father, and pounded him on the back. Then, carefully setting his Hawken rifle aside, he'd picked up Jessie and swept her off the ground. Smells she'd never imagined assailed her senses—bear fat, the tangy scent of pine, and the smoke of a thousand fires.

Jessie had shrieked in fear, but somehow the fright had turned quickly to open laughter. To her own great surprise, she wasn't afraid of this giant with weathered skin and eyes the color of winter skies. Instead, she fell madly in love with the man. Jebediah read the affection in her eyes and grinned his approval.

"Yer got yourself a beauty there, Alex," he said softly. "Goin' to break some ol' boy's heart, and that's a fact."

"I reckon she will at that," Jessie's father agreed.

Later, Jessie finally understood who Jebediah was—that his name was spoken with those of others of his kind—men like Joseph Walker and Jim Bridger and Edward Rose. When Jessie asked her father what he'd done, he simply told her, "He's a mountain man, child . . ."

She knew her father well, and the way he'd said the words told her a lot. Alex Starbuck didn't pass out respect to other men lightly.

He can't be gone, she thought to herself, *not Jeb. Ordinary men couldn't bring down Jebediah Baker . . .*

"Jessie, are you all right?"

"I—yes, Ki, I'm just fine." She shook her head and sighed. "Mind just wandering some. Oh, look—there's Hamilton. Right up there."

She stopped and peered past the big Baldwin engine. Twenty yards along the track, the Utah & Northern came to a halt. Making his way through rusty stacks of rails was a heavyset, middle-aged man in a black worsted suit, ivory shirt, and black bowler. The full white duster that covered his suit flapped lightly in the chill morning breeze. He spotted the pair and waved, then quickened his pace and bounded toward them, his broad features stretched in a grin.

"By God, it's good to see you folks!" he boomed. He greeted Ki warmly, hugged Jessie, and held her off to look her over. "You're not getting any uglier," he said somberly. "You know that, don't you?"

Jessie laughed and gave him a mischievous wink. "And

2

you're the same old devil I remember, John Hamilton. I suppose you're still terrorizing all the women in Montana?"

"*What* women, Jessie?" Hamilton shot her a sorrowful frown. "There's maybe forty thousand people in the whole damn territory, young lady. I'd say right off about *eight* of 'em are fine-looking women. Pardon. Nine, now that you're here."

"If there's eight or eight hundred, I'll bet you know where they all are this minute. My father said once in Denver—"

"Ah, yes, well . . ." Hamilton colored and cleared his throat. "Ki, it's good to see you again, sir. I trust you've been well?"

"Yes. Just fine, John." He grinned at the man's discomfort. "I'd like to stretch my legs a bit, if you two don't mind. I know you've got a lot to talk over."

"Won't take you long to look around," Hamilton said soberly. "Thirty or forty seconds ought to do it." He pumped Ki's hand once more. "We'll be at Morgan's store at the end of the gully. Can't miss it—only other place with four walls is the stable."

"I'll find it," Ki told him. "See you there soon." He gathered up his satchel and Jessie's and wandered off. Hamilton guided Jessie away from the train. Ahead, the tracklaying gang worked noisily to extend the way another few yards. Jessie had to agree—there was little to see here at all. There was a scattering of tents and frail shacks along the rails, cut by a dozen muddy trails. She was certain there were as many team horses as laborers in the camp.

"Sorry about this place," Hamilton told her. "Can't even offer you a hotel room, Jessie. We'll be moving out fast. Be a lot more comfortable—*and* safer—camping on the trail."

"John, I've seen a few railroad towns before."

"So have I, but this one's sorrier than most." He helped Jessie over a narrow plank that someone had laid across the mud. "They're talking about forming a town company and sellin' lots. Calling the place Dillon after the president of the line." He shook his head in disgust. "You ask me, the whole bunch'll move on to Butte when the rails pass by. Who in hell'd want to live here?"

They made their way over the flats, past the embers of morning fires and tents blackened with smoke. The tracklayers they passed were Chinese; the supervisors and railroad men were all white. The Orientals kept their eyes to the ground,

3

but the others watched Jessie with open hunger. They saw few women, and none at all like this one. The heavy leather jacket and faded denims failed to hide the lush curves of her body and the startling beauty of her face. Her skin was slightly tanned, the color of honey and cream. Strawberry-blond hair fell freely past her shoulders. The hair framed green eyes, a straight, aristocratic nose, and a full and generous mouth.

If Jessie noticed the bold appraisals, she ignored them. Hamilton, though, met the men's eyes with a challenge and authority that turned them away.

Morgan's store was nothing more than four walls of scrap lumber, a rough plank counter, and a plain dirt floor. Hamilton nodded a greeting to the owner, and led Jessie past a hanging blanket to the rear. A pot of hot coffee steamed on the stove, and Hamilton filled two tin cups of the scalding liquid.

"Take the chair," he said wryly. "Far as I know, it's the only one south of Virginia City." He squatted on a keg and blew on his coffee. "I want to say it, Jessie, and get it out of the way. I knew Alex Starbuck twenty years, and worked for him most of that time. He was the finest man I ever knew. I'd have come for the burying if you'd wanted. I guess you know that."

"I do, John, and I'm grateful," she said softly. "When he was killed, what I needed most of all was to know that men he trusted were holding down the fort. I thank you for your letter. It meant a great deal." She sipped her coffee and set it aside. "Now—what happened to Jebediah? I know they hung him in Mule, but there's more to it than that. Your message made that pretty clear."

Hamilton let out a breath. "Yeah, there's more to it, all right." He pulled his bulk erect and glanced past the hanging blanket and back to Jessie. "I'll just hit the high spots and you can ask questions. Jebediah and four or five other old-timers have been roaming around the Montana Rockies ten or twelve years. They work up the Lewis Range to Canada, down to the Blackfoot River, or over to the Missouri and Fort Benton. Some say they've riled up the Blackfoot or the Flatheads on occasion. Maybe it's true, I don't know. They're all men seventy and more years old, and old habits are hard to break. Mountain men and Injuns are bound to mix it up some, till they're both

4

dead and gone. Mostly, from what I hear, they keep to them-selves and follow the old ways. They don't want anything to do with the miners or anyone else."

"Then what was Jebediah doing in a place like Mule?"

Hamilton's broad features were set in anger. "I didn't get there till a week after it happened. Near as I can put it together, he wasn't doing a damn thing 'cept buying a little flour and bacon and whiskey. There's been trouble up and down Clark Fork and on the Nine Mile. Two miners got their throats cut in O'Keefe Canyon. Another was killed and chopped up bad at the mouth of Cedar Creek. And just before they hung Jeb, a feller was shot in the head north of the St. Regis River. Folks were stirred up when Jeb Baker rode in. Those miners were looking for someone to hurt, and he was it." Hamilton paused, and looked intently at Jessie. "Here's the rest of it, the part I know's true but can't prove. Hanging Jebediah Baker was no accident. Someone saw him coming and picked him out special. Jeb was a scapegoat. I'm sure as sin he was."

"And you know who was responsible, John?"

"Damn right I do," Hamilton said darkly. "Just as sure as I'm standing right here. It was Pierce Cavanaugh, Jessie."

"Pierce Cavanaugh . . ." Jessie nodded and sipped her cof-fee.

Hamilton nodded approval. "I see you know the name."

"I've read every report you sent on Montana Territory over the years," said Jessie. "Cavanaugh's name has cropped up more than once."

"Huh!" Hamilton spat on the ground. "Kinda like saying the devil's name crops up now and then in hell."

From what Jessie remembered, Pierce Cavanaugh had made a fortune mining gold in the first big strikes of the sixties, and hadn't slowed down since. Now he controlled a large portion of the mining in western Montana, and had a talent for squeez-ing out competitors who tried to grow. So far, he hadn't hurt the Starbuck holdings. Hamilton would never take credit, but Jessie knew he was responsible for holding the man at bay.

"And you think Cavanaugh had Jebediah killed? Why, John? You said he was a scapegoat, but—"

"I think Cavanaugh's behind the deaths of those miners. I don't know *why* he had 'em killed. They sure didn't have a thing he wanted. But I know this corner of Montana, and I know Pierce Cavanaugh, Jessie. He killed them, then put out the word that the mountain men were responsible. When old Jeb came to town, some of Cavanaugh's boys were on hand to see that things went the way he wanted 'em to go." Hamilton looked meaningfully at Jessie. "You don't mind the morning breeze, might be a good idea if we did some walking. That all right with you?"

Twenty yards or so past the store, the land rose slightly above the valley. Jessie could see the completed tracks stretching south, following the old emigrant trail and the stage road down to Ogden, where the Utah & Northern joined the Union Pacific.

"I know old Morgan pretty good," said Hamilton, "but there's no use getting careless now. The rest of this story isn't for anyone's ears but yours and Ki's."

"If your message meant what I think it meant, John . . ."

"It did," Hamilton said sternly. "I wouldn't have gotten you up here 'less I was certain." He looked Jessie squarely in the eye. "There was an old Crow woman who carried food to the men in the Mule jail. At the time, there wasn't anyone else in there but Jeb. I guess he figured what they'd do, that he wouldn't be getting out alive. Anyway, Jeb knew some of the Crow woman's people, and she sure as hell knew him. He told the woman to get word out to his friends not to come seeking blood. That was the way he put it. Seem's he's got a grand-daughter up in the hills, and didn't want anyone going after her."

Jessie raised an eyebrow. "A granddaughter? I never even knew he'd taken a wife."

"Your father likely knew—if Jeb ever thought to tell him. The wife and daughter died of smallpox some years back. The girl's name is Yellow Wing, and she's about three-quarters Sioux, I guess." Hamilton kicked at the dirt with his boot. "The other message was for you, Jessie. Jeb knew I was around, though we hadn't seen each other for a good five years. He said—and these are the exact words he told the old woman— 'Tell John Hamilton to let Alex's girl know. The ones that killed him are loose up here.'"

"My God, John!" Jessie stared at Hamilton and took a deep breath. "Are you *sure* that's what he said?"

"The Crow woman had no reason to lie."

"No, no, of course she didn't. Jebediah knew about the cartel, then," she said thoughtfully. "My father must have told him long ago. He knew enough about the Prussians to know they were responsible for his death—the message is clear about that. But how would he know they were up to something in Montana Territory?"

Hamilton shook his head. "I can't answer that. Doubt if anyone can now. Mountain men see a lot of things other folks don't. They just don't go around *talking* about it, is all." He looked away and squinted into the sun. "After I got Jeb's message, I started thinking. If the Europeans *are* pulling something up here, Cavanaugh's the man they'd likely use. He's got the organization and the power—and no scruples anyone's ever noticed."

Jessie looked thoughtfully at the man. "If you're right, Jeb's death could have served Pierce Cavanaugh two ways, John. He used him as a scapegoat to cover the miners' deaths, and because he *knew* Jeb was onto something! But—what is it they're after? Silver? Cattle?"

Hamilton shook his head. "I wouldn't pretend to tell *you* about the cartel, Jessie. God knows, you and Ki have come up against them enough to know what they're like. But I do know this neck of the woods—better'n most, I don't mind saying—and what I'm telling you is true. Montana's getting ready to explode. There isn't a handful of people here now, but that's going to change, and change fast. In the next couple of years, why, you'll see a—"

The sharp crack of a pistol cut off his words. Hamilton and Jessie turned at once as angry cries rose from the cluster of tents below. The side of a lean-to collapsed and a man went flying into the mud. Another staggered out behind him, a big man hot on his heels. The two went at it, trading fierce blows. Suddenly the man who'd sailed through the door picked up a piece of scrap lumber to use as a club, and joined the fray. The smaller man ducked, dropped to his haunches, and turned to fight the pair at once.

"My God, it's Ki," Jessie cried out abruptly. "John, those bastards are beating him to death!"

7

Chapter 2

Ki walked along beside the tracks, taking long strides and breathing in the morning air. He was grateful for the chance to get outside and stretch his legs. The Utah & Northern was still a construction train and carried only a single passenger car. On the long haul up through Idaho Territory, Ki and Jessie had shared the ride with Texas cowmen looking for range, and sour-faced railroaders drunk from a week in Ogden. Halfway through the night, the railroaders had announced they didn't like cows at all. And they sure as hell didn't like men who had cowshit on their boots. The Texans had taken exception to these remarks. A few cracked heads and broken bottles later, both parties had settled down for the night.

Jessie had slept, her head lolling on Ki's shoulder with the rhythm of the train. Ki had stayed awake. Every man in the car had stripped Jessie with his eyes. More than one, Ki knew, wondered how much trouble it would be to toss this fine-looking woman's traveling companion off the train.

Ki kept close to the train, avoiding the tents and shacks to his right. He wore an old leather vest over his plain cotton shirt, faded blue denims, and ankle-length Wellington boots. The boots were his only concession to the trip. He preferred no shoes at all, or at most a pair of comfortable, rope-soled slippers. He was a lean, angular man, very much like a dozen others along the tracks.

Still, men glanced up and looked him over. Ki ignored them and kept walking. He'd seen the look before, and knew what it meant. He wore no hat, and his straight black hair hung to his collar. His cheeks were sharp planes that trailed to the firm line of his jaw. His eyes were dark as river stones, tilted slightly

8

upward at the corners. He looked the same as the others—and he didn't. The eyes, the hair, the unusually high cheeks told the men along the tracks a different story. The workmen laying rail ahead of the train looked a lot like the man passing by. So what the hell was a Chinaman doing dressed up like a white, walking just as straight and tall as you please?

The flatbed cars to Ki's left were stacked with rails and timber ties. The four farther back were rust-colored boxcars full of supplies for the Utah & Northern, and goods to be shipped overland to Virginia City or up to Butte and points north. Teams hauled wagons of every size and shape through the mud, backing up to load freight off the train.

Ki started to circle the tangle of wagons for higher ground, then stopped in his tracks as a man bellowed a curse in his direction. A wild-eyed mule suddenly bolted up the slope, dragging a flatbed wagon. Ki stood his ground, shouted at the mule, grabbed its harness below the bit, and jerked hard. The animal tried to shake him free, but Ki held on. He turned the rig around and led it back to its owner.

The man was still sprawled on the ground. He was a short, stocky man in his sixties, and Ki saw at once that his left leg was stiff and useless. A young boy in baggy overalls and a shapeless hat was doing his best to get a crutch under the old man's arm.

"Here," Ki told the boy, "take the mule a minute." He handed the reins over and lifted the man by his shoulders, then placed the crutch firmly under his arm. "There—are you all right now?"

"Right as I'm goin' to get," the man growled. He squinted curiously at Ki with watery eyes. "Thanks, mister. I'm obliged. Goddamn animal tries to kill me ever' time it gets a chance." He offered Ki a firm grip. "Name's McCabe. Will McCabe. You come in on the train?"

"Yes. My name is Ki, Mr. McCabe."

"*Key,* huh?" McCabe raised a shaggy brow. "That all the name you got?"

Ki grinned. "I'm afraid that's it."

"Well, don't matter." McCabe spat on the ground. "Way I see it, it's not a man's name but how he wears it that counts most." He called over his shoulder, "Angel, give me ol' Billy and get the last of those boxes on the wagon. I got to wet my

9

whistle 'fore my throat turns to dust." He shot Ki a wink. "I can offer you hot coffee at my tent. An' maybe a little something to go in it."

"Well, thank you," said Ki, "coffee'd be...uh, yes..." He stared past Will McCabe's shoulder, suddenly aware that the boy named Angel wasn't anywhere close to being a boy. Taking the reins from McCabe, she tossed her hat aside and let bright flaxen hair tumble freely over her shoulders. Ki caught a glimpse of hazel eyes, a freckled nose, and the corner of a grin before she turned and stalked back to the freightcar's door. He followed her long stride with new interest. Somehow the overalls didn't seem shapeless anymore.

"Her name's Angela," McCabe said flatly. "Call her Angel for short. She's my niece and she's a good girl, mister."

"Yes sir, I'm certain of that," Ki said carefully. McCabe was no fool and he'd seen the way Ki had looked the girl over. "Does your offer of a cup of coffee still hold?"

McCabe laughed at Ki's expression. "Hell yes, why not? Don't blame you for looking—just don't look too damn hard."

McCabe and his niece had set up camp some thirty yards from the tracks. While Angel made coffee, her uncle eased himself painfully to the ground and lit a cheroot. McCabe told Ki they'd come down from the Big Hole River to get mining supplies off the train.

"Don't know why I bother," the old man grumbled. "There ain't enough trace in that goddamn hole to fill a tooth—an' I can't hardly walk, much less handle a mine."

"What happened?" Ki asked. "If you don't mind my asking?"

McCabe slapped his stiff leg. "'Bout half the mountain come in while I was down under it." He glanced across the camp at his niece. "Be deader'n last summer if she hadn't pulled me out. That's one brave girl, I'll tell you. Just like her mother, my kid sister, rest her soul."

Angel brought coffee, and for an instant their hands touched. The girl met his eyes once more, then turned quickly aside and busied herself at the wagon. Even under McCabe's watchful eye, Ki couldn't help noticing the incredibly slim circle of her waist, the pointy little breasts that strained the coveralls' straps. She was scarcely seventeen, he decided, but age had little to do with being a woman.

"Whole country's changing," McCabe was saying. "I seen it right from the start, and it ain't even begun, I'll tell you that. You can take that to the bank, young feller." He paused, and nodded down the hill. "Railroad's the reason. Going to bust this territory wide open. Utah & Northern will get to Butte this time next year. Northern Pacific'll hit us up east at the same time. Won't be long 'fore we'll have more lines than an ol' lady's face."

"What's going to bring people here?" Ki asked. "Farms and cattle? I know silver's still good, but that isn't enough to start a boom."

McCabe's eyes flashed. "Gold and silver both'll be around for quite a spell. But there's something here a whole lot bigger'n that—"

"Uncle Will . . ."

Both Ki and McCabe turned. It was the first time he'd heard the girl speak. Her voice was stronger, more commanding than he'd figured. It didn't seem to match her slender form and quiet manner.

"I'm *sure* your guest isn't interested in a lot of boring talk about mining," she said evenly. "He doesn't look like a minin' man to me. You're not, are you, sir? What is it brings you up to Montana Territory?" She shot him a charming smile and Ki answered it in kind. He hadn't missed the girl's urgent glance at McCabe. Whatever he'd meant to say, Angel had warned him off fast. He muttered into his coffee and looked at his hands.

"Business," Ki said casually. "The lady I work for has investments in Montana."

"What kind of investments?" Angel asked. "Oh, now if that's none of my business, just say so," she added contritely.

"Her name's Jessie Starbuck," Ki explained. "She's got some cattle and mines up here. And you're right, Miss McCabe. I *don't* know a lot about mining."

"Goddamn," said McCabe, giving Ki a startled look. "If it's the Starbuck I'm thinking about, you're traveling in rich company, son."

"Jessie's a fine woman," Ki said simply. He looked up at Angel. "From what your uncle tells me, you two share some of the same good qualities."

Angel frowned. "And just what do you figure those'd be?"

"Courage, for one. And I'd guess you're not a lady who

11

holds back from saying what's on her mind. Jessie isn't either."

Angel colored, then covered a grin with her hand. "I think I'll get some more water," she said quickly. "Might want to make up a little more coffee." Grabbing up a pail, she tossed back her hair and walked down the ravine toward the tracks.

"Lord God, I owe you another one, boy." McCabe threw back his head and laughed. "Ain't easy to get that child's goat. But you sure went and did it!"

"She's a very fine girl," said Ki. "I, uh—mean that with all respect, of course."

"Oh, of course you do," McCabe said dryly. "Partways, at least." He shot Ki a wink. "Hell, son, I ain't always been old. And it's nothing against you personal. If it 'pears like I cluck over the girl like a goddamn hen over her chicks, you're right." He nodded over his shoulder toward the tracks. "I don't have to tell you what fine, upstandin' gents you find in a place like this. And up on the river, in minin' country, it don't get better, it gets worse."

"I understand," said Ki.

McCabe looked thoughtfully at his hands. "Angel's got no manners, 'least none that show. But she looks after me like I look after her. That, uh, business I was about to get into back there, concerning mines and such—I'd consider it a favor if you'd forget about that."

Ki shrugged. "Consider it forgotten, Mr. McCabe." He wondered why the old man was so concerned. Whatever he'd meant to say, Angel had cut him off fast. Ki hadn't the slightest idea where the conversation had been headed.

"What I *ought* to do," said McCabe, "is stop all this minin' shit and go on down to Denver or somewhere and sit in a rocker."

Ki grinned. "Is that what Angel wants you to do?"

"It's been mentioned a couple of times," McCabe growled.

"Somehow I don't picture you in a rocker."

"No?" McCabe cackled and showed his teeth. "Ain't that amazing. Neither do I." He shook his head and made a face. "Going to have to, though, an' real soon. She won't leave me up there alone, and it's sure no place for a young girl. She needs more schoolin' and pretty dresses, and folks she can—"

McCabe stopped abruptly as a short, startled cry reached his ears. "Shit, that's her!" The old man's face went slack.

12

"Damn it, what was I sayin' just now? This ain't no place for a—"

Ki was on his feet and gone, following Angel's path down the ravine. He saw her almost at once, a flash of yellow hair that vanished quickly through the door of a lean-to bar. A man gave a raw, low-pitched laugh. Angel cursed him soundly until a hand over her mouth cut her off.

Ki raced toward the hut. A crude plank door slammed in his face. He stopped, twisted slightly on one foot, and drove the other through the door. Wood splintered and exploded about the room. Three men looked up in surprise. Two held Angel over the bar while the third tried to tear away her clothes. Ki never stopped moving. His right hand came up in a blur, fingers thrust out stiffly. The blow caught the man at Angel's left below the nose. At the same time, Ki spotted the barrel of a Colt coming swiftly out of shadow below the bar. His left hand shot out in a knife-edged chop. The pistol exploded with a deafening roar in the small room. The gunman screamed and stared at his shattered wrist. Ki grabbed his collar, pulled him over the bar, and tossed him through a wall into the mud.

Angel shouted a warning. Ki saw the blow coming, but couldn't stop it. He caught the flash of a three-day beard and gray eyes as a fist landed solidly on his temple. He staggered back, shaking his head to clear his vision. The man came at him, raining punishing blows at Ki's belly. Ki backed through the ruined door and rolled, came to his feet, and met the man in a crouch. The fellow came at him like a bull and Ki ducked, digging his heels in mud and launching himself low at the attacker's legs. The man swallowed a curse, stepped to one side, and pounded the side of Ki's head. Ki spat blood, stumbled, and fell on his back. The man bellowed and kicked out, driving Ki's face into the mud. Ki choked and rolled free, lashed out with his foot, and caught the man solidly in the chest. The man gagged as air left his lungs. Ki sprang to his feet, stiffening his hands into iron-hard wedges to finish the other off. He caught the slight grin on the man's features, saw gray eyes flick to the right, and cursed himself for a fool. The first man he'd downed was back on his feet, and Ki had forgotten all about him!

Something hard struck his back, sending him headlong into the mud. He sensed the next blow and threw himself aside. A

13

boot glanced painfully off his ribs. Ki gritted his teeth and came to his feet, wiping dark ooze out of his eyes. The two circled him warily, the gray-eyed man to the left, the other to the right. Ki saw now that the bastard had hit him with a piece of the splintered door.

Suddenly the man moved, faster than Ki would have guessed. The club sliced air only inches from his head. Ki danced aside and dropped to his haunches in a crouch. The man came at him, whipping the weapon before him in a fast and deadly arc. Ki stepped back and saw the gray-eyed man coming at him from behind. He turned and let the big fist graze the edge of his shoulder. The other man laughed and thrashed out savagely with his club. Ki twisted in the mud, grabbed the man's arm below the weapon, and jerked him neatly off the point of his hip. The man yelped and hit the ground hard. Ki kicked him solidly in the head, twisted on the balls of his feet, and leaped away.

The gray-eyed man now watched him with cautious respect. He shifted to his left, taking slow and easy steps. Ki watched his eyes, the tendons in his neck. The man kept moving, arms pressed close against his sides, fists covering his face and chest like a boxer. Ki backed off and the man moved in. Ki stumbled away, as if he feared to let the other get close. The man grinned, feinted to the left, and came in swinging a solid right. Ki dropped his head and shoulders and came up fast, inside the man's guard. The man grunted and aimed a hammerlike blow at Ki's head. Ki's stiffened fingers drove into the man's throat like spikes. He cried out in surprise and covered his face. Ki hammered away relentlessly. The man staggered and fell away. Ki hit him hard across the mouth with the edge of his hand. The other stood an instant, blood coursing down his face. Then his eyes went dull and he fell on his face in the mud.

Ki stepped back and drew a welcome breath. Angel peeked cautiously out of the shack, her hazel eyes as big as saucers.

"Are you—are you all right?" she asked.

"Oh sure," Ki said wearily. "I'll be fine in a couple of weeks." He heard a familiar laugh behind him, and turned. Jessie and John Hamilton were standing on the bluff just above. Ki imagined how he looked, covered as he was from head to toe with black mud.

"Any way I can leave you five or ten minutes without you

14

finding trouble?" said Jessie. Her green eyes flicked to the girl and back to Ki. "Right. I, ah, guess maybe there isn't."

"Jessie," Ki said calmly, "right now would be a very good time to simply say nothing at all."

Chapter 3

John Hamilton had stayed alive for a number of years by smelling trouble before it happened. He didn't like the crowd of sullen-eyed men gathering around the ruined shed. Phrases like "slant-eyed bastard" and "goddamn chink" were beginning to make the rounds.

"Be a good idea if you put off takin' a bath till we get this place behind us," he told Ki. "I've got horses at the stable. You and Jessie go get 'em and start riding north. I'm going to have me a word with that young lady and her uncle."

Ki didn't argue. He could sense trouble as well as Hamilton could, and knew that leaving the railhead fast was a good idea. Any more trouble would put Jessie in the middle, and he didn't intend to let that happen.

"I'm sorry," he told her. "There wasn't anything else I could do. They would have hurt the girl."

"Don't you dare apologize for that," Jessie said shortly. "What's the matter with you?"

"I don't know. Maybe I'm just tired and mad all at once."

"You didn't sleep all night," said Jessie. "You sat up watching out for me."

"I guess so."

"There's no guess to it. A fellow ought to get a little sleep before he takes on three big bastards in a fight. Seems to me you should've learned that in samurai training somewhere."

Ki stopped and shot her a look. "You're making fun of me, aren't you?"

Jessie laughed aloud. "Of course I am. I can't hug you and tell you I'm glad you're all right. You're too damn dirty!"

Ki rode a chestnut stallion and led Hamilton's saddled gelding. Jessie followed on an animal that was the twin of Hamilton's mount. She led a coal-black pack mule. Both the mounts and the mule had been ready and waiting in the stable. Ki decided Hamilton was a man who didn't like to get caught out in the open. Glancing cautiously over his shoulder, he clucked the mount gently ahead, and moved past the last of the scattered tents.

"Hey, over there to the left," Jessie said.

Ki looked past her and saw a wagon making tracks straight for them, leaving the railhead behind. Will McCabe and Angel sat up front; Hamilton rode in the bed, his short legs dangling off the back, a shotgun cradled in his lap.

McCabe brought the rig to a halt and Hamilton hopped off, handed the weapon to McCabe, and pulled himself into the saddle. "Convinced these folks it might be a good idea to ride along," he said evenly. "Boys back there are going to take a little spell settling down."

"Ki, I'm obliged to you again," said McCabe. "By God, if you hadn't been there, we'd—"

"Uncle Will..." Angel laid a hand gently on his arm. "I reckon I can do my own thanking." She looked straight at Ki, and for a moment the hazel eyes bored right through him. "Thank you. That was a very wonderful thing to do."

"I was just...there, Miss McCabe." Her gaze warmed him clear down to his belly. He thoroughly enjoyed the sensation, but wished the girl would save a look like that for another time.

"Let's put some miles behind us," said Hamilton, turning his mount in a tight circle. "No use pressing our luck."

Hamilton rode them hard a good hour, then settled into an easygoing pace. He was sure no one in the railhead camp would bother to follow, but, as he confided to Ki, "I'll be a lot more certain a week from Tuesday."

At noon they stopped for a cold meal at the edge of the valley, bringing the wagon and the horses under the shade of lodgepole pines. Ki found an icy stream and cleaned himself up, rinsed his muddy clothes, and spread them on branches to dry. When they were back on the trail once more, he wore a loose cotton shirt, scuffed denim trousers, and his old leather vest. The wet Wellington boots had found their way into his saddlebag, and his feet were comfortably bare.

"I never saw a man who didn't wear shoes," said Angel.

17

"I mean, there's nothing *wrong* with it. Just never saw it before."

"I'm only half American," Ki said solemnly. "The barefooted half is Japanese."

Angel swept corn-yellow hair off her brow and gave him a look. "That isn't any kind of explanation and you know it."

Ki grinned. "No, it's not." He looked down at the girl from his mount. Her skin was the color of fresh cream, her lips pale pink under the sun. He wondered what she'd do if he asked her to leave the wagon and ride behind him, but he kept the question to himself. He had no desire to rile her uncle, and Will McCabe was clearly listening to everything they said.

"Most men keep their hands bare," he told the girl. "That makes sense because they use them. They wrap their feet in leather, because all they ever do with them is walk. Sometimes I use my feet to fight. It's easier to do that without boots. Besides"—he grinned—"they dry a lot faster when you get them all muddy."

Angel didn't answer his smile. "Is—is that what you do, Ki? I mean—you just fight?"

"No," he said gently, "only when I have to, Angel. That's part of my job. To take care of Jessie as well as I can."

"Oh. I see . . ."

The question she wanted to ask was on her lips, but he knew that was as far as it would go.

"We'll talk later," he said. "Is that all right with you?"

"Yes, that'd be fine," she told him. Angel lowered her face quickly. She knew already that he could read her thoughts in her eyes.

"Will McCabe's asked us to stay the night at his place," said Hamilton. "If it's all right with you, Jessie, I told him we'd be grateful. He's not far north of the Big Hole River. I want to cross the pass over the Divide early tomorrow. McCabe's will be as good a place as any for a start."

"Fine," Jessie agreed. "You know the country, John." She turned and looked at Ki. For the moment the three of them were riding together, ahead of the slower wagon. "He told you he had a mine up there, right? What kind of a mine, Ki?"

Ki shook his head. "Gold or silver, I guess. He didn't act as if it was doing very well."

18

Hamilton gave him a knowing look. "Might be it is, and might be it's not. Miners always tell you their digs aren't worth a nickel. Not too bad an idea, either."

Ki looked thoughtfully at the man. "As a matter of fact, he *was* sort of cagey about that. McCabe was going to tell me something, but Angel stopped him. We talked about the railroads coming and opening up Montana. McCabe said it wasn't cattle or silver that would open up the territory. He said there was something bigger than that."

A broad grin spread across Hamilton's features. "I had an idea Will McCabe was a lot more'n your average miner. Well, I'll be damned!" He shook his head and looked from Jessie to Ki. "I'll bet a double eagle to a dime the old man's talking 'bout *copper*. Hell yes, he is. McCabe thinks he's found him a copper vein."

Ki looked puzzled. "Copper? What's so valuable about copper?"

"Not too many people figure it's worth the trouble," said Hamilton. "Going to be something, though, whether they know it or not." He turned to Jessie again. "I wrote you a long letter at the start of the year, remember? Asked you to let me take some gold and silver stock and put it into copper?"

"I remember," said Jessie. "And I said go ahead. But I'll admit it was because I trust your judgment, John. You said copper'd go up, but you didn't go much into why."

Hamilton's eyes flashed with excitement. "Ee-lectrical industry," he said softly . "Goin' to be bigger'n anyone imagines, and copper's the key. I've been picking up claims for you on the quiet, mines where the silver's played out and there's a good copper showing. There are others doing it too."

Hamilton paused and squinted above the horizon. The afternoon sun had turned the Bitterroot Mountains to the west a smoky blue. Shadows stretched across the valley and cut sharp planes through the Divide, looming ahead. "Things are changing fast," he said evenly. "Just remember that, Jessie. Things are by God goin' to happen . . ."

Will McCabe's cabin was set on a bare, rocky ridge four miles above the river. There were woodlands to the east, but the land around the cabin was scraped raw. It was clear enough to Jessie that the old man had sunk a good dozen shafts over the years.

19

Whatever he was after, looking for it hadn't been easy.

Jessie was more than ready for the long day to end. Soon after supper, she said good night and went to her room. Angel was tending the big stone fireplace and Ki was outside checking the horses. Will and John Hamilton scarcely noticed Jessie leaving. They were still at the table under a dim kerosene lamp, smoking and swapping yarns about Montana.

The knife-edge rim of the Divide was only a few miles to the north; even before the sun disappeared, a chill wind settled into the valley. By the time Jessie made her way to bed, the small, unheated room was cold enough to frost her breath.

Perching on the side of her bed, she pulled off her cordovan boots, then leaned back to peel her tight denims down her legs. Standing again, she slipped the flannel shirt over her shoulders, past the full swell of her breasts. For a moment she was naked except for the red garter holster that circled her thigh. As she quickly crossed the room, the full autumn moon turned her honey-gold flesh a satiny white.

Jessie wrapped one of Angel's robes about her shoulders, made her way back to the bed, and pulled the rough sheet and woolen blankets up to her chin. She could still hear the drone of male voices through the wall as McCabe and John Hamilton solved the territory's problems.

Sleep didn't come easily. Jessie thought of Jebediah Baker, and wondered how often the old man had crossed the high mountains and broad valleys of the West. In the days when he was young, a man could pack out of St. Louis upriver and disappear in a nearly uncharted land. Many had never returned, but Jeb had fooled death a hundred times and lived to tell about it. He'd survived harsh winters, hunger and privation, and Indians who'd give their right arm to mount his scalp before their lodge. For more than sixty years he'd battled the cruel, unforgiving land, and given as good as he got.

It's not right at all, thought Jessie. *A man like that ought to go out different than other men . . .* The image of Jebediah with a rope around his neck made the blood run hot in her veins. They'd murdered him without giving him a chance, the same as they'd done to her father.

Thoughts of Alex Starbuck brought her fully awake again. She sat up in spite of the cold, listening to the wind rattling the glass in the bedroom window. Why did the good men have

20

to die, when so many worthless bastards were walking around fat and happy? She'd evened the score a little, but the men who'd ordered her father's death were still alive. Alex Starbuck had fought them all his life, but they'd finally gunned him down on his own Texas ranch. Jessie had watched the life go out of a man she'd always figured would live forever...

In his youth, Alex Starbuck had built a vast empire by helping to open the Orient to trade. His ships had brought him money and power, and his charm had won him a fiery young bride with flaming hair. Soon, Starbuck discovered that there were men who were determined to rule the lucrative markets of the East. This powerful European cartel would stop at nothing to eliminate any who stood in their way. Alex had fought back, meeting fire with fire. Ships were sunk and cargoes sent to the bottom. Men died on both sides, and finally Jessie's mother, Sarah, was struck down. Alex, in the only act of his life that ever shamed him, had struck out at his enemy's son. The old Prussian count had bided his time, and finally taken his revenge.

Jessie had inherited her father's vast empire and the grave responsibility that went with it. The faceless men of the cartel were still there—determined, now, to rid themselves of Alex Starbuck's daughter.

Jessie leaned back against her pillow and stared at the half-darkened room. If Jeb Baker was right, the cartel was ready to strike again, this time in Montana Territory.

"The railroad's going to open up the country," Hamilton had told her. "And every damn miner, shopkeeper, and businessman in Montana'll try to carve himself a good-sized piece of the pie."

Jessie felt a sudden chill at the thought. Silver was still worth digging out of the earth, and men who looked to the future were ready to turn copper ore into gold. Great herds of cattle were moving north, and farms were sprouting up in the rich, fertile soil. Men were hungry for new money—and the cartel had the money to spend. Montana Territory was ripe for the picking. The nation's Northwest was the key to the country's future. Whoever ruled those lands could rule the nation.

"They'll try," Jessie muttered to herself. "By God, they'll swallow it whole if they can!"

Chapter 4

Ki listened to Hamilton and McCabe for a while after supper, told Jessie he'd check the horses, and slipped quietly out the back door. After the heat of the cabin, the crisp night air felt good. He still wore no shoes, and his worn leather vest was inside. He didn't feel the cold sweeping down from the mountains to the north. Part of a samurai's training was learning to yield discomforts of the body to the stronger will of the mind. Pain slowed your reactions, took your mind off what needed to be done. If you were constantly trying to keep warm or fill your belly, it gave an enemy with discipline the edge. And that was something Ki was determined to keep for himself.

For a moment he breathed the chill air and let his eyes grow accustomed to his surroundings. The moon bathed the harsh, rocky terrain in cold light, softening its sharp planes and angles. He watched a small animal poke its head out of a hole, leap from cover, and bound away. He heard the girl open the cabin's back door, then close it softly behind her. Turning, he watched her walk toward him, a small slender figure in a plain cotton dress, a heavy fleece jacket wrapped tightly about her shoulders.

"You ought to be careful in the dark," she laughed quietly. "Uncle Will's got holes out here that even he's forgot about."

"So I noticed," said Ki. "Did Mr. McCabe do all this by himself?"

"Oh yeah," Angel said wearily, "all by himself. And before that, he did the same thing down in Bannack, and before *that*, in Colorado somewhere." She paused and studied Ki a long moment, her eyes catching sparks from the moon. "He's a good man, Ki. A real good man. Ma raised me as well as she could, after Pa got sick and died. She passed away when I wasn't more than ten, and Uncle Will took me in like I was

22

his own. Hadn't ever *seen* me before Ma died. Didn't even know he had a niece, for that matter."

"You're right," Ki agreed. "That's quite a responsibility for a man to take on. I'd say he's done a fine job, seeing how you turned out."

"Well now, I thank you for that. 'Course, you don't have the slightest idea how I did or didn't turn out," she said wryly. "But I thank you just the same. Come on—maybe you're not freezing, but I am. Let's walk." She hooked her arm in his and leaned in against him, then led him west, down the path away from the cabin.

"I like Jessie," she said after a moment. "She's a real nice lady, you know?"

Ki didn't miss the tone of her voice. "Sounds to me as if that surprises you, Angel."

Angel bit her lip. "Damn it," she said soberly, "anything I hate, it's a man who can read me that easy, and you surely can. All right. I'm sorry for what I was goin' to ask you back on the trail and didn't. I don't hardly know you, Ki. Whatever's between you and her isn't any of my business."

Ki stopped and turned her gently around to face him. "I told you the truth, Angel. I work for Jessie and she's my friend. A very good friend. I've vowed to take care of her. To protect her as best I can."

"Vowed?" Angel raised an eyebrow at the word. "That's kind of a funny way to put it."

"It's a long story," he told her. "Maybe we'll have the time to talk about it someday."

Angel asked no more questions. Instead she nodded and led him toward the big wooden building at the end of the path. Ki had been inside when they'd arrived that afternoon. The structure was one-quarter barn, a neat and orderly section up front with a hayloft, room for horses and Will McCabe's mule and wagon, and the usual stable gear. The other three-quarters was in wild disarray. There were burlap sacks full of ore, tangles of rope and chain, broken block and tackle, and rusted mining equipment.

"I don't know whether you believe this or not," said Angel, "but Uncle Will knows *exactly* where everything is in this mess. If I moved one old piece of junk, he'd have a fit."

Ki grinned. "I believe it. Every man's got his own way of

23

keeping things straight." He rested his hand on a sturdy wooden table. A metal rod as thick as his thumb was clamped in a vise. The end of the rod had been recently sawed clean. A keg nearby held a dozen or so rods cut in roughly three-foot sections. Ki lifted one free, hefted it in his hand, and put it back. "I don't know much about mining," he told the girl, "but I'd guess there's about everything a man would need right here."

Angel laughed and brushed a tumble of yellow hair over her shoulders. "According to Uncle Will, it's the other way around. The thing he needs right now is the thing that *isn't* here." She leaned against the wall and gazed absently past him. "I'm glad Mr. Hamilton's here. Uncle Will doesn't ever get a chance to just talk to another man." She glanced down at her hands, busy with the fringes of her jacket. "You . . . got a girl somewhere, Ki? Someone real special?"

"No," he told her. "No one special. I guess you have to stay in one place for a while to have someone like that."

"Think so, huh?" Angel forced a little laugh. "Lord, if *that's* true, I ought to have a hundred special fellas. I sure do stay in one place, that's for sure!"

"Not too much chance to socialize up here, I guess." Ki moved a step toward her. The small circle of her mouth opened slightly. The big hazel eyes looked into his.

"No. No, there surely isn't." She walked to the kerosene lamp by the door and turned the wick down low. "Uncle Will says there's no use keepin' a bright light in the stable. Mules don't do a lot of reading."

"That's a fact," said Ki. He watched her turn to face him, knowing exactly what he'd see. It had been there between them, unspoken, since they'd met at the railhead that morning. Before, Ki had been uncertain whether to let it happen or not. Angel was very young; he wasn't sure now that she was even seventeen. And then there was Will McCabe, who'd warned him off firmly but politely.

"Works two ways, you know," Angel whispered. "I can read you good, too."

"I don't doubt that at all," Ki said dryly. He reached out and she came to him quickly, pressing herself firmly against him. He wrapped his arms around her and drew her close. Angel's slender form shuddered at his touch.

"Oh Lordy," she sighed, "I wanted it to happen so bad!"

24

"Angel, I know. I wanted the same thing."

"Hush now," she scolded him, pressing a finger to his lips. "It's all right, Ki. I'm a growed-up girl and I know what I'm doing. You're thinking maybe I'm not, now aren't you? I've— I've been with a man. A boy, I guess, not hardly a man. But he was nice to me and...oh yes, *yes!*"

Ki cupped her cheeks between his hands and brought her face up to his. Her mouth opened eagerly, the moist flesh of her lips unbelievably soft and tender. For a moment she let the tip of her tongue flick cautiously over his mouth. The instant he met her probing tongue with his own, she gave a startled little cry and ground her lips against his. Ki thrust himself hungrily into her warmth, tasting every sweet and secret hollow, stroking her mouth wider with every touch. Angel's fragile body smoldered against him. She threw back her neck, drinking in his kisses with a quick and desperate hunger. Ki ran his hands through a mist of golden hair, letting his fingers trail down the column of her throat to the soft curve of her shoulders. Angel's breath came in rapid bursts. Her body seemed to writhe with a purpose all its own; gentle curves and angles searched out his muscled frame. Hard little breasts pressed against him, burning through the fabric of his shirt.

When she paused to catch her breath, her face was slick with moisture, her pale skin flushed with excitement. Ki smelled the musky aroma of her flesh, the clean scent of her hair. Her hazel eyes were enormous, a startling shade of amber sprinkled with gold.

"That was . . . some kinda kissing," Angel said shakily. She buried a little laugh against his shoulder. "You know what? I'm not cold at all anymore." She gave him a mischievous wink, pushed him gently away, and took his hand. "I think we'd better get up there in the loft, is what I think," she whispered. "'Fore my legs give way for good."

Ki glanced past her shoulder and raised an eyebrow. Angel shook her head. "Uncle Will's got seegars, good corn whiskey, an' someone to listen to his yarns. He isn't comin' out in the cold to check the barn."

Ki didn't argue. Angel caught up her skirts in one hand and scampered up the ladder to the loft. Ki caught a glimpse of slender legs, the flash of a lovely thigh. When he reached the top himself, he found her nestled in a corner on a soft mound

25

of hay. The pale light of the lamp down below left the loft in half-shadow. He crawled to her and took her in his arms and kissed her gently. Her dark eyes held him, wide with wonder as he touched her throat softly and worked the buttons of her dress. She reached down to help, her small hands tangling hopelessly with his. She giggled with delight and laid her hands demurely in her lap, watching him intently, the pink tip of her tongue between her teeth.

Ki slowly bared one shoulder and then the other, finally slipping the dress down to her waist. Without taking her eyes from his, Angel raised her hips and let him slide the dress over her bottom and down her legs. She wore a soft cotton chemise under the gown. Seeing her like this, Ki thought she looked more than ever like a small, helpless little girl, a child who'd climbed up in the loft to spin out her dreams. She smiled then, touching the corner of her mouth with the tip of her tongue in a plainly wanton gesture. A tangle of flaxen hair fell lazily over her face, leaving one hazel eye searching boldly over his body. The little-girl image vanished abruptly. Ki felt his manhood swell painfully against his trousers.

Angel came to her knees and blew back her hair. "You haven't finished unwrappin' your package," she said softly. "Reckon I'll just have to do it for you . . ."

As Ki watched, she drew the chemise over her head. The cloth whispered into shadow and disappeared. Arching her back like a cat, she rested her hands on the hay behind her and drew in a breath. The motion hollowed her belly and gave her pointy breasts a saucy tilt.

Ki licked dry lips, marveling at the sight of her slender young form. She was a small and fragile creature, a girl made of velvet-soft curves and lazy angles. In the shadow of the loft, her naked flesh was the color of dusty gold. Her waist was so slender he was sure he could circle her with his hands with inches to spare. He let his eyes drink her in, from the ripe peaks of her nipples to the dark line of down that vanished between her thighs.

"Is that—is that *all* you're goin' to do?" Angel teased. The words seemed to catch in her throat. "I'm going to go plumb crazy if you don't do a whole lot more'n just look!"

Ki grinned. "Looking at you sure gives me a lot of pleasure. Don't know if I could stand anything much stronger."

26

Angel's eyes widened in mock alarm. She caught his broad grin, made a face and stuck out her tongue. "All right," she said coolly, "we'll do it your way, mister. You don't *have* to touch me at all. I'll just kinda—*describe* what's happening and you won't need to bother." She closed her eyes and rested her hands lightly on her thighs. "Right now I've got this real warm and buttery feelin' all over. It's curling 'round inside me and moving up real slow. Right . . . right up here . . ." Throwing back her head, she let her palms slide under her ribs to cup the firm swell of her breasts. She let out a sigh and ran the tips of her fingers over her nipples. "Lord, Ki, I can't tell you what it feels like now! My little ol' tits are tight and tingly, and the warm's like syrup runnin' hot . . . sliding through my belly down to here . . ." Still on her knees, she spread her thighs slightly to let her hands come to rest between her legs.

"Oh God," she moaned, her face twisted with pleasure. "I'm—I'm all wet, Ki. All the warm's coming out and I'm hot as a furnace! I'm goin' to—"

Angel exploded with laughter as Ki swept her up in his arms and tossed her roughly on her back. She shook long legs in the air as he smothered her naked body with his kisses. Starting at her lips, he let his mouth trail past the column of her neck to the rigid points of her breasts, down the length of her belly to her thighs. Angel gasped as his tongue teased the warm and downy nest between her legs. He lingered there, savoring soft flesh, teasing her tender parts with the tip of his tongue. Finally he kissed every inch of her lovely legs, finishing with tiny bites on the tips of her toes.

He left her then, and stood. Angel sprawled naked on her back, gasping for air as he stripped off his shirt and trousers and tossed them aside. He stood above her, hands against his sides. Angel looked up and squinted into shadow.

"Ki, you just goin' to stand up there or— Oh my *Gawd!*" She sat up abruptly, eyes wide as saucers at the sight of his rigid member. "I—I sure was right," she said with wonder, "I got me a *man* this time. You sure as hell aren't no boy!"

Ki stepped forward, took her hand gently in his, and squeezed it around his erection. Angel closed her eyes and moaned. Ki eased her back on the hay and kissed her softly, scarcely brushing her lips with his own. He bent to kiss her breasts, drawing the hard little nipples into his mouth. Her breath began to quicken, faster and faster as the fires within her grew. He stroked her firm young flesh, letting his fingers trace the fragile curves of her ribs to the flat plane of her belly. Angel groaned and thrust herself against him. At his touch, her willowy legs parted to welcome him in. Ki kneaded the sweet, feathery nest, letting his fingers stroke the honeyed flesh. Angel trembled, her slender body singing with pleasure. Ki moved quickly between her thighs. Angel cried out, snaked her hands between them, and drew his manhood inside her. Her body went rigid, arching beneath him like a bow. A ragged cry escaped her lips and he stilled it with his mouth. Angel groaned, her body slick with moisture. Her throat went tight and her face twisted with pleasure.

Ki felt liquid fire begin to thunder through his loins. Angel sensed his readiness and cried out with joy against his shoulder. For an instant they clung together, balanced on a razor-thin edge between torture and release. Ki plunged himself inside her again and again. Angel slammed the curve of her mound against his groin, raked her nails across his back, and scissored long legs around his waist. A fiery spasm of pleasure enveloped them both. She shrieked with delight as he spilled himself inside her.

Angel lay in his arms, the warm flesh of her body next to his. One lovely leg was draped lazily over his torso; her head was nestled in the hollow of his shoulder and he could feel the heat of her breath against his throat. He stroked the tousled hair and she purred and snuggled closer, sliding a satiny breast under his arm.

"Oh Lord," she sighed, "I think I've been loved real good, you know?"

"That's funny," Ki said solemnly, "the same thing just happened to me."

"It did?" Angel grabbed his arm and pulled herself onto his chest. "Well now. Imagine that." Her hazel eyes sparkled with mischief and a grin curled the corners of her mouth. Ki glanced past her shoulder and decided he'd never seen a lovelier sight. Light from the lantern below painted her flesh a silken gold. The delicate line of her back curved to an incredibly tiny waist, then rose in a graceful arc to a firm little bottom. He felt his member stirring back to life. Angel felt it too, and thrust herself brazenly against him.

"Oh dear," she murmured. "I do believe somethin' real peculiar is happening, Ki."

Ki didn't answer. Instead he grabbed her shoulders and tumbled her off his chest. Angel threw back her head and closed her eyes. Yellow light danced on her thighs and traced the slender columns of her legs. Ki let his hands slide under her bottom to cup the swell of her buttocks. Lifting her slightly off the hay, he bent to kiss the warm cleft between her thighs, letting his mouth brush lightly over a mist of tawny down.

"Ahhhh, *Ki!*" Angel arched her back and went rigid. Small fingers slid down her belly to join his own. Her body jerked in quick little spasms of delight. Ki's lips teased her, coming closer and closer to her pleasure—close, but never quite touching.

"Please," Angel gasped. "Oh, Ki, I—when you did that a minute ago, you—I never dreamed of a man kissin' me there before!"

"No? And you want me to do that, Angel?"

"Yes, *yes!*"

Ki let his lips find the soft petaled flesh. His tongue flicked gently at the proud rosy bud that was the crown of her pleasure. Angel's thighs trembled. Ki thrust his tongue deeply inside. Angel thrust her flat tummy up to meet him. Her fingers gripped his hair, pressing his face hungrily against her warmth. Ki probed deeper and deeper. Angel moaned and clasped her thighs about him. Her body thrashed in uncontrollable tremors of delight.

Ki could feel her orgasm mounting, thundering through every velvet tendon of her body. She cried out, pressing herself desperately against his mouth. He reached up, grabbed her thighs firmly, and flipped her over on her belly. Angel cried out in surprise. The plush little bottom twitched before him, swelling his rigid member until it ached. The musky taste of her flesh was still on his lips. He grasped her thighs and spread them wide, then thrust his length inside her to the hilt.

Angel have a high, joyous cry that died in her throat. Ki braced his knees, clutched her waist, and drew her to him. Angel answered with a raw and wanton hunger. Ki plunged harder and harder, no longer afraid that this fragile young body would break. Angel's deep need matched his own; the fire between her thighs urged him to drain her, to take everything she had to give.

Once more, Ki felt himself climbing toward an intense, almost unbearable peak of pleasure. Angel thrashed against him in spasms of pure joy. They soared on the crest of their release as if they were one, then burst free together in a white-hot explosion that left them shaking and gasping for breath.

Angel fell limply on her belly. Her back was slick with moisture, dotted with a million tiny pearls. Ki turned her over and took her in his arms. Her eyes were dark and lazy, her small mouth slack with pleasure.

"You are a very special woman," he whispered. "That was loving the way it ought to be."

"Oh, Ki," she sighed, tears suddenly blurring her eyes, "you don't even *know*, do you? I—I told you a feller gave me loving, but—God, we were just kids playin' at being grown up, you know? It wasn't—it wasn't like this at all!" She snuggled closer, under the warmth of his shoulder. "I didn't even *dream* there was anything like this!"

Ki grinned. "You could have fooled me. I guess loving is natural for some women."

Angel searched around for her chemise, and shook it free of hay. Ki helped her pull the garment over her shoulders, giving a sigh of regret as her taut little breasts disappeared.

"I'm going to have to wash *every*thing in ice-cold water 'fore I get in bed," she said darkly. "Sure as hell, if I don't, Uncle Will'll smell lovin' all over me in the morning and we'll both get shot."

He handed her her dress, and slipped into his trousers and shirt. "Angel, Will McCabe already knows you're grown. He might not want to think about it, but he knows."

Angel stopped, one arm in the sleeve of her dress. "I know he does," she said gently. "And I know what you're tryin' to say—that I'm not a little girl anymore and I need a life of my own." She shook her head in sudden anger. "What do you want me to do, Ki? Just up and leave him out here? I couldn't, even if I wanted to, and I don't! Oh hell, that's not true, either. Part of me does and part of me doesn't."

"I know." He leaned over and kissed her lightly. "And I admire you for feeling the way you do."

"Do you?" She forced a little laugh. "Well don't admire me too much, friend. There's times I'd like to scream bloody murder and run as far from this place as I can get." She shook

30

her head and covered her face. "And *that* makes me feel plumb rotten. It purely does, Ki."

"You mustn't," Ki told her. Her took her shoulders and brought her roughly to him. "It's natural to feel the way you do."

"Is it?" She shook him off and blinked back tears. "He's all I've got. And I'm all he's got, too."

"I know."

"Maybe you do and maybe you don't."

"You owe him. But he owes you too, Angel. I'm not saying you should just leave. You couldn't do that, and you shouldn't."

Angel sniffed. "What *are* you saying, then?"

"Just that Will McCabe has the same feelings you do, Angel. He wants something better for himself, whether he's ready to admit it or not. And he wants something better for you. He told me that this morning."

"He—he did? Really?"

"He did. Angel, Will McCabe's been around a long time. He knows you're a woman—he's not sure yet that *you* know, is all. And he—"

Ki's words were lost as a sharp, thunderous explosion shook the earth. Bright light lit the rafters, and the building shook beneath them.

"Ki, my God, what's *that!*" Angel clutched his arms, her eyes wide with sudden fear.

"Stay right here," Ki snapped. "Don't move—don't do anything at all!"

Angel cried out, but Ki was gone. He leaped from the loft, scarcely touching the ladder, and bolted out of the barn. An awesome, searing ball of fire brought him up short. He shrank back instinctively, shielding his face with his hand.

"Jessie!" The name was a hoarse cry of pain. He raced for the burning cabin, knowing there wasn't a chance she was alive. No one, nothing, could live through that inferno....

A rider appeared suddenly to his left and Ki threw himself aside. A pistol roared twice, digging up gravel at his back. He sprang to his feet and bolted for the barn in a crouch. Angel met him inside, her face as pale as death. Ki picked her up and tossed her roughly to the floor. The pistol cracked again, ripping splinters off the wall. Ki cursed, pressed himself flat, and risked a look out the door. The rider was coming straight at him, kicking his mount and waving his Colt in the air.

Ki glanced wildly about the barn, his heart pounding against his chest. His eyes caught McCabe's worktable—the vise, the keg full of straight iron rods. He ran in a crouch for the keg, grabbed up a handful of the rods, and sprang for cover. Angel screamed as the horse and rider burst into the barn. He jerked the mount in a rough half-circle, hunched his shoulders, and leveled the Colt at Ki.

Ki moved in a blur. His hand slammed straight out from his shoulder and the rod whipped end over end. The pistol exploded, and Ki felt lead tug at his sleeve. The gunman gave a strangled cry, stared dumbly at the rod embedded in his chest, and slid limply out of the saddle.

Angel brought a hand to her mouth. Her knees started to go, but she grasped the stable door and held on. As Ki ran past her, he told her to blow out the lantern and keep low, and then he slipped quickly out of the barn. The cabin was a sheet of white flame. Ki heard a burst of laughter and saw two riders circling the fire. A terrible cry of rage tore from his throat and he ran for the nearest man. The rider turned, saw him coming, and raised a rifle to his shoulder. Ki sprang aside, twisted on his feet, and launched a rod in the gunman's direction. The man bellowed in surprise as the weapon whipped past his shoulder. His horse pawed air and he wrenched it frantically away.

The second rider spurred his mount and raced at Ki from the right. Ki turned to meet him, grasping a rod at both ends. He crouched and let the rider come. Hooves flashed in the light of the fire and spittle flecked the animal's mouth. The rider bellowed and lashed out savagely with his boot. Ki sprang in the air, whipped the rod over his shoulder, and brought it down hard. The gunman howled as his kneecap shattered. He tried to hang on, but the pain twisted his body out of the saddle. His good leg caught in the stirrup and his back slammed hard against the ground. The horse broke into a run, dragging its rider over the rock-strewn earth.

Ki turned quickly, knowing the other man was still a threat. Three shots thundered to his left. Ki went to the ground, glanced up quickly, and saw John Hamilton framed against the fire. His portly figure was covered from head to toe in scorched longjohns. He stood his ground in the open, methodically firing one round after another at the last surviving rider. Hamilton

32

knew his weapon, and the gunman dug his heels in hard and bolted off. The rifle sagged at Hamilton's side and he turned to Ki.

"You all right, boy? I think we're rid of that bastard."

Ki staggered toward him. "John! Jessie, is she—?"

"I'm all right, Ki," Jessie said wearily. "Just barely, though." Ki turned and stared as she walked out of shadow beyond Hamilton. Her hair was as red as the flames behind her. Her face and white robe were streaked with soot, and the ivory-handled derringer was clasped in her hand.

Ki ran to her and took her in his arms. "God, Jessie, I thought you—"

Jessie held him close. "I know. I thought the same thing about you." She closed her eyes and shook her head in despair. "It was dynamite, I guess. They—they must've tossed it right up against the cabin. John and I were on the other side. We had about a second to get out, and—oh God! Poor Mr. McCabe and Angel! They never had a chance!"

Ki gripped her arms. "Angel's all right. She wasn't in the cabin, she was with me. Out there. In the barn."

Jessie stared and let out a breath. "Ki! Thank God for that! At least one of them's alive." Her face twisted in pain and she looked straight at him. "Ki, you'd better find her. Don't let her come up here alone."

Ki left Jessie with John and stalked from the burning ruin back to the barn. Angel saw him coming, cried out, and ran into his arms. Ki didn't have to tell her. The terrible, empty look in her eyes told him she already knew.

Chapter 5

They rode northwest for the pass just after first light, keeping the high ridge to the east at their backs. Anyone trailing them would have to get above them, and Hamilton figured it wouldn't be all that easy to get a horse over country like that. If they followed from below, they'd have to face bright sun for half a day.

"We won't hear from 'em again," Hamilton said darkly. "They aren't all that anxious to earn their pay. Besides, I figure it's just a *him* and not a *them*. If we saw three, that's likely how many there were."

"It didn't have a thing to do with that business at the railhead," Jessie said absently. "I thought for a while that was it, but it's not so, is it?"

"Hell no, it's not." Hamilton spurred his mount and made a face. "Those were hired guns, Jessie. We've got to figure it was Cavanaugh's boys. And if it was, that tells us a lot I'd just as soon I didn't know. The son of a bitch knows I came down to get you—wouldn't be a lot of trouble to find out. Gold dust and whiskey still gets mouths to flapping, no matter how careful you are." He paused and shook his head. "I think he's branded himself, Jessie. Maybe he got to that poor ol' Indian lady, hell, I don't know. But I'm betting he knows Jeb Baker tipped us off. Why else would he come in after us like that? Unless he figures we know him for a cartel man."

"I don't like the answer any more than you do," said Jessie. "But it makes sense, John."

"'Course, I could be way off track. Maybe Pierce Cavanaugh doesn't know a damn thing. He never needed much excuse to gun me down. Maybe it's just him and me."

"Huh-uh, that's not it, and you know it," Jessie said flatly. She looked past Hamilton and out over the valley. Clouds swept shadow up the hills and over the sawtooth ridges. "It's them,

34

all right. The Prussians and their friends. I don't *have* to see 'em. I can smell 'em already from here . . ."

They had buried Will McCabe under a cairn of ore trailings near the entrance to his mine. John Hamilton spoke a few words over the grave and then they headed out north for the pass.

Ki wished Angel would cry. After the first awful realization that her uncle was dead, she showed no emotion at all. Instead, she rummaged busily through the barn, gathering up enough worn-out work clothes, old boots, and horse blankets to outfit Hamilton and Jessie. Neither of the two had salvaged anything from the fire.

Not once, Ki noticed, did Angel even glance at the burned-out cabin. It was almost as if the place didn't exist. When he told her very gently it wasn't a good idea to stay on at the place alone, Angel didn't argue. John promised to send a man down to look things over. Jessie said she'd help any way Angel wanted, after she had a little time to think things over.

Ki sat with her in the wagon, his own mount trailing behind. Angel stared straight ahead as if he weren't even there.

"I'm not going to tell you everything's going to be all right," Ki said softly. "It will be, but that won't do you a lot of good now. Just do the best you can. It's going to hurt, and you might as well let it."

"Ki, I wish to hell it would," she said dully. "Trouble is, I don't feel a thing. Not anything at all."

"Well, that's natural enough."

"Is it?" She turned on him abruptly, her eyes sparking with anger. "It's *all* right if I can't even remember what he looks like? If all I—if all I can remember 'bout last night is lovin' you, feeling my skin all naked next to yours? My God, Ki!" Her face twisted in pain. "What kind of person am I to be thinkin' of something like that, when he's—"

"There's nothing wrong with what you're feeling," he said firmly. "You're covering up the bad with something good. That doesn't mean you don't care. It just means you care much more than you'll let yourself feel."

Angel didn't answer. After a while, Ki left her with her thoughts. Time, he knew, would do a lot more healing than talking would. He stayed by her side to guide the wagon over Lost Trail Pass, keeping the rig steady over the treacherous cut

35

through the Divide. He was too busy to enjoy the breathtaking scenery—pines so dark and rich a green they seemed nearly black, and bleak granite peaks that scraped all the color out of the sky.

They made camp early on the Bitterroot River, cold and exhausted from the trip. Half an hour after supper, an autumn storm swept out of the north, splitting the night with ragged forks of lightning and chilling rain. Ki held Angel close under blankets and heavy canvas beneath the wagon. She shivered against the cold, her slender form seeking out his warmth. Near the height of the storm, he heard her start to cry. He held her but said nothing. Finally, when her breathing found a soft and easy rhythm, he drifted into sleep.

In the morning she was gone.

She'd taken the mule and a bridle and a blanket. Ki searched around the circle of the camp, but the rain had pounded her tracks out of existence.

"I've got to find her," he told Jessie. "She can't just wander off alone out there!"

"Ki . . ." Jessie laid a hand on his arm. "You can bring her back, but you can't make her stay. Not if she's made up her mind."

"Made up her mind to do what?" Ki said darkly. "She doesn't *know* what she's doing right now!"

"Yes she does," Jessie told him. "She's doing what she thinks she has to do. She's gone home."

"There's nothing back there to go home to. Nothing."

"There is in her mind. Leave it that way, Ki. All right?"

Ki didn't answer. He stared into the bleak, chill morning, past rain dripping off heavy branches. After a while he pulled his jacket around his shoulders and went off to saddle the horses.

The town of Mule lay in a valley under steep, wooded hills shaped like the humps of a camel. Clark Fork meandered crookedly past the far edge of town. A few miles to the east was the Flathead River. To the west was Iron Mountain and the Bitterroot Range. Through a break in the pines, Jessie saw a cluster of mining structures perched precariously on the steep grade overlooking the town. Below were swaybacked cabins, a boardinghouse, and several saloons. The hillsides were raw

36

and eroded from years of digging. Everything was the color of soot and rust.

"Nice, huh?" Hamilton guessed her thoughts. "Take the Union Pacific and see the majestic West."

Jessie shrugged. "I've seen better and worse, I guess." She urged her mount off the trail and onto a muddy street. Two miners with dark beards stepped out of a cabin to watch her pass. "I'll settle right now for a half-clean room and a hot meal. I guess there's a store of some kind in town."

Hamilton nodded. "Nothing fancy, but we can get you some clothes." He pointed at the raw, two-story clapboard building just ahead. "That's Miz Ferguson's place. Bad-tempered old woman, but she keeps decent rooms and runs the cafe next door. We'll get you and Ki set up and walk over to Keller's store. It's up there past the livery. I rent a little office near Keller's—got a desk up front and a room and a bed out back. Comes in handy when I'm up this way, or when I send a man in on Starbuck business to— *Goddamn, look at that!*"

Hamilton jerked his mount in hard and sat up straight in the saddle. "Bastards!" His face went livid and his big hands curled into fists. "Son of a bitch burned me out—damn his sorry hide!"

"John—"

Hamilton didn't hear her. He swung out of the saddle, grabbed his Winchester, and slogged angrily through the mud. Jessie glanced at Ki, who nodded his understanding, passed his reins to Jessie, and slid to the ground. He caught up with Hamilton as he stomped through the charred ruins of the small building. The older man kicked out savagely at a thick piece of metal.

"Right there's my goddamn *bed*," he said darkly. He glanced past Ki, sniffed the air, and glared. "Smells a couple of days old. Likely put a torch to it soon's I got out of town."

"Cavanaugh, you think?"

"Hell yes, Cavanaugh. Cavanaugh's people, that is. Pierce doesn't dirty his hands with work like this." He paused, looked narrowly at Ki, then glanced at Jessie in the street. "You and Jessie figured I'd start a war or something, huh?"

"We wouldn't blame you if you did."

"You planning on helpin' me or stoppin' me? Shit, forget it. This isn't the time. Come on, looks like I need a room, and some clothes too."

Hamilton arranged for quarters at Mrs. Ferguson's, then led them down to Keller's store. Jessie bought several flannel shirts, a pair of leather gloves, a heavy lumberman's coat, and a flat-crowned Montana Stetson. After rummaging through the goods, she found two pair of denims small enough for her figure, and lace-up timber boots that almost fit. She also found a large, moth-eaten, second-hand carpetbag to carry it all. Ki purchased an extra pair of denims and a coat similar to Jessie's.

Hamilton seemed to know Keller well, and the two men grumbled at each other until the storekeeper came up with an English worsted suit that Hamilton figured was worth wearing—and big enough to fit his portly frame. A young boy totaled up the bill, while Hamilton retired to the back room with his friend. Jessie saw his face when he returned. His eyes were as cold as marble, his features set in anger. Jessie started to speak, but changed her mind.

Hamilton wouldn't open up until they'd changed at the boardinghouse and ordered food at the Bitterroot Cafe. When the platters of steak and eggs arrived at the table, he set down his coffee and glared.

"He's here," he said bluntly. "Right here in Mule, by God."

"Who's here?" asked Jessie.

"I think he means Cavanaugh," said Ki.

"Damn right I do." Hamilton glanced at his steak and shook his head. "Jessie, this isn't startin' out good at all. Cavanaugh wouldn't come up here personal if he wasn't up to something. It isn't his way."

Jessie picked up her knife. "John, we already *know* he's up to something. Why does it surprise you to find him here?"

"No, you're missin' the point." He brushed a hand impatiently through his hair. "You don't know the man. He's capable of anything, Jessie, but he keeps his hands clean. Likes to call all the big boys his friends. Puts on suppers for men like Horace Tabor in Denver; plays cards with Charlie Goodnight at that fancy new Cheyenne Club." He shook his head firmly. "Getting close to a place where he's stirring up trouble is out of character for Pierce. And I damn sure don't like it."

Jessie said nothing, but Ki could read the concern in John's eyes. "It's Jessie, isn't it?" he said shortly. "He's out in the open because of her."

38

"I don't know. Maybe." Hamilton backed off, then nodded stubbornly at his plate. "Yeah, all right. I can't say for certain, but I'd guess that's the answer." He looked squarely at Jessie, his broad features set in determination. "Damn it, I should've had more sense than to bring you up here at all. Once I knew Cavanaugh was involved . . ."

"Hey, wait a minute, now." Jessie put her fork aside. "I *am* here, and I'm not runnin' back to Texas, if that's what you're thinking. Cavanaugh's such a—a *gentleman,* John . . . if he's so particular about what people think, he won't likely shoot me down in the street."

"He didn't personally toss that dynamite that killed Mc-Cabe," Hamilton reminded her. "But Will McCabe's dead all the same, and you didn't miss joining him all that much."

"All right. You made your point. You got anything in mind?"

"Already got something started," Hamilton told her. "Keller over at the store's going to send one of his boys downriver a few miles to the nearest telegraph. Fort Missoula's 'bout fifty or so miles southeast. Tomorrow sometime, one of my poker-playing friends, Captain Douglass, will drop by Mule unexpected with half a troop of cavalry." Hamilton grinned. "That ought to keep Pierce Cavanaugh in line, and give us a little time to think."

"And you'd like me to do what? Sit in my room till then?"

"Yeah. I'd like that a lot."

"So would I," Ki added.

Jessie sighed and spread her hands. "All right. I have to admit that what you said makes sense. I just don't like hiding," she said shortly. Bright flecks of gold sparkled in her eyes, and Ki knew exactly what they meant. "Damn it all, John, I'm going to get to the bottom of Jeb's murder, and if Cavanaugh's mixed up in something bigger, I'm going to do what I have to to stop him. All right, it's a good idea to call in your friend. I'm certain Pierce Cavanaugh has plenty of his own people in town—and he's sure as hell got Mule's fine citizens well trained. But after tomorrow, then what? We can't keep our own personal cavalry troop on hand forever."

Hamilton sighed. "Damn it, Jessie Starbuck—with all due respect, let's get through tonight and tomorrow *first,* all right?"

Jessie laughed at the man's discomfort, leaned across the table, and squeezed his hand. "Fine, John. You're right as you

39

can be, and I'm sorry. I'm bitin' off more than I can chew, that's pretty clear. We'll hole up and regroup." She pushed her plate aside and forced a smile. "Anyway, that was a fine steak, and I just thought of somethin' you forgot. If Cavanaugh's so picky about keeping his hands clean, we shouldn't be complaining that he's here. Why, we're safe as we can be as long as he's in Mule."

Hamilton looked as if he'd tasted something sour. "Makes sense the way you put it. How come I don't feel any easier at all?"

Back on the street outside the cafe, Jessie saw that the skies were clouding up again. Ragged wisps of gray scraped the mountains and darkened the sky. The temperature had dropped ten degrees since they'd been inside.

"Be dark in an hour," said Hamilton. He sniffed the air and nodded. "Going to storm all night, looks to me."

"Fine," said Jessie. "Maybe Cavanaugh will keep his friends inside and we can get a little sleep."

"Maybe," Hamilton grunted. "Don't count on it, though." He shot Ki a cautious look. "I know you don't like firearms, son. But tonight'd be a damn good time to make an exception. I can loan you a pistol."

"Thanks," said Ki. "Tonight I think I'll take you up on the offer." He didn't want the weapon, but he knew Hamilton would rest easier if he had it. Under the circumstances, it couldn't hurt. He still had a handful of *shuriken* throwing stars that he'd retrieved from the fire. Other than these, everything else had been lost. A fine, tempered Japanese bow had been in a chamois wrapping lashed to his satchel. All he'd found of the weapon was a charred piece of wood. His *tanto* blade was somewhere in the ruins, but he'd been unable to find it. If trouble came, he'd make do with what he could find. Except for the bow, which couldn't be replaced outside of Japan, he could do without the rest. He still had his hands and feet, and for a samurai warrior, those were the most dangerous and reliable weapons of all.

By the time they reached the boardinghouse again, heavy droplets of rain had begun pelting the valley. From the shelter of the door, Ki glanced up the muddy street. Mule was nearly deserted. With the coming of the storm, the town had faded

40

to two colors: drab gray and somber black. Suddenly, lightning seared the sky, splitting a tall pine up the hill. The frame building shook as thunder rolled in over the mountains and the rain came down in force.

Hamilton left them at the top of the stairs and turned a corner to his room. Ki followed Jessie into her quarters and paced the floor. Jessie leaned against the door and folded her arms.

"Can't be too many gunmen in here," she said dryly. "This place isn't exactly a suite in the Windsor."

"You don't think Pierce Cavanaugh's a threat?"

"Of course I think he's a threat. I just don't think he's a threat tonight."

"Uh-huh. Well, keep your Colt handy," said Ki. "You've got it with you, haven't you?"

Jessie bit her lip. "I've got the derringer, Ki. I lost the Colt in the fire."

"Damn it, I'm sorry." The custom-made .38 on the .44-caliber frame had been a present from her father. It had been a fine-looking weapon, slate-gray, with peachwood grips. "You should have said something. I would have looked for it."

Jessie shrugged. "I looked all I could. We had other things to do." She forced a smile and kissed him lightly on the cheek. "Go on, get to bed. We could both use some sleep."

Ki nodded, left her, and waited till he heard the key turn in the lock. He locked his own room next to hers and took out the key. Lightning flashed and threw his shadow against the wall. He didn't bother to light the lamp. Pulling the blankets off the bed, he made himself a roll next to the wall. Jessie's bed was only inches away through the thin wall. He'd know if she needed any help.

He was tired, and sleep came quickly. Once he awoke and sat up for a moment. An unfamiliar sound had sifted through the light veil of sleep. He listened a moment, then pulled his blankets about him. Whatever it was, it didn't come again. He thought about Angel, wondering if he'd done the right thing by letting her go. That line of thought was too painful to follow.

He awoke at once to the urgent knock at his door. The rain had settled down to a lazy drizzle; the first patch of morning was dishwater-gray against the window.

"It's me," the voice said frantically through the door. "Keller,

41

from the store. For Christ's sake, open up!"

Ki threw open the door and took one look at the store-keeper's ashen face. "What is it?" he demanded. "What's wrong?"

"It's John Hamilton—" The words stuck in his throat. "And don't ask me what happened. Jesus, you're goin' to have to see that for yourself!"

Chapter 6

"Ma'am, this isn't anything a lady ought to see," said Keller. "If I was you, I'd wait back here."

"Thanks," Jessie told him. "You're probably right, but I don't think I can do that."

"Well, suit yourself." Keller shrugged, led them out of the boardinghouse and a few doors down the street, then cut back through an alley behind the livery. A muddy path wound up the hill above the town. Some thirty yards ahead, a cluster of lanterns winked dimly through the drizzle. Men stood in a tight circle, looking at something on the ground. They glanced up as Jessie and Ki approached, miners with paste-white flesh, eyes circled in weary shadow. The men nearest the path stepped aside to let them through.

It took a moment for Jessie to understand fully what she was seeing. Her eyes knew what was there, but her mind refused to put the pieces together. The colors were all wrong—reds too bright and whites a sickly blue; things glistened wetly on the ground, beaded with pearls of rain . . .

"Oh Christ, no!" The words strangled in Jessie's throat. Bile rose up in her throat, and Ki grabbed her to keep her from falling.

"All right," he told her firmly. "Come on, there's nothing more we can do."

She let him turn her away down the path. Closing her eyes didn't help. She could still see the horse cut nearly in half, the man's legs somehow still in the stirrups, his body no more than a grisly stump above the waist.

"What—what did they do to him?" she asked calmly. "I want to know, Ki. I want to know exactly what happened."

Keller, walking beside them, shot a questioning look at Ki.

"Go on," Ki said shortly. "Tell her."

"Miss Starbuck, they, uh . . . near as we can tell, they come and took John out of his room and brung him up here. Tied his hands behind him, and you can"—Keller cleared his throat— "you can see where they wired his feet in the stirrups. I reckon they just strapped a couple of sticks of dynamite 'round his waist and lit the fuse and slapped the horse off in a run. Likely happened with all that thunder goin' on, and no one heard the noise. Uh, ma'am, I'm sure it was real quick. Don't imagine John felt a thing."

"The hell he didn't!" Jessie turned on the man with a fierce and terrible anger. "You can bet they told him exactly what they were doing. Made him sit there helpless while they lit the fuse!"

Keller blinked and backed off. Jessie shook free of Ki's grip and faced the circle of miners. "I don't suppose any of you men have the slightest idea who did this, do you? I expect everyone was snug in his bed." The men looked down at the ground. Jessie cursed under her breath and turned away.

"I'm sorry," she told Keller. "I had no business turning on you. I know you were John's friend."

Keller shook his head. "No offense taken, miss. He was a real good man. I'll, uh, take care of ever'thing up here."

"Thank you. I appreciate that."

"Mr. Keller"—Ki looked over his shoulder to make certain none of the others could hear—"John told us at supper last night he'd asked you a favor. You were going to send your boy to get a telegraph message off to Fort Missoula."

Keller colored and clamped his jaw shut. "Yeah, he . . . did say somethin' 'bout that . . ."

"What?" Ki stared and grabbed his arm. "Damn it, man, you didn't do it, did you? You didn't send it!"

"I was going to," Keller protested. His head seemed to shrink into his shoulders. "Some of Cavanaugh's boys was . . . you know, hangin' around the store when John left. I was going to do it later."

"But you didn't," Ki said bluntly.

"No, I . . ." He glanced at Jessie and looked away. "All right, I got scared. My boy's only twelve, miss, an' he's all I got. If those bastards even thought I was helpin' John—"

"It's all right, Mr. Keller," Jessie said gently, "we can't hold you to blame. And I'm grateful for what you've done."

44

"I'm real sorry 'bout all this," Keller muttered. "I want you to know that." He jammed his hands in his pockets and hurried off down the hill.

Ki and Jessie made their way back to the boardinghouse. "Go up and get your things and mine," Ki said sharply. "I'll get the horses. We'll ride south and try to make Fort Missoula."

"Ki . . ." Jessie stopped and turned him around.

"No, Jessie." Ki's eyes narrowed to slits. "We're alone in this town, and no one's going to raise a finger to help us, don't you see that? They took Jeb Baker out and hanged him, and now they've murdered John. Whatever law they've got in Mule, Pierce Cavanaugh owns it. He's here in town, Jessie. And John Hamilton read him wrong. He's not worried about what his fancy friends think. He's out in the open now. If he'd kill John like that, he's not too concerned about how Jessie Starbuck disappears."

"Uh-huh. And I wonder why that is . . ."

"What?" Ki shook his head in dismay. "My God, Jessie, who *cares* why?"

"I do," she said, brushing rain off her cheek. "Pierce Cavanaugh's either desperate or real confident, Ki. He's up to something big here and doesn't want anyone to stand in his way. That's why he's breaking all his rules."

Ki said irritably, "We can figure out what he's up to when I get you safely out of Mule."

"Why? What for? If he wants to do me in, we'll just make it easier out on the trail. Once we get out of town—"

Ki turned and gripped her shoulders until she winced. "Jessie," he said firmly, "I have always done what you asked. My life is yours, I don't have to tell you that. This time, though, I will not obey you. I'm sorry. You will do what I say."

Jessie shook her head in alarm. "I know you're just trying to take care of me, but damn it, it doesn't make sense! If we ride out of town, he'll kill us for certain!"

"Go on," Ki said angrily. "Get your things and meet me in front of the boardinghouse!" He turned and stalked away down the hill before she could read the message in his eyes. Another moment, he knew, and she would see it. They knew each other well, and she'd see it plainly and know exactly what he was doing. They'd kill her in town, and he wouldn't be able to stop them. On the trail, though, he could even up the odds—delay them, lead them away from her, and kill them quickly without a sound, leaving enough of them dead to give her a chance to get away. He couldn't let her see that until it was time. If she knew he was going to die to let her live, she'd never allow it. She'd stand by his side and fight it out. And that wasn't the way he wanted it.

He saw them out of the corner of his eye, knew who they were before he even got close to the livery. There were two of them, leaning against the stable as if they stood there every day. One was heavyset and older than the other, wearing a worn black suit and a shirt buttoned up to the neck. His face was like dough that hadn't risen right—small holes bored through puffy flesh for eyes, a crooked seam of a mouth. The other man was young, lean to the point of emaciation. A shapeless black overcoat hung from his frame like a tent. His slack features were hidden under a grease-stained hat. Both men wore tarnished town constables' stars. The big man carried a pistol; his friend didn't seem to be armed, but Ki wasn't convinced of that yet.

He ignored the pair completely, pretending he hadn't seen them. Inside the damp stable, he paid off the boy and had him saddle up the horses. Before he walked the mounts outside, he opened his jacket and tucked Hamilton's pistol farther back along his waist. Nodding to the boy, he took the reins and walked his horses into the muddy street.

"Hold on a minute, mister."

Ki stopped and looked curiously at the lawman. "Are you talking to me?"

The man grinned, raising pads of fat on his cheeks. "Shit, you see anyone else on the street?"

"I'm listening," Ki said plainly. "What do you want?"

The young man snickered. The big man quieted him with a look. Ki let his eyes flick over the pair again. The fat man carried a Schofield Smith & Wesson in a California holster. His friend had something under the bulky coat. Ki wasn't certain what it was, but it was there.

"Nothin' serious," the lawman assured him. "Just like to know who's in town, what kinda business they got in Mule."

"I don't have any business here," Ki said bluntly. "I'm leaving town right now."

"Well now, don't hurry off," the big man drawled. "Not

46

'fore we get a chance to talk."

"Fine." Ki stood his ground. "What would you gentlemen like to talk about?"

The lawman scratched his jaw. "Seems kind of peculiar, you and the lady leavin' town 'fore your friend's buried proper."

Ki swallowed his anger. The bastard was sure of himself and wanted Ki to know it. He was saying John's murder was no concern of the law in Mule.

"Is that all you wanted to say? Is it all right with you if I move along?"

"Oh, well, sure." The lawman shot him an easy grin. "Don't see why not."

Ki nodded and turned away.

The slender man moved, whipping his overcoat aside—and the twin barrels of a sawed-off shotgun came up fast to cut Ki in half . . .

Ki, though, was no longer a target. Their eyes, the flesh around their mouths, the way they moved, told him what they meant to do. They were too lazy to take him the other way. A shot in the back was quicker and safer.

Dropping his reins, Ki twisted on his feet, grabbed the big man's collar and pulled him to him, turned him roughly around, and squeezed the beefy neck in the crook of his arm. The man cried out and clawed for the Smith & Wesson. Ki kneed him in the back and the fleshy arms jerked up in pain.

"Go on," Ki warned the man with the shotgun. "Your friend will die, and I promise you you'll never fire your second shot."

The man's jaw fell. "Karl—what you want me t'do?"

"I want you to drop the fuckin' shotgun, Sam'l!" the big man choked. "Drop it, damn you!"

"No, don't drop it, Samuel," Ki said. "Just turn the stock around easy and give it to me."

Samuel did as he was told. Ki took the weapon, loosened his grip on the big man's throat, and pressed the barrel against his neck.

"J-Jesus, mister, be careful with that!"

"Oh, I'm always careful," Ki said. With his free hand he eased the pistol from the constable's holster and dropped it in the mud. "Now, Samuel, suppose you pick up those reins and bring the horses along. If you still want to try something, I'll save a shell for you, after I take off the top of Karl's head."

47

"Not goin' to do a thing," Samuel said tightly. "Not a thing, mister!"

"Good. Just keep walking down the street."

"You aren't going to get out of town," Karl growled. "Shit, mister, he won't let you do that."

"Now just which *he* are you talking about, constable?"

"Uh, no one." Karl caught himself and shook his head quickly. "Didn't say a damn thing."

Ki walked sideways, keeping as close to the buildings as he could, one eye on the street at his back. Two men came out of a building across the street, saw what was happening, and stopped to watch. A small crowd was gathering on the corner by the saloon. Ki recognized Keller and some of the miners who'd been with him up on the hill. The rain came down in a fine mist, veiling the drab structures across the road. The men on the corner stepped in the street to give Ki room. He watched them closely. He hadn't forgotten there were men in Mule who'd been glad to hang Jeb Baker, once Cavanaugh's friends had put the notion in their heads.

He passed the corner and let out a breath. Jessie was waiting on the boardinghouse porch. No one bothered her, or even looked in her direction. She saw him then, and started toward him. Ki shook his head and she stopped.

"You ain't going to make it, boy," the lawman said calmly. "It isn't going to happen."

"Then I'd start worrying if I were you," Ki snapped. "If I even feel you breathing too hard—" Ki's head jerked around as the three men appeared out of an alley across the street. He knew who they were without asking. They were tall, broad-shouldered men who moved with an easy gait. Two wore dark English suits and bowler hats. The third, a bareheaded man with sandy hair, wore pale riding breeches, knee-length boots, and a brushed-leather coat. They wore their tailored clothing well, and clearly didn't belong in a godforsaken place like Mule.

"Now that's what I was saying," the constable told Ki. "Them three don't give a shit if you blow my head off twice. Long as they get you too."

"Shut up," said Ki. He jammed the twin barrels in the man's neck. "You, Samuel—get up close and give me those reins."

Samuel obeyed without a sound. Across the street, one of

48

the men in the bowler hats leaned in to speak to the man in riding clothes. The man nodded, stepped out where Ki could see him plainly, and opened his jacket wide. Moving slowly, he pulled out a silver-plated Webley revolver. He grinned crookedly at Ki, raised the pistol in both hands, and leveled it at Jessie's head.

"No, *don't!*" Ki's heart stopped.

"Up to you, friend," the man called out.

Ki let out a breath, stepped back with a curse, and handed the shotgun to Karl.

"What did I tell you, son?" The man shook his head as if he were sorry for Ki's bad luck.

Something moved at the edge of Ki's vision. He tried to duck, but the blow plunged him painlessly down into darkness . . .

Jessie didn't move.

It took all the strength she could muster to watch them haul Ki unconscious down the street, head and shoulders dragging in the mud.

If they're waiting for a woman to start screaming and tearing her hair, they're by-God not going to get it!

The curious miners and townfolk drifted away, disappointed the show was over. The man across the street slipped the Webley in his jacket and picked his way toward her through the mud. His two friends waited, paying no attention to Jessie now. The sandy-haired man stopped a few feet away.

"Miss Starbuck," he said plainly, "Mr. Pierce Cavanaugh would like you to drop by and see him. He's in the last cabin out of town. I'll send a rig over to pick you up."

"I'll walk," Jessie said flatly. Her green eyes turned the man to ice.

"Fine. Suit yourself." The man turned and walked back across the street. Jessie took her satchel and Ki's back up the boardinghouse steps and left them in the inside hall. Mrs. Ferguson popped out of her room, sniffed the air, and looked Jessie over.

"Ain't going to be no problems, is there?" she demanded. "Don't want any trouble in my place, young woman."

Jessie stuck a finger in the old lady's face. "You even talk to me about trouble, I'll burn this sorry place to the ground.

49

You got that, ma'am?" Mrs. Ferguson's eyes went wide. She brought a hand to her face and retreated quickly to her room.

Jessie paused only an instant in the hall. Slipping the ivory-handled derringer from the waistband of her jeans, she checked the twin loads and dropped it in the pocket of her jacket. Back outside, she headed north, keeping her head low and into the wind. The rain had tapered off, but the wind was chill and wet. For some reason she couldn't imagine, a plank sidewalk started two blocks down the west side of the street. There were no other walks in town. Jessie shrugged and crossed over. As she bent to scrape her boots, voices up the street caught her attention. She straightened and saw a flatbed wagon drawn by two weary mules. As the wagon passed, men went silent and backed off. In a moment, Jessie saw why. There were three stiff bodies in the wagon, each wrapped tightly in canvas.

Keller came up behind her. "What is it?" she asked. "What's happened, do you know?"

Keller shook his head. "I got an idea, but I hope to hell I'm wrong. Word came down from the north last week there was cholera in some of the camps. Looks like maybe they was right."

"Cholera?" Jessie's eyes went wide. "Are you certain?"

"Sure as I want to be. Doctor I know up at Lew's Gulch come by on Thursday. Said he'd seen a couple of men 'fore they put 'em in the ground. Said it was cholera, for sure."

Jessie took off her hat and brushed fiery hair off her shoulder. "I'm sure John didn't know. If he had, he would have said something about it."

Keller looked away. *"I* sure didn't tell him," he said testily. "Or anyone else, Miss Starbuck. Isn't the kind of story you want to spread around unless you're sure." He paused and looked up the street. "I'm sorry 'bout your friend. He isn't hurt any. I checked at the jail. You're uh, headed up to see Cavanaugh, aren't you?"

"Yes, I am." Jessie raised a brow. "News sure travels fast in this town."

Keller glanced over his shoulder. "Be careful," he said quickly. "The man's a goddamn snake." Leaving Jessie with a nod, he hurried across the street to his store.

The cabin was easy to find. It was two stories high, solidly built, and nestled in a grove of dark pines. Smoke curled out of the chimney and disappeared in heavy branches. Neatly fashioned split-log steps led up the steep hill to a broad front porch. A dozen pairs of weather-bleached antlers were mounted on the outside wall.

The man in riding clothes opened the door the moment she stepped on the porch. "Come in, Miss Starbuck," he said politely. "Mr. Cavanaugh's waiting. Mind if I take your coat?"

"I'll keep it," snapped Jessie.

"Please." He shook his head and stopped her. "Afraid I'll have to insist."

"Now look, damn it!" Jessie's green eyes flashed. The man didn't move. She peeled off the coat and threw it in his direction. He ran his hands expertly over the fabric, found the bulge of the derringer, and gave her a lazy smile.

"You try pattin' *me* down like that," Jessie warned him, "you're going to have yourself a problem."

"Won't be necessary," he said calmly. "This way, please."

Jessie followed him through the narrow entry into a big, sprawling parlor. The room was well furnished and neatly kept. Bear rugs and Indian blankets covered polished pine floors. Several good paintings adorned the wall. Heavy sofas and chairs in plush red velvet were arranged in a semicircle about a crackling fire. Jessie wondered idly who owned the cabin and its fixtures. It was certainly out of place in Mule. Likely a mine owner, she decided—a friend of Cavanaugh's, or someone in his pocket.

Jessie glanced around, suddenly aware the man had left her. She resisted the urge to back her bottom up to the fire and get it warm.

"Be damned if I'll make myself at home," she muttered aloud. "Wouldn't give the bastard the satisfaction."

"You talk to yourself. That's *funny!*"

Jessie turned, startled, and saw the girl curled up in a chair by the fire. She hadn't made a sound, and the chair's high wings had masked her presence.

"I'm sorry," said Jessie, "I didn't see you there."

"That's all right." The girl smiled and blinked enormous china-blue eyes. "No one ever does. I'm Marcie. Who're you?"

"Jessie. Jessie Starbuck, Marcie."

"You're sure pretty," said the girl. "'Bout the prettiest lady I ever saw."

"Well, uh, thanks. You're very pretty yourself, you know."

Marcie giggled and bit her lip. "Guess we're *both* pretty, then." She stretched languorously, for an instant baring a firm little breast tipped a dusky shade of pink. Jessie knew the act was deliberate. The girl was young, almost a child, but there was nothing childish about the way she controlled her body. Her skin was pale, so delicate and translucent that Jessie could follow the fine blue tracery of veins down her throat to the swell of her breasts. Wheat-colored hair, curled in tight little ringlets, framed doll-like eyes, a turned-up nose, and a wide, sensuous mouth. The dark blue gown was much too large for her slender figure; much too rich and elaborate for any occasion short of a full-dress ball. It struck Jessie with a chill that she was a little girl playing grown-up, and that the game had somehow gotten out of hand.

"You here to talk to Pierce?" Marcie asked. "He's 'round somewhere. I'll get him if you want."

"No, that's all right. I'll wait, Marcie." *He knows I'm here,* she told herself. *Leaving me with Marcie, letting me see what she is and who she belongs to is part of the act.*

"I can get you something to drink," Marcie suggested. "How 'bout that? You like brandy? *I* do. I can get us some of that."

"No, I'm fine."

"Well, then . . ." Marcie sprang out of her chair. "I'll just have some myself, if it's all the same with you." She danced in a little circle, full skirts billowing about willowy white legs. Jessie saw that her tiny feet were bare. She stopped at a heavy wooden cabinet, opened the door, and poured herself a full snifter of brandy from a cut-glass decanter. Grinning at Jessie, she brought the glass to her lips. Amber liquid curled down the corner of her mouth onto her breasts. Marcie giggled, touched a finger to her flesh, and brought the droplet to her tongue. Suddenly her eyes went wide and she froze, her finger to her lips. Jessie turned and saw the man standing behind her.

"We are not supposed to have refreshments unless we're asked," he said smoothly. "Are we now, Marcie?"

"I . . . forgot, Pierce." Marcie's voice was tight with fear. "I sure won't do it again."

"Fine, fine. Now sit down and be still, honey." The man smiled and looked at Jessie. "I'm Pierce Cavanaugh, Miss Starbuck. I hope Marcie's kept you company."

"We got along just fine," said Jessie.

"Good, good. Let's talk some, shall we?"

Jessie couldn't take her eyes off the man crossing the room. He was a tall, elegantly handsome man in his forties, with a full head of raven-black hair. The sharp planes of his face were lightly tanned, his features open and honest. The deepset brown eyes were warm and friendly, and his mouth seemed to curl in a natural smile. For a moment Jessie caught herself relaxing in his presence. She swallowed hard and shook her head in disbelief. Lord, for an instant she'd forgotten what he was and what he'd done, forgotten the real terror in Marcie's eyes!

"I'm sorry you've had some . . . problems since you've been in town," he said evenly. "Maybe there's some way I can help."

"Wh-what?" Jessie shook her head in annoyance. "Mr. Cavanaugh," she said coldly, "save your manners for someone else. I'm not interested in playing games. It's a waste of your time and damned insulting to me. Two good men have been murdered in the last couple of days. A friend of mine's in jail, and I've got a good idea he's going to have some kind of accident real soon. I think maybe you could talk that constable into letting him go before that happens. Maybe you'd do that and maybe you wouldn't. I don't know—might be *I'm* due for one of those accidents before Ki. That's what I'm asking you straight out. If we can bargain, give me some terms and I'll try to meet 'em."

Cavanaugh almost smiled. He dropped his arm casually over the back of the sofa. His fingers brushed Marcie's bare shoulder, and the girl went rigid. "You come right to the point, don't you? Good qualities in business. From what I understand, you've done well with your father's interests."

Jessie stuck out her jaw in defiance. "Come on, mister. Can we work this out or not?"

Cavanaugh looked at her without expression. "Suppose you and Marcie here spent an afternoon together on that bear rug before the fire. Would you agree to terms like that?"

Jessie's stomach turned over, but she held his eyes without flinching. "If—if that's what you want, then yes. I would." She didn't dare look at Marcie. "What kind of guarantees do I get that Ki and I go free?"

Something cold and dark flickered in Cavanaugh's eyes. It was there for an instant, then gone, the benign and friendly manner in its place. "You're assuming too much, Miss Star-

53

buck. We weren't bargaining for both you and the Oriental. This is just for him. We'll have to think of something else for you."

"Damn you, I—"

Cavanaugh smiled wanly and waved her off. "Be sensible, Miss Starbuck. Please. If I wanted you for something like that, why, I'd simply have you do it. I don't have to bargain, now do I?" He stood and shook his head. "You're in no position to make deals. I didn't ask you here for that. I simply wanted to tell you I do not wish you to interfere in my affairs. Go back where you came from and do whatever you like. But I don't want Starbuck doing business here. Montana Territory is closed. All I want from you is your absence. Get out of Mule, ride south, and keep going. That's the deal I'm making, and the only one I'll offer. That's fair now, isn't it?"

Jessie shot him a narrow look. "And Ki. He comes with me."

Cavanaugh shook his head. "He goes, but not with you. He leaves after I'm certain you're out of my hair." He caught Jessie's disbelief and smiled. "Please. I have no interest in the Japanese, Miss Starbuck. I just want you gone. Leave, and your friend will be just fine."

Again there was that open, winning smile, the deep brown eyes that said she could trust Pierce Cavanaugh with her life.

"All right." Jessie stood and faced him. "Agreed." She forced a smile while her heart hammered dangerously in her breast. "I'll do as you ask. You don't mind if I buy a few supplies for the trip?"

"I don't really care what you do," he said gently. He nodded his dismissal. "Good*bye*, Miss Starbuck."

Jessie turned away and walked across the room. She didn't bother saying goodbye to Marcie. The man in the riding boots was waiting in the entry. He handed her the coat and moved to open the outside door. Jessie grabbed the jacket and swept past him. She walked down the split-log steps and started back to town. It was all she could do to keep from breaking into a run.

She stopped at the livery and got her horse. The constable had returned the two mounts after hauling Ki off. She left the animal in front of Keller's store, looped the reins around a rail, and stepped inside. Keller looked up and blinked, clearly surprised to see her.

"I want some traveling supplies," Jessie told him . "A canteen, some flour, bacon, and beans. Pans to go with all that, and some coffee and a pot. Anything else you can think of." John Hamilton had brought those items with them on the trek up north, but she had no idea where they were and didn't care. The buying was all for show, and she didn't give a damn what she got.

"I want something else too," she announced, leaning toward him over the counter. "I want a weapon and some shells. Preferably a Colt."

Keller looked nervously at his hands. "I, uh . . . that wouldn't be a good idea, Miss Starbuck."

"For who?" Jessie snapped. "You or me, Mr. Keller?"

Keller turned red. "Look now, I'd do anything I could," he said miserably. "I got to live here, miss."

"You have my sympathies," Jessie said tightly. "Forget it. Just dump that stuff in a canvas bag." She dug a double eagle out of her denims and slapped it on the counter. Without glancing at Keller again, she threw the sack over her shoulder and stepped outside. Tossing her purchases over the saddle, she mounted up and rode back to the boardinghouse. Bounding up the steps, she found her satchel and Ki's where she'd left them. Mrs. Ferguson came quickly out of her room and took a stance in the middle of the hall, arms folded across her bony frame.

"I'm sorry," she said stiffly, "I'm goin' to have to ask you to leave the premises, miss. I can't have folks 'round here who—*awwwwk!*" the old lady backed off in horror. "Get your hands off me! What are you *doing!*"

Jessie dragged the lady, kicking and flailing her arms, back into her quarters and set her roughly down in a chair.

"Now," she said calmly, "you're going to get your wish in about a minute, lady. First, though, we're going to talk about weapons. You got anything on the premises? A pistol, a Winchester, I don't much give a damn."

The old woman's eyes got wide. "I—I—I wouldn't know what you're talking about," she said primly. "I'm a respectable widder lady an' I run a decent place. And I do *not* hold with firearms of any kind."

"Fine." Jessie searched quickly about, found a long shawl, and began binding the woman's hands to her chair. "I'll just have to tear this place apart and make sure. I'm not too neat, but I'll do the best I can."

"Oh Lord God!" the woman moaned, "it's—it's in the closet there. Take it. Don't kill me, please!"

"Nobody's killing anyone," Jessie said wearily. She walked to the closet and pushed the curtain aside. A twelve-gauge, double-barreled Parker breech-loader stood against the wall. Beside it was a fair-sized bag of shells. Jessie picked up the gun and the shells, tossed them on a table, and stalked back to the wide-eyed woman in the chair.

"Wh-what are you going to do?" she asked, staring fearfully at Jessie. Jessie didn't answer. Instead she went to the old lady's bed, tossed a pillow out of its case, and wrapped it around the woman's mouth.

"Someone'll let you loose," Jessie told her. "I'm sorry about this—I don't usually go around abusing old ladies. But I don't trust you, ma'am, or anyone else in this town. I keep wondering how they got John Hamilton out of his bed and out of this house without you helping."

She looked at Miss Ferguson and shook her head, then gathered up the gun and the shells and shut the hall door behind her. She didn't much blame the woman or anyone else in Mule for running scared. But when in hell was the town going to stand up on its hind legs and bark back?

Chapter 7

Jessie walked hurriedly out of the boardinghouse to her horse, stumbling to make her efforts appear clumsy. It wasn't all that hard with the load she had to carry. The carpetbag she'd bought at Keller's when she'd first arrived in Mule was tucked under one arm, along with a roll of blankets. Over her other shoulder she carried the unwieldy sack of supplies she'd just purchased. She didn't see Cavanaugh's men but she knew they were there. She hoped that what they'd see was a woman so eager to escape with her life that she wouldn't take time to make a proper riding pack. Maybe they'd grin, watching her tie the carpetbag and the blankets on wrong, then loop the canvas sack on the saddlehorn. Jessie prayed that was exactly what they'd see, that they'd miss the shotgun broken at the breech and jammed awkwardly into the sack.

Mounting up, she pulled the horse around and spurred it south. A few moments later she was out of Mule, following the freighters' trail that had brought her into town. She kept to the road ten minutes, then kicked the horse up the slope and disappeared into the trees. They'd be waiting farther down, far enough out of town to make certain none of the townsfolk saw them take her, deep enough in the wilds to keep her grave from being found.

Christ, does Cavanaugh think I'm enough of a fool that I'd believe he'd let me go? That Ki has a chance in hell of going free?

Jessie lowered her head and drove the horse uphill, ignoring the wet branches that whipped and stung her legs. At the top she paused and searched the way ahead, then turned the mount back north, keeping to the thick tangle of brush that marked the ridge. A mile farther on, the cover began to thin. Jessie reined in and leaned forward in the saddle. Mule lay in the valley down the slope. She could make out the backs of the livery, the boardinghouse, and the cafe. Down the street a ways was the jail. Three horses were stabled in a makeshift corral out back. A thin plume of smoke curled up from a tin chimney. Jessie dismounted, set her carpetbag and blankets in the crook of a tree, and laid the canvas sack on the ground. She retrieved the twelve-gauge Parker, loaded it and snapped it shut, then filled her pockets with shells.

Nighttime would be a lot better; someone was bound to see her riding down the slope. Ki, though, would surely have an "accident" long before dark. And Cavanaugh's men were likely wondering where she was already.

"The hell with it," she sighed. "It happens right now or it doesn't happen at all." Mounting up again, she urged the horse down the slippery ridge. A gully and scattered scrub partially hid her halfway down, but the last leg was right out in the open. She hoped that if anyone saw her, they'd take her for just another rider hunched down against the drizzle.

She guessed it was after noon, but there was no way to tell from the sky. At the back of the jail, she looped her reins over a rail, swung out of the saddle, and slogged through mud to the back door. Turning the knob slowly, she found that it wasn't locked. Breathing a sigh of relief, she pushed it open quickly and stepped inside.

The two town constables were playing cards. A third man stood gazing out the front window at the street. Jessie recognized him from his fancy black suit and black bowler. He was one of Cavanaugh's men who'd been present when they'd hauled Ki away.

All three men looked up at once. The stocky lawman with the doughy face was halfway out of his chair, his right hand snaking up his leg.

"Don't," Jessie said sharply, bringing the Parker up to her shoulder. "That'd be real dumb, now wouldn't it?"

The lawman froze and eased himself down, resting chubby hands on the table. "You use that and you'll have the whole town in here, lady."

"That's right." Jessie shot him a smile. "It's a shame you won't be here to see it. Now, real easy, mister . . ." She pointed the shotgun toward his head. "Stand up and let your gunbelt

58

loose. The rest of you just practice slow breathing."

"She can only get two of us, Karl," the smaller lawman blurted.

"Shut up, you goddamn fool," snapped Karl. The man in the bowler hat laughed. When Karl's belt clattered to the floor, Jessie motioned the other man to stand. He eased the short-barreled Colt out of his belt and laid it gently on the floor. Jessie turned to the man in the bowler. He shook his head and shrugged.

"Sorry, I'm not armed," he said with a smile. "I'm just a businessman, Miss Starbuck. I never carry a weapon."

Jessie's green eyes flashed. "I'll give you three seconds," she said soberly. "Then I swear to God I'll kill you."

The man's eyes went wide. "Now look . . ."

"One . . ."

"All right, damn it!" His smile went slack and he carefully opened his coat.

"Well now," Jessie said evenly, "just what kind of 'business' are you in, mister?"

The man clamped his jaw shut. Under his arm was a half-pouch leather shoulder holster. Nestled inside was a silver-plated Smith & Wesson .38. He unfastened the rig, slipped the coat off his shoulders, and let the garment and the weapon fall to the floor.

"Fine," said Jessie, turning her full attention back to the lawman. "Now let's go and see about your prisoner." A door led down to a short hall to the jail's two cells. Ki stood up from his cot and grinned.

"Must be visiting hours," he said. "Nice of you to come by, Jessie."

"Yes, isn't it?"

Karl opened the cell door and Ki pulled the three roughly inside. The big man resisted, and Ki slammed him against the wall hard enough to force air out of his lungs. "Don't tempt me," he said harshly. "I remember what I owe you, friend. All of you, get out of your clothes. Strip down. Do it!"

The gaunt little constable blinked in horror. "W-with *her* watching?"

Jessie laughed. "Haven't had breakfast, or I would. Don't think I could take it on an empty stomach." She turned and walked back to the small office and gathered up the scattered weapons. In a moment Ki joined her with a bundle of clothes and boots.

"They're tied and gagged," he reported. "I'll drop the rest of this stuff outside. If they want to follow, they can do it naked."

Jessie glanced out the front window. A freightwagon was slogging up the street; no one else was out in the weather. Stuffing her collection of weapons in the constable's saddlebag, she gathered up two Winchesters and a box of shells. Ki carefully opened the back door. Jessie threw one of the rifles in the mud and kept the other. Ki chose a dun-colored gelding from the railing and followed Jessie back up the hill.

"Have you figured out where to go?" Ki asked her.

"Uh-huh. Any way but south. Pierce Cavanaugh's got some boys waiting for me down the road. Most likely they're headed back this way by now." Kicking her mount, she urged it up the hill, pushing the animal until it reached the shelter of the trees. Collecting the goods she'd left behind, she passed on a few essential items to Ki and left the rest.

"I put a pair of your trousers and a shirt in my stuff," she told Ki. "Sorry I couldn't take more, but I didn't want 'em seeing me take your bag too."

Ki nodded and waved her off. Jessie glanced back down at the town. "To answer your question," she said, "I haven't the slightest idea where to go. We'd never make Fort Missoula. That's out. Best thing to do is lose ourselves fast, and worry about where later." She gestured over her shoulder. "Northeast, maybe. Up toward the Mission Mountains. It'll be rough going, but not any easier for them than it is for us."

Ki frowned. "If I remember, the Flathead reservation's up there. We're not all that far from it now."

"Good," Jessie said firmly. "I'd rather argue with Indians than with Pierce Cavanaugh."

They headed down the far side of the ridge, circling north and then east to give Mule a wide berth. Back on level ground at the head of the valley, they quickened their pace, crossing the other end of the freighters' road and riding hard northeast.

Ki heard them first—horses crossing a shallow stream far to their right. Gesturing quickly to Jessie, he led them due north toward a high ridge of granite that thrust out of the trees like naked bone.

60

"Either they outguessed us," he said shortly, "or they sent two parties." He silently cursed the wet earth that left their trail clear enough for a greenhorn to follow. "If we can make it to that ridge, we can stop and try to slow them down."

"'We,'" Jessie said firmly. "That's the right word. Not 'you.'"

Ki shot her a curious frown.

"Look, friend," Jessie said gently, "I know what you had in mind last time we tried to leave Mule—you slow 'em up and *I* run. I just wanted to get it clear that's not the way it's going to be. I won't even—"

"You're the stubbornest woman I ever saw," Ki said irritably. "Come on, let's get out of here."

They waited another moment, then guided their mounts down the side of a rocky draw. Long ago the depression had been the bed of a shallow river. Brush covered the draw, but past that, the gravelly surface was bare clear to the ridge, a good two hundred yards in the open.

"They'll be coming through that grove where we stopped," Ki told her. "They'll spot our tracks and know what we're doing. Let's move on before they think of sending flankers to cut us off."

Jessie nodded, heeled her horse, and scattered rock as she bolted from cover. Ki followed, glancing once over his shoulder, then bending to the saddle. The two hundred yards seemed a hundred miles. Wind whistled about Jessie's ears. Her mount's hooves clattered against the loose, treacherous rock, and the animal snorted harshly as the way ahead grew steeper.

The first shot whined off to her left, scattering shards of granite. Ki shouted a warning and Jessie veered sharply to the right. Now rifle fire cracked all about her. She crouched over the horse's neck and kept going, fighting to keep the frightened beast from tossing her off. She gripped the reins tightly in her fists, cursed the animal aloud, and made it take the low spine of rock at the top of the ridge. The horse whinnied in protest, took the jump, and nearly fell. Jessie swung out of the saddle, grabbed the Winchester, and crouched undercover to the edge of the ridge. Levering in a shell, she loosed a volley at the gunmen below. Ki's horse leaped the spire to her left. She heard him cry out, and then he was tumbling out of the saddle to the hard rock floor.

"Ki!" Jessie dropped her rifle and ran to him. Blood covered the side of his head, and she thought he was gone. He groaned once, tried to get up, and sank back to the earth. Jessie wiped blood away and saw that the bullet had grazed bone just above his right ear. She found a bandanna in his pocket, wound it around his head, and scrambled back for the rifle.

Just take it easy, she told herself calmly. *They've got to come out in the open to get up here, the same as we did.*

She quickly circled the granite spire, popping up now and then to deliberately draw fire and get a count. The top of the outcropping was five yards square at the most. Men could ride or climb three sides, but not without crossing bare ground and climbing a twenty-degree slope. She could cover one side with little trouble—but certainly not all three.

The rear of the spire was something else. It was a bridge to higher ground, well covered by rocks and stunted pine. It led off to safety, to thick forested slopes and knifelike ridges. All she had to do was get there, and Cavanaugh's men would play hell trying to catch her. Even if they tried to cut her off, to circle around and take her, they'd be hours getting to it. She could cross the natural bridge and be gone in three minutes. Right. Just lift Ki unconscious onto his horse, heft his dead weight into the saddle, and lead him across . . .

Sounds from below cut off her thoughts. Moving quickly to the rim, she peeked through a crack in the stone. Her heart nearly stopped at the sight. Three men were running a zigzag pattern up the hill. Another few seconds and they'd have been right in her lap!

Jessie took a deep breath, held it, and let it out slowly. The vee of her sight found the first man's shoulders. The Winchester fired and the gunman went down. Covering fire found her, but Jessie didn't move. Calmly holding her position, she followed the two retreating figures downhill. One took cover, and she squeezed off a shot at the second. Ricocheting lead dusted his heels. Her second shot caught him in the thigh and sent him rolling awkwardly over rock. Jessie rolled on her back, inched a few yards to her right, and studied the hill below. Nothing. No one was trying the other slope. A grin tugged at her lips, but the thought of what had happened sobered her quickly. They knew, now, that she was alone atop the spire, that Ki was dead or hurt and they only had to deal with her. They could concentrate their fire and keep her down; she'd get a few, but she wouldn't stop them.

Grasping the rifle in her fist, she made her way back to Ki. The blood had stopped, and his breathing was slow and steady.

"Come *on*, damn it," she said tightly. "Ki, for Christ's sake, wake up!" She put her hands under his shoulders and tried to lift him, knowing already that it was hopeless. Somehow she had to get him on a horse and over the bridge. If she had a rope, a strong leather cord, anything, she could tie it to his shoulders and use her horse to haul him into the saddle. Maybe she could—

"Looks to me like you gone and squirreled yourself right off the top of your tree, 'thout leavin' yourself nowhere to jump."

"*What!*" Jessie spun around and stared. The man leaned both arms on the long barrel of his Sharps. He towered over her not six feet away, a tall, angular man in dark buckskins and a worn leather cap.

"My God," Jessie breathed, "where did *you* come from?"

"My ol' mama, I reckon. Same as you." A grin creased his bearded face. "I'm Joseph Glass, an' I 'spect you'd be Jessie. That first shot of yours wasn't half bad for close up, you bein' a woman and all. You any good at far off?"

Jessie shook her head in wonder. It seemed like a hell of a time to discuss her marksmanship.

"Look, how do you know my name?" she demanded. "Who are you? You just suddenly appear out of nowhere, like a—"

"Might be we ought to move out an' talk later," the man drawled. He walked over and squatted next to Ki, quickly studied his wound, then picked him up easily and laid him gently over the saddle. "Mount up and take your friend's reins," he told Jessie. "I'm going to have me a look."

Jessie nodded, swung into the saddle, and brought her horse close to Ki's. The man named Glass made a circuit of the spire and walked back to the horses.

"They're talkin' it over. Couple more minutes, they'll be a-comin'." He mounted up and turned toward the rear of the rocky knoll, the natural bridge that would lead them onto the steep, wooded slopes. "Just keep to the middle like me," he said without turning around. "They can't see nothin' from down there."

63

The bridge was less than twenty feet wide, covered on both sides with a tangle of brush and stunted pines. Jessie followed Glass, keeping her own mount and Ki's in the man's path. The slope on either side dropped off abruptly for a good two hundred feet. She was glad that thick cover masked the edge, and she instinctively pressed her legs into the saddle and kept one eye on Ki.

They were well over the bridge and into the cover of tall trees when a volley of angry shots sounded behind them. Glass raised his hand for Jessie to stop. Slipping off his mount to the forest floor, he stood and listened. The shots came again, and this time she could hear men shouting.

"One bunch is comin' up the easy side on horseback," he said, almost to himself. "Same as you did. Others are on foot, climbin' up from the west." His pale blue eyes looked past her. "I spotted 'bout eight altogether."

"That's about right," she agreed.

Glass nodded, took off his cap, and set it on a branch. "Mind if I borrow that Winchester and some shells?" He nodded toward the big Sharps rifle that hung in a leather scabbard on his saddle. "No use takin' a cannon to kill squirrels."

"Go right ahead." She hesitated, then grinned. "To answer your question back there, I'm not bad at hitting things far off."

"I 'preciate the offer," he said politely. "But I don't believe this'll require any help."

Glass disappeared into the trees. Jessie dismounted, soaked a bandanna in water from her canteen, and cooled Ki's face. He groaned once, opened his eyes briefly, and closed them again. Jessie leaned against a tree and waited. A jay spotted her quickly and squawked an angry challenge. In a moment the sharp crack of the Winchester echoed off the mountain. She counted the shots—five of them in all, well spaced, as if Glass were having target practice. Men's voices reached her, high-pitched shouts of alarm. There was brief answering fire from a pistol, and then silence. She knew what had happened, imagined how he'd done it. Cavanaugh's gunmen had charged the slope, found her gone, and figured out that she was over the bridge. They'd waited for the men on foot to get their horses. Glass would have waited as well, letting them all start over in a bunch. When the first rider was on him, he'd started hitting those in the rear and working his way forward. The men who got away would be those who'd lagged behind. She didn't think it likely that Glass had missed anyone who came under his sights.

Jessie shook her head. The survivors would have a hell of a story to tell Pierce Cavanaugh. They couldn't know about Glass, but they knew Ki was hit. Her reputation with a rifle was going to earn her fame she didn't rightly deserve.

When she looked up again, he was there. She hadn't heard him coming. He handed her Winchester back to her and said, "Much obliged for the use of the weapon, miss. Now let's get moving. We'll stop for a spell a ways out and let your friend get on his feet."

"You all right?" Jessie asked anxiously. "Lord, Ki, you don't look good at all."

"I'm fine," Ki said darkly. He pulled himself erect, leaned against the tree, and waited for the nausea to go away. "I feel like a fool. That bullet creased my skull right in the same spot where that constable clubbed me. I have to find a fresh place to get hit."

"Be a good idea if you just quit gettin' hit anywhere, you know?"

Ki eased himself down and gingerly touched the bandanna around his head. Joseph Glass squatted over a small fire across the clearing. A sheer granite cliff rose up behind him. The cliff was covered with gray- and rust-colored splotches of lichen. The bald rock wall sheltered a narrow natural trail that twisted for miles along the side of the mountain. Ki was certain it would be nearly impossible to find, unless you stumbled right on it. Or if, like Glass, you knew exactly where you were going.

He hardly knew the man, but he respected what he saw. Glass said little and moved with an easy animal grace, wasting no motion at all. Ki knew instinctively that he was at home in his surroundings. He could see and hear things other men never noticed—the way grass bent, the pitch of a bird's call. These were talents a man couldn't learn out of a book. Ki admired such qualities, for he shared more than a few of them himself and knew they took a lifetime to learn.

He sipped hot coffee and let a grin tilt the corners of his mouth. Most likely, Glass had never heard of Japan's elite

65

warrior class. Yet in many respects this mountain man followed the *kakuto bugei*, the true samurai way. And if Ki knew Glass for what he was, it was clear the man knew him as well. When they'd met earlier in the day, the bearded man had taken his measure. A look had passed between them and nothing more.

Ki walked with Jessie to the fire and filled his plate. Glass waited until they were finished, then wiped his dark beard and nodded ahead.

"Where we are, in case you're wonderin', is in the Bitterroot Mountains. Canada's maybe sixty, seventy miles north, if you was a bird. Hell of a lot more if you ain't. That's the Rockies off to the west."

"And we're going where?" asked Jessie.

"North a little ways. Not too far. It's gettin' on evening, but I want to keep ridin'." He glanced in Ki's direction. "You feel like sittin' a horse?"

"Yes. I'll be fine."

"All right. Let's get to it." He stood and began hiding the remains of the fire. In moments they were on the trail again.

They rode in silence through the dusk, Glass guiding them single-file along the narrow path. Once he nodded at Ki, and Ki dropped back to check their rear. Glass slowed his pace and Jessie moved up beside him.

"That was no accident," she said abruptly, "you being up on that spire. How long had you been watching us, friend? I'd like to know, if you don't mind."

Glass shot her a shy grin. "Tell the truth, I been hangin' around a couple of days outside Mule. Sort of lookin' things over."

Jessie blinked in surprise. "You were there, when I got Ki out of jail?"

"Yep. Followed you out of town and watched those fellers come buzzin' out after you like hornets stirred with a stick."

Jessie held his gaze. "Did you—did you see them kill a man on the hill the night before? They blew him up with dynamite. He was a friend of mine."

"No, I didn't." Glass pursed his lips. "Heard it, though. I was bedded down 'gainst the storm. Saw you two up lookin' the next morning." Glass shifted in the saddle and gathered his thoughts. "I was out past the Flatheads, down the Sun River," he said evenly. "When I got back here, they told me what

66

happened to Jeb. Yellow Wing—that's his granddaughter—she wanted to go on down and get blood, but Jeb's partners wouldn't let her. This Crow squaw got word to some fellers we know and said Jeb didn't want it that way." He shook his head and frowned. "Sure as hell wasn't easy, keeping that little gal down."

"I know about that part," Jessie told him. "John Hamilton—the man they killed last night—John talked to the Crow woman and got word to me."

"Jeb was a fine man," Glass said distantly. "Don't come any better. Dyin' like that ain't right. Not for Jeb Baker. I figure Yellow Wing's about right. Blood calls for blood."

"You evened the score back there a little," Jessie reminded him.

Glass looked right through her. "Don't reckon that's so, way I see it. I figure there's a feller somewhere hasn't paid his share."

Jessie nodded thoughtfully and studied the man beside her. She'd ridden with him half the day before she'd realized he was a good deal younger than she'd imagined. The farther they got from the carnage he'd left behind, the more the harsh lines around his eyes seemed to soften. To Jessie's great surprise, she saw that there was a man scarcely older than herself behind the heavy black beard and weathered features. The firm line of his jaw and the hawklike nose were as if shaped from stone. The pale blue eyes looked hauntingly familiar, and she realized with a start that she'd seen them before. They were Jeb Baker's eyes, sky-blue touched with grains of flint, eyes that seemed ever searching restlessly about, looking for distant peaks and rivers.

"You heard about me from the Crow woman?" Jessie asked. "Is that how you knew who I was?"

"Knew before that," said Glass. "Jeb talked about your father some. Had a lot of respect for the man." He turned and ran a hand through his beard. "Mind if I get a mite curious? What're you and your friend doin' up here—it ain't just Jeb, now is it?"

"It has a lot to do with Jeb. But you're right, there's more to it than that."

Glass caught her hesitation. "Don't feel obliged to talk, if you don't have a mind to. Ain't my business."

67

"No, it's not that, Joseph." She realized it was the first time she'd called him by his name. "I want you to know. I really do. The truth is, I'm not at all sure what I'm after, except that it leads back to the men who had Jeb murdered. I'm hoping you can help me with that."

"Yeah? An' how's that?"

"I think Jeb was killed for several reasons. I think the fact that he came down to Mule that day was real convenient for the men who got him hanged. Miners had been murdered up in the hills, and they needed a scapegoat for that. But that's not the big reason Jeb was killed. He knew something he wasn't supposed to know." She paused and looked at Glass. "Do you have any idea what that might have been? Did he say anything to you?"

Night was closing in fast, and she couldn't make out his features in the dark. "Can't say for sure. I'll think on it some." He sniffed the air and studied the ground ahead. "Better tell your friend to pull on back here now. Gettin' close to where we're going. Be a good idea if those ol' boys in camp figured he was ridin' in with me."

Darkness covered the eastern slopes of the mountains. Jessie rode directly behind Glass, with Ki close behind her. Now the high rock walls seemed to close in around them. More than once, Jessie had to duck to keep from hitting her head. There was room for one horse on the trail, but not an inch left over.

Finally the narrow defile opened up and she could see a patch of stars through the trees. Glass paused, waited a long moment, then rode on ahead. The trail twisted steadily downward, then slowly bottomed out.

"Evenin', Henry," Glass spoke into the dark. "Gettin' a mite cool for this time of year."

"Is for a fact," a voice spoke to Jessie's left. She stared into the night but saw nothing. A few yards farther on, she smelled smoke, and then a dim yellow glow appeared through the trees. The fire painted shadows upon a great slab of stone. Three faces looked up from the circle, two old men and a raven-haired young woman who Jessie realized must be Yellow Wing.

Glass signaled for Jessie and Ki to stop. "I'll take your horses," he said quietly. "You can bed down over there, if you don't mind." He pointed toward a ponderosa pine well away from the others and the fire. "I'll bring you somethin' to eat, and we'll save the innerducin' till morning. These folks ain't real good at meetin' strangers."

"Any way you like," Jessie told him.

"Yeah, well..." Glass nodded absently and led off the mounts, after Ki had removed their packs. After a while, Glass appeared at the fire, squatted down, and filled two plates and brought them back.

"Pretty good elk stew. There's some wild onions in there, too."

"I can smell it," said Jessie, eagerly accepting the plate. "I like it already."

"I don't want you to get the wrong idea," said Glass. "You're as welcome as you can be. Thing is, we don't ever bring folks up to this place. They didn't know you were comin'."

"Then maybe you shouldn't have brought us," said Jessie. "We're grateful for what you did, Joseph. But we don't want to cause any trouble."

Something flashed in the man's eyes. In the half-light, Jessie couldn't read his expression. "I can handle it, I reckon," he said evenly. "See you all in the morning."

Glass walked back to the fire, and Jessie and Ki finished their meal in silence.

"It looks as if everything you hear about mountain men is true," Ki said finally. "They like to be left alone."

"They'll come around," said Jessie. She watched Joseph Glass and the figures by the fire. The men crowded in around him to talk. The half-breed girl, she noticed, didn't move in Glass's direction. "They were Jeb Baker's friends. That ought to make a difference."

Ki didn't answer. Jessie set her plate aside and spread out her blankets under the tree. In a moment he heard her steady breathing and knew she was asleep. He curled up under his covers and watched the fire. One by one, the figures stood and faded into the darkness.

He awoke once, suddenly alert to an unfamiliar sound. Without moving, he let his eyes flicker over the clearing, past the dying embers to the rocky wall beyond. For an instant he saw the girl. She was watching him from the shelter of a tree, not ten feet away, her face and figure in shadow. He blinked once, and she was gone.

69

Chapter 8

To her great surprise and relief, Jessie found she didn't have to worry about the mountain men's acceptance. After introductions at breakfast, they vied openly for her attention, acting more like boys than old men. Jessie was taken with them all. Other men's measures didn't concern them in the least. They scorned any life but the one they lived, and pitied the poor devils who spent their days in dreary cities. What good was a fortune, if you didn't have the mountains and the sky?

There was Rooster-John Fielding and Henry Clark, and another man known simply as Philadelphy. At first Jessie found it hard to tell them apart. They were dressed alike in buckskins worn to a greasy shade of black, patched and mended a hundred times and molded to fit their sinewy frames. All had weathered faces and sported full white beards. Philadelphy and Henry Clark had flowing manes to match. Fielding, though, doffed his cap and proudly showed her the scarred flesh of his bald head.

"Assiniboine chief took my scalp on the Milk River," he grinned. "Chased that ol' red bastard twenty years afore I caught him."

"Don't listen to him," drawled Philadelphy. "Got drunk at rendezvous, the way I heard it. Some ol' Blackfoot woman with no teeth done the scalpin'."

"By God, that's a lie an' you know it!" Rooster-John bellowed. "Miss," he pleaded, "that's a plain untruth, is what it is."

The other mountain men roared with delight at their friend's discomfort. Jessie bit her lip and pretended to ponder the problem. "Seems to me I've heard about you and Blackfoot women. But it didn't have a *thing* to do with scalping."

Philadelphy and Clark groaned. Rooster-John beamed with

70

pride, and Jessie knew she'd made a friend for life.

"You sure got the ol' boys goin'," Glass told her later. "They think you're somethin', Jessie."

"You must've buttered them up good last night," Jessie grinned. "They weren't at all what I expected. What in the world did you tell them?"

Glass gave her a curious look. "I didn't do no butterin' up a-tall," he said soberly. "I told them who you were and what happened, and that's it. Jessie, those fellers don't take a whole lot to what other folks tell 'em, even someone they know. They're cantankerous ol' coons, and stubborn as mules—but they judge a person honest and say right out what they think." Glass caught himself and grinned. "Hell, didn't mean to get all fired up. I sound like a preacher on a stump."

"That's all right," she told him. "I do understand what you're saying."

Movement caught her eye and she glanced past Joseph to the far side of the clearing. Yellow Wing was coming back from the creek, carrying a leather bucket of water. She was a young, reed-slender girl with coal-black hair braided in two strands over her shoulders. She had the proud, sharply planed features of her Sioux ancestors, and skin the color of dark wild honey. Jessie thought she'd be a real beauty, even without the striking effect of her eyes. Instead of the dark brown of her mother's people, she'd captured the bright, sky-blue color of her grandfather Jeb. Set amid her Indian features and the tone of her skin, the contrast was startling.

As Yellow Wing passed, she looked up and saw Jessie talking with Joseph. Her eyes turned to ice and she glanced quickly away.

"Now what am I going to do about that one?" Jessie sighed. "You see how she was at breakfast? Didn't even answer when I said hello. And she didn't like me talking to those old fellows at all."

Joseph looked at his hands and frowned. "I'm sorry. I kinda figured this'd happen."

"Why? It's none of my business, but I'm asking anyway. Is it me being *here*, Joseph—or bein' here with you?"

Glass colored all the way down to his neck. "Damn it, that's not it at all," he said sharply. "There's nothin' like that between me and Yellow Wing."

71

"Lord, why not? She's a real beauty, for sure. And you're not all that ugly yourself."

Glass stared, then burst out laughing. "By God, woman, you don't mind sayin' what you're thinking, do you?"

Jessie feigned surprise. "Why, you're confusing me now, Mr. Glass. A minute ago you said being straight out was the mountain man's way."

Glass shot her a painful grin. "Didn't say nothin' about a *woman* behavin' like that. It's, uh . . . it ain't natural . . ."

Jessie rolled her eyes. "Now there's a man's answer if I ever heard one." She shook her head and nodded across the clearing. "All of which tells me nothing at all about her."

"Nothin' to say," Joseph sighed. "She's like that a lot. It ain't you and Ki, it's everyone, Jessie. She never had much to do with outsiders. Jeb was her whole life, everything she needed. Now that he's gone, there's nothin' but me and them three. We're the closest thing she's got to family, and sometimes she acts like we ain't even around."

"You don't think I should even try?"

"Suit yourself," he muttered. "Reckon you will, if you've a mind to."

Jessie tried to find Yellow Wing, but the girl had a talent for making herself scarce. Instead she spent the rest of the morning with the three mountain men. They were heading out east the next day, bound for the far slopes of the Rockies. Joseph had already tried to learn where Jeb might have gone, what he'd seen that would cause Cavanaugh to want to kill him. None of the old men had an answer.

"He seen something," Henry Clark told her. "'Bout a week 'fore he went down for supplies. Already told Joseph that."

"But you don't know where he went?"

"Coulda been anywhere," Philadelphy put in. "Henry's right, though. The old hoss had something on his mind. He was chewin' on it for sure."

"But he didn't say anything?"

"Nope." Philadelphy drew a Bowie knife out of his belt and began honing it over a worn whetstone. Jessie noted that the weapon had a carved bone handle, and a blade half as long as her arm.

"Got a notion it wasn't far," said Henry. "Maybe up north."

"Why you think that?" asked Rooster-John.

"Dunno. Just do. Got me a feelin'."

"Hmmmph!" Rooster growled. "You ain't had no *feelin'* in thutty years."

"Sure as hell have," said Clark. He gave Jessie a broad wink. "Had one jus' this morning, when this pretty here brushed my laig after breakfast."

Rooster-John and Philadelphy howled. Jessie laughed with them, and tried not to show her disappointment. Jeb's friends would do anything they could to avenge his death, including marching down to town and cutting out Cavanaugh's liver. But they truly had no idea where Jeb had gone and what he'd seen. Whatever it was, he'd kept it to himself and taken it to the grave.

"It can't stop here," Jessie told Joseph later that day. "I won't let it, damn it."

"Said I'd help if I could," Joseph said. "Don't know what we can do if we got no idea where he went. It's a big country out there."

"I know. It's not your fault, Joseph."

"You said one of the men thought he'd gone up north," Ki put in. "Do you think that's so?"

"Maybe." Glass shrugged. "Might be somethin' to it, and might be Henry's just guessin'. And, hell—north *where?* There's a lot of that direction to take in."

Jessie squinted into the sun. It was late afternoon and Glass had walked them past the clearing into the trees. A stream rushed by down the slope, white water frothing through boulders as big as houses.

"If there's nothing up here," she told Ki, "we'll have to go back. Pick it all up somewhere else. Get some help, maybe. See if we can get to someone in Cavanaugh's organization. Find out what they're up to." She stared bleakly at Ki. "Damn—that's what *he'd* do, right?"

"Getting in that way would take time," Ki told her. "Even if that was what you wanted to do."

"Which I don't. Ki, we've got to keep trying. Start from scratch somehow, even if we have to use some—"

Jessie caught Joseph's eye and stopped. Turning, she saw Yellow Wing standing silently behind her. She looked right at Glass and no one else.

"Joseph," she said evenly, "will this place the woman seeks

73

bring blood to my grandfather's killers?"

"Why, I think maybe it might," said Glass.

"Then I believe I know where he went. I don't know why, or if he saw what you're looking for. I cannot go there myself, but I will tell you what I know."

They left at first light the next morning, riding northwest along the steep slopes of the mountain. The country was rugged, but some of the prettiest Jessie had seen. Autumn splashed the land with bright color. All around them, the leaves of quaking aspens flashed like millions of gold coins in the breeze.

"Hard to fault what Henry and the others were saying," Jessie told Glass. "Couldn't be a finer place to be."

"Still good," Glass muttered. "Won't be that way forever. And that's the God's truth." He urged his mount over a rocky crag and pointed to the mountains on the horizon. "That's where we're headed. Used to be Kootenay Indian country. A hundred years or so ago, they lived up here and over in Idaho and up in Canada. Changed their habits some when the horses came. Been a lot of Indians up here. Nez Percé, Flatheads, Kalispels. Blackfoot too, I reckon, wandering a little west, looking for trouble."

"The place we're going," said Jessie, "it has something to do with the reason Yellow Wing wouldn't come."

"Has a lot to do with it," Glass replied. "If it's the place I'm thinking about, it's Kootenay sacred ground. A burial place. Yellow Wing wouldn't go near it."

Jessie shook her head. "It doesn't make sense, does it? What would Jeb Baker have seen up there that'd get him killed?"

"Beats me," said Glass. "Guess all we can do is look and see." He headed down the slope to lower ground, and Jessie followed. The day was lazy and warm, all the more pleasant after the dreary siege of rain. As Jessie rode, she laced a leather thong through the brim of her Stetson so she could let it hang free on her back. She shook a tumble of thick amber hair over her shoulders and stretched her arms wide. The sun felt good, and she wished she had a shirt a bit lighter than the heavy men's flannel she'd bought from Keller. "Poor old devil," she said under her breath, thinking of Keller again. Like every soul in Mule, he'd bent under the threat of Cavanaugh's power. The whole town had lost the will to fight. And once that happened, standing straight again didn't come easy.

"Jessie, ride up here beside me real slow..."

The urgency in Joseph's words cut through her thoughts. He was sitting perfectly still, peering through a thick grove of aspen. He nodded slightly and Jessie followed his glance. Past the trees was a clearing. Five Indians on horseback were moving west. They were all young men. Two wore calico shirts, the others were bare to the waist. The last man in line led a scrawny cow on a rope. The animal's ribs were showing, and its hipbones stood up high.

Glass waited until the Indians had passed, then silently motioned Jessie on ahead. He kept them in cover as long as he could, then crossed the open space at its narrowest point. Neither spoke until they were back in the shelter of the trees. Glass took off his cap and offered Jessie his canteen.

"Poor bastards," he said darkly, "no fight in 'em, but no use lettin' them know we're here." He caught the question in Jessie's eyes. "Flatheads. Off the reservation back southeast. Stole that poor worthless cow from some settler."

"What are they going to do with it?"

"Take it out and eat it. Likely bones an' hide an' all. Same thing's happenin' all over. Goin' to be a bad winter, and the Indians all know it. Buffalo's disappearin' fast. Hunters are comin' home empty-handed, and the goddamn Indian agencies don't have a thing to give 'em. Lot of Blackfeet, Piegan, Flathead, and Sioux are goin' to starve before spring."

Glass paused, looked at Jessie, and shook his head. "Talk to folks down in Denver or somewhere, you'd figure all the Indians up here was goin' to lay down tomorrow and die. Real convenient-like. 'Cept the U.S. Army ain't heard about that. They're too damn busy buildin' forts to keep 'em back—Fort Assiniboine last year up in the Bear Paw Mountains to watch the Blackfeet, and Maginnis just this year, south of that."

"John Hamilton told me there were four thousand Sioux up in Canada with Sitting Bull," said Jessie. "He said the Nez Percé are joining them. You think there's anything to that?"

"You mean do I think the Sioux'll come howling back down after scalps?" Glass made a face. "Won't ever happen. Poor devils will come back and starve with their brothers."

Jessie caught the expression in his eyes. "You think about that, don't you, Joseph?"

"What? Indians starving? Yeah, I think about it. I been

75

hungry more'n once." He kicked his horse and waved Jessie on. "Come on, let's get up that rise while the sun's in the clouds. Want to see if those fellers really went where they were headed."

They found the spot late in the afternoon, a narrow valley high in the foothills under towering stone cliffs. There was no sign left that the place was sacred ground. Still, both Jessie and Glass felt it at once—a somber, oppressive quiet they hadn't experienced the moment before.

"Joseph, are you sure this is it?" asked Jessie, aware that she was speaking in a whisper. "What would Pierce Cavanaugh be doing in a place like this?"

"I don't know. But it's the right spot for certain." He swung out of the saddle and let his eyes sweep the rocky borders of the valley. Jessie joined him and they walked, leading their horses. In a few moments Glass waved her to a stop and squatted on the ground.

"Rain washed a lot of stuff out, but there was people here, all right. Lots of 'em. Come down here, look at this." He parted the sparse grass and pointed to a series of shallow depressions. "See that? Wagon tracks. And horses and footprints all over the place." He stood and frowned thoughtfully over the valley. "Hold the mounts, Jessie, and don't move around from where you are. Don't want to mess up sign any more than it is."

Jessie nodded, took the reins, and watched him move off to the south. He walked from one side of the valley to the other, always moving away, crisscrossing the field. At the far end he turned and started back, then disappeared among the rocks a long time. Finally he came back to Jessie, took a long swallow of water, and wiped his head.

"All right," he told her, "this is what we got. Forty, fifty men was up here. They stayed a couple of days, set up some tents, ate and slept and did some talking. Met a lot in one big tent over there by the line of brush. They cleaned up pretty good, but I found some burned garbage buried in the gully. There's a piece of newspaper from up in Canada. And some tins from there, too. Probably a lot of food from here, but they didn't leave any to tell."

Glass paused and squinted down the valley. "All the wagons

came from the north. We can figure on Canada, I reckon. They were heavy comin' in and near as heavy leavin'. They all went south, by two or three different ways. While they were here, all the wagons were bunched up off to the side of the camp, the way freighters'll line up. One thing I can't rightly figure— the ground where they stood's got lots of salt in it."

"Salt?" Jessie looked puzzled. "Why? What for?"

"Got no idea, but that's what it was." He shifted his feet and frowned. "Found somethin' else too. Right over there in that hollow overlookin' the valley. That's where Jeb was lyin', watching whatever was going on. I found his moccasin tracks where he came in. He watched half a day, then took off back to where he left his horse. There's a creek meanders off west behind those rocks. He got out quick and rode south."

Jessie raised a brow. "He got out *quick,* you said?"

"Uh-huh." Joseph's face clouded. "Hard to believe it, but old Jeb must've got a might careless. Someone saw him up there. Found *their* tracks, too. Couple of tame Arikaras that was with the party of whites. They went after Jeb, but he had a horse and they was on foot. He hightailed it out and likely lost 'em 'fore they got back for mounts."

"My God, Joseph!" Jessie's eyes went wide. "That's why they killed him when he came down to Mule. They knew who he was!"

"Oh yeah," Glass said grimly. "If the Indians got a look at him, they'd of known he was Jebediah Baker."

"And they told whoever they were working for. Cavanaugh's people."

"If that's who was here."

"It was," Jessie said firmly. "I don't have any doubt about that. But what did he *see,* Joseph?" Anger and frustration strained her voice. "We don't know any more than we did. Wagons and Indians and—and salt? What the hell does *that* mean?"

"I don't know, Jessie." He shook his head and swung back in the saddle. "Come on, we got a long ride back."

Chapter 9

Ki didn't much like the idea of staying behind, but Jessie asked him to, and Glass said he'd consider it a favor. Philadelphy and Henry Clark and Rooster-John were leaving shortly, and Joseph didn't want Yellow Wing left in camp alone.

"For God's sake, don't tell her that's why you're staying," Glass warned. "That girl don't figure she needs a keeper. I'll tell her your head's hurtin' bad—which I don't figure's too much of a lie."

Ki agreed, mostly because he had a lot of confidence in Glass. He could take care of Jessie as well as any man could—next to himself. And he knew Glass wouldn't be taking her at all if he figured on trouble.

He liked the mountain men, and talked to them all he could until they packed up and rode out of camp. After that, there was little to do but sit under a tree or talk to the horse. Being in camp with Yellow Wing was a lot like being alone. The girl went out of her way to avoid him. When Ki tried to join her to fix his meal, she stood abruptly and left. Wherever he went, she followed him cautiously with her eyes.

Finally, Ki made a point of not looking at her at all. She was a pleasure to watch, for sure, a girl who stirred his feelings more than a little; still, he had to respect her wants and leave her alone.

Shortly after noon he walked down the rocky slope that led to the swiftly flowing stream below camp. Walking north, he found a small pool on the far bank, crossed over, and took off his clothes and plunged in. The water was ice-cold and chilled him to the bone. Still, he forced himself to stay; the water brought his blood back to life and numbed the steady throbbing in his head. He thought about washing his clothes, but decided against it. The sun wasn't warm enough to dry them as quickly as he wanted.

He was pulling himself out of the water when he heard it . . .

He stopped abruptly, cocked his head, and listened. The sound was clear and he knew exactly what it was, even above the noise of rushing water. A horse blew air nearby—somewhere upstream to his right.

Ki went rigid, every muscle in his body tightening in the presence of danger. An enemy was nearby—no, more than one, now. He couldn't see them but he could feel them—*kime*, the samurai's carefully developed sixth sense, told him where they were. The one upstream was sitting his horse. Another, on foot, was standing on the smooth rocky slope below camp. And somewhere there was another.

Ki's heart hammered against his chest. *He's got her—he's got Yellow Wing!*

It took all the will he could muster to stay where he was, to keep from bolting up and running to help her. Instead he drew his clothes off the bank and slid back into the water. If they'd killed her, there was nothing he could do. If she was alive, he could help her by staying alive himself.

Taking a deep breath, he moved underwater to the far edge of the pool, near the bank. A dead tree had fallen into the water. Debris swept down by the rains had caught in its branches. Ki surfaced slowly, letting his eyes and nose break the surface. He was just where he wanted to be, tangled in the half-submerged branches. Leaves and dead grass clung to his hair and cheeks. Ki didn't disturb them. He listened, moved an inch to the left, and peered beneath the tree.

An Indian was less than six feet away. His spotted pony stood in the stream while he studied the water, the bank, every inch of land close by. He was a short, stubby man with broad features and dark eyes. His loose black hair was held back by a dirty red headband. He wore old cotton trousers and a threadbare blue shirt. He held a Henry rifle next to his body, his finger curled around the trigger.

Ki waited.

The Indian finally turned and left, riding off downstream. Ki didn't move. He was listening for hooves on stone and knew the rider had moved only a few yards off. The water numbed his body, and he kept himself from shivering by sheer force of will. After he knew the Indian was gone, he waited another quarter-hour. Finally he slid naked out of the water and onto the bank, crawled on his hands and knees into the woods, and forced his arms and legs back into his wet clothes.

Ki sat in the high branches of a spruce and watched the rocky ravine that ran below the cluster of aspen. If he was right, they'd come out close to the spot where a gray spire of granite broke the surface. They'd taken the lower trail, moving off quickly northeast. There was no way he could beat them on foot, following the way they were taking. He did the only thing he could. It was that, or lose them altogether. When they circled off around the side of the mountain, he started laboriously over the top. He was cut, bloodied all over, and his legs burned with the pain of exertion. If he was wrong, it was all for nothing. Even if he was right, maybe they'd beat him to the spot and pass on. And how would he ever know?

He'd wasted no time in camp, pausing only to leave a message scratched hastily on the sheer rock wall behind the fire. He could put the pieces together easily enough. The men that Glass had left alive had gone back to Cavanaugh, and Cavanaugh hadn't given up. Ki had to admire the man for using Indian trackers. No one, he was certain, could have found the mountain men's camp except an Indian or one of their own. Most likely, they'd had a little luck and spotted the three old-timers down the trail. They wanted Ki and Jessie, and finding no one on hand but Yellow Wing would make them anxious. Where were they? And where was the *other* mountain man, the one whose tracks were all over the place?

Two things had helped him, Ki knew. First, there had been only one horse in camp. One horse, one girl. The Indians figured everyone else had ridden off. Second, there was the fact that he'd walked to the water over rock that left no tracks. They'd looked in the woods and by the stream and then left, moving quickly out of the camp. Ki didn't blame them. They hadn't found the tracks Jessie and Glass had left on the trail; the three mountain men had left camp the same way and covered their own sign. The Indians knew there was another mountain man on the loose, and they didn't care to wait around and meet him.

Ki came suddenly alert. Movement caught his eye down below. Seconds later they appeared. He gave a long sigh of relief. Three Indian trackers and the girl. Her hands were bound behind her. The last man in line led her mount after his own. Ki watched another moment, then climbed down from the tree. At least they'd slowed their pace, which meant they were feeling more at ease. He'd still have to run himself to death, but he wouldn't have to climb any mountains.

It was well into the night when he heard the men's voices and saw the glow of their fire over the ridge. Ki stopped and sank to the ground. Everything hurt. His lungs were on fire and his muscles shook. The sky whirled dizzily overhead. When he could bring the stars into focus, he decided it was well after ten, maybe closer to eleven. He'd been pushing himself hard for a good seven or eight hours. He knew what his body could do, and that he'd come very close to draining it dry.

How long had the Indians been in camp? Three or four hours, he decided. Easily that, and maybe more. The knowledge brought a sense of foreboding. If they'd had the girl that long, he might already be too late.

Ki thrust the thought aside and forced his body erect. Gritting his teeth against pain, he made his way up the ridge, crawled between the trunks of two trees, and peered into the camp.

He took in the scene in a glance. The Indians had their own small fire at the far edge of the clearing. Past them were the horses, their own and maybe ten more. Beyond the mounts and into the trees were four sturdily built flatbed wagons covered with canvas. Closer, nearly directly below Ki and behind a scattering of tents, was a bigger, brighter fire. It was the kind of fire white men made if they weren't used to sleeping outdoors. Seven men were around the fire, and Ki instantly recognized three. They were the men he'd met in the street in Mule. One had aimed a pistol at Jessie. Another he'd tied up naked in the jail.

Past the fire, nearly lost in the shadow of the trees, two men stood close together. Ki bit his lip in thought. He'd never seen Cavanaugh himself, but from the way Jessie described him, this was the man. Ki couldn't see the other man's face. He was short, heavyset, his suit a peculiar cut.

And where in hell was the girl? Ki wondered. As near as he could tell, she wasn't anywhere in sight.

It took him a painful ten minutes to work his way around

81

the camp, past the fire and the tents, to the thick stand of pines. He'd kept his eyes on the two, Cavanaugh and the other, watching their silhouettes against the fire. Now they were no more than a dozen feet away. He could have walked up to Cavanaugh and killed him before he could move, then vanished before the men by the fire came to their senses. It was a tempting idea, except he'd be no closer to freeing the girl—wherever she was, he reminded himself grimly. Maybe he'd have to drag the bastard off somewhere and ask him.

"Couldn't be helped, damn it," Cavanaugh was saying. "The Starbuck woman and the Jappo were gone. What were the Indians supposed to do, stay there and wait?"

"I am not talking about the others, Herr Caff-anaugh," the heavyset man said in a thickly accented voice. "I am talking about the girl. The saffages should never haff brought her here—not from a camp of men like that!"

"No one's going to follow those Indians," Cavanaugh grunted. "They're damn good at what they do. Besides," he added, "now that we've got the half-breed girl, we can use her to find out some things."

"Ah? And what can she tell us, Caff-anaugh?" He puffed on a long cigar, and Ki saw his face in its glow. Heavy brows and deep, searching eyes. "What can she say that we do not know already?"

"What the Starbuck woman's up to, maybe. Where she is now."

The short man gave a nasty little laugh. "A saffage? She would know things like this?"

"Hell, I don't know what she knows," Cavanaugh said irritably. "We can ask her and find out."

"Ah. You haven't questioned her yet?"

"I was kind of waiting for you," he said easily. "Thought maybe you'd like to lend us your . . . medical experience."

The man chuckled, a sound that went all the way up Ki's spine. "Perhaps. It may be I could be of some serfice."

"If you want, I'll have my boys bring her over to your tent. She's back there with the Indians now."

"They . . . haven't *used* her, haff they?" Ki caught the alarm in his voice. "If they've, ah, dirtied the girl . . ."

"No one's touched her," Cavanaugh assured him. "And she's a very pretty girl, by the way. Quite young."

The man paused and glanced back at the fire. "I will be leaving before morning. Can you keep your schedule, Caff-anaugh?"

"We'll have everything out before daylight. And I brought you a message from my people on the Missouri. Everything got there fine. They'll be moving south about the same time we will."

"Good. Timing iss essential. You understand this, yes?"

"I understand just fine," Cavanaugh said tightly. "I've been in business awhile too, Doctor."

"This Starbuck woman—she has been a thorn in our side before. I don't like her mixed up in this."

"She'll be taken. I said she would be, didn't I?"

"You had her once, I remind you. And the Oriental as well."

"And I'll have them both again," Cavanaugh flared. "Be-sides, she doesn't know a damn thing. She can't hurt us."

"She has hurt us considerably in the past."

"Well, I wouldn't know about that."

"*I* would," the man said coolly. "And I am saying this to you. It must be done. It must be taken care of, Caff-anaugh."

Ki moved off quietly, making a wide circle toward the far end of the camp. He had to find Yellow Wing and get her out, cut loose a couple of mounts and get moving before Cavanaugh came to get her. He wished he could have waited and heard more, maybe learned what they were moving to the south. He shrugged off the thought and moved deeper into the woods. There was no time for that. He'd stayed and listened too long as it was.

He found her almost at once, nearly stumbling over her legs in the dark. He blinked in surprise and decided his luck was changing. She was sitting on the ground, her arms stretched awkwardly behind a tree. Ki turned her chin up, making sure she knew who he was. She nodded and gave him a wide-eyed stare as he pulled the gag from her mouth. Using one of his razor-edged *shuriken* throwing stars, he quickly sliced through her bonds. He pointed toward the Indians' fire through the trees, then pointed again in the direction of the horses. The girl understood. She rubbed the circulation back into her arms and followed him to deeper cover. He glanced once more to-ward the fire, then started through the brush.

"Wait." Yellow Wing grabbed his arm and shook her head.

"Don't you know anything about horses? Don't sneak up behind them. Go where they'll see you coming."

"But so will everyone else."

The girl stuck out her chin in disdain. "I'll do it. You watch for trouble."

Before he could stop her, she was gone. He crouched in the dark, guarding her approach to the mounts. In a moment she was back, leading two Indian ponies with woven grass bridles. One of them, he noticed, was hers. "See?" Her blue eyes blazed challengingly. "That is the way to get horses."

"Fine," Ki said nervously. "Let's talk about it later." He walked beside her as she led the mounts through the trees. "There's a ravine back there, over the ridge," he told her. "Once we get past it . . ."

"I know where it is. I saw it when we came in."

"Good."

A thought suddenly struck her and she stopped him. "Where is *your* horse? I wasn't thinking. I didn't need to take two!"

"Yes you did," Ki said flatly. "I don't have a horse."

"How did you get here, then?"

"I walked. Ran, mostly."

"You did?" The girl raised an eyebrow.

"Look, we'll discuss this later. Right now we—*look out!*" Ki threw the girl roughly to the ground. An Indian came at him out of the dark. A knife flashed and tore through his sleeve. Ki turned aside, grabbed the Indian's arm in both hands, and levered the warrior's weight off the point of his hip. The Indian yelled and went down. Ki stepped in quickly and kicked out with his heel. The Indian let out a breath and went limp.

Yellow Wing shouted a warning, and Ki spun around fast. Both of the other two Indians came at him at once. There was no time to strike out, no time to step away. Ki simply dropped and lowered his head. The Indian cursed in surprise and sprawled over Ki's shoulder. Ki let him go, sprang to his feet, and twisted on his heels. He lashed out desperately as the next man threw himself through the air. His foot caught the Indian over the heart. He sucked in a breath and staggered back; Ki pressed in relentlessly, chopping the dark features again and again, lashing flesh and bone with the edge of his hand. Finally the man dropped to the ground. Ki turned in a crouch, expecting to find his second assailant ready for more. Instead, the man lay still on his back.

"What happened?" he asked the girl. "All I did was trip him."

"Yes. All *I* did was cut his throat," Yellow Wing said shortly. She jammed the man's blade in her belt and swung lightly onto her mount. "The others are coming," she said calmly. "It would be a good idea if we left."

Ki grabbed the horse's neck and threw his leg painfully over the bare back. Shouts rose up from the camp. A volley of gunfire clattered through the trees, but Ki saw they were firing in the wrong direction.

"I don't believe you *ran* all the way here," the girl said suddenly. "I know that is a lie. An Indian could do it, but you couldn't."

"Yellow Wing, I don't give a damn what you believe," Ki said harshly. He dug his heels hard into the pony's flanks and bolted off into the dark.

85

Chapter 10

Glass wanted to get them back before dark, but they'd spent so much time in the northern valley that the camp was still hours away when night fell.

"I'd go in like we did last night," he told Jessie, "but that ain't too good an idea 'less those old coons are at home. Nothin' bigger'n a tick prowls around that place if they're in. Awake, sleepin', it don't make any difference to them."

"You're very fond of them, aren't you?" said Jessie.

Glass gave her a curious look. "I *like* 'em, if that's what you mean. Don't know about *fond*. They're real good men, I'll tell you that."

"That's what I meant," Jessie said evenly. In the future, she decided, she'd have to watch her choice of words. Glass loved those three old men like he'd loved Jeb Baker. But that wasn't the way he would put his feelings into words.

They slept and started off early in the morning. An hour after dawn they were crossing the rushing stream below camp. Glass led Jessie onto the trail toward the entry, then suddenly reined in his mount.

"What is it?" Jessie saw his face grow hard.

"Christ, I don't rightly know. Whatever it is, it ain't good." He urged his horse to the side of the trail, leaning out of the saddle to study the ground. He slipped his rifle out of its case and motioned her forward, moving ahead through the narrow path and into the camp.

"Trouble, just like I figured." He swung off his mount and swept the rifle about the clearing. "Stay right here," he told her.

Jessie looked over his shoulder and caught her breath. "Oh Lord, Joseph, look there!"

"I see it," he said stiffly. Morning sun glanced off the high stone wall behind the ashes of the fire. Ki's message was scrawled with a charred stick:

3 IND.

TOOK GIRL

FOLLOWING

3–4 AFT.

"That helps." Glass nodded his approval. "He knows we don't need to be guessin' about when this happened." Glass cursed and kicked at the ground. "They didn't try to cover their tracks. Three Indians. Arikaras."

"Is it—are the tracks the same as the ones up north?"

"Oh yeah," Glass said sourly. "He was here. Feller with a sewed-up moccasin on his right foot."

Jessie's heart sank. "Then they were looking for me. They took Yellow Wing back to Cavanaugh."

"Uh-huh. And your friend Ki took off after 'em. On foot."

Jessie looked startled, then remembered. "There was only one horse in camp!"

"He walked off in the woods. Maybe down to the stream. They came in and got her while he was gone." He mounted up and nodded. "Let's get goin'. They got maybe fifteen or sixteen hours' head start. And that's too goddamn much!"

Glass followed the Indian's sign with no trouble. They were headed northeast and making little effort to cover their tracks.

"Sassy bunch of bastards," he told her. "More'n likely saw Philadelphy and Henry and Rooster-John pull out. Knew they was packed for a trip and figured you and me was gone for a spell, too."

"They didn't worry about Ki?"

Glass gave her a half-grin. "Been thinkin' about that. Ki didn't do a lot of stompin' around. I reckon they figured he'd already rode out, too. Way they're ridin', they don't think anyone's on their trail."

"You don't see Ki's tracks, do you?"

"Not yet. They'll be here, though, up ahead." He looked thoughtfully at Jessie. "That friend of yours ain't any green-horn, is he? Son of a bitch is climbin' *mountains* after them Injuns. Christ A'mighty."

"He's a good man, Joseph."

87

"Already knew that," said Glass.

The country grew rougher with every mile. Knifelike ridges of granite crisscrossed the way, often turning the trail into a maze. Ahead, east and west and directly behind, rugged mountains thrust out of the earth.

He's on foot in this, Jessie thought. *Lord, it's bad enough on a horse!*

Around noon, Glass waved Jessie to a stop. A moment later he left her, crossed a dry stream, and stepped off his mount under the trees. A hawk circled high, winging in close to a pinnacle of stone, nearly brushing rock with its wings. When Jessie looked back, she gave a start. Two Indians on spotted horses stood across the stream bed from Glass. They looked right at her, dismounted, and walked up to Joseph. Neither of them resembled the poor Flatheads they'd seen leading their bony cow up north. They walked straight and proud, holding their heads high as they talked with Glass. They scorned the white man's clothes for buckskin leggings and leather shirts. One wore a bright beaded vest. Jessie couldn't help noticing a U.S. Cavalry sergeant's stripes on his shoulder. Both had bone-handled knives in their belts and carried new Winchester rifles.

After a while the Indians turned and mounted up and guided their horses off through the trees. Glass waited until they were gone before he climbed on his horse and made his way back to Jessie's side.

"Said my woman was right pretty." He grinned broadly. "Wanted to know if you was for sale."

"Uh-huh. And what did you say?"

"Said I was honored that they'd ask, but just couldn't part with you for any price."

"Well now. I do appreciate that. What else?"

"What?"

"What else did they say about, ah . . . *your* woman?"

"They said, uh . . ." Glass's face reddened and he looked at the sky. "That's about it . . ."

"You are a liar, Joseph Glass." Jessie threw back her head and laughed, and Joseph gave her a sheepish grin.

When they were on the path again, he scratched his beard and leaned back in the saddle. "Those two are Oglala Sioux," he told her. "Damn far afield, but from the looks of things, they've got their reasons. One of 'em says he's a cousin of Crazy Horse, and I wouldn't doubt he's right. You catch sight of them stripes?"

"I saw 'em."

"I 'spect he came by 'em honest down on the Greasy Grass, the Little Bighorn. That little set-to with the Seventh Cavalry."

Jessie repressed a shudder. "He doesn't seem worried anyone'll see them."

"Him?" Glass laughed. "That's Red Elk. The other one's Little Hawk. Neither of 'em gives a damn what a white man sees. They're not reservation Indians. Refused to go in. They're headed up north to join the others in Canada."

Jessie rode in silence a long moment, then looked curiously at Glass. "You just...walked up to them, Joseph. You didn't expect any trouble."

"I got no quarrel with 'em. They know who I am."

"I see."

"And besides—well, hell, you couldn't know that, could you? Yellow Wing's mother was one of their own. An Oglala Sioux. Kin to Crazy Horse, too. Her and Red Elk's likely related one way or other."

"Of course." Jessie shook her head. "I keep forgetting she's part Sioux."

"More'n part, really," Joseph said distantly. "If that little gal'd been there, she'd of taken on Custer by herself."

Jessie laughed, then caught the look in his eyes. "What is it, Joseph? What's wrong?"

"Nothing, I don't guess—or nothing we can do anything about. I asked those two if they'd seen the Arikaras, and they hadn't. But they ran into a couple of Nez Percé down south. The Nez Percé was scared 'cause the whites down there say there's cholera east of the Divide. Lot of folks on the road, pullin' up stakes and runnin'. The Nez Percé weren't fools and got out of the way. Figured if anything was wrong in Montana, someone'd decide the Indians was to blame."

"Cholera?" Jessie bit her lip in thought. "Joseph, I told you when I was in Mule, I heard—"

"I know," he said darkly. "And that means it's *west* of the Divide, too. Might be there's an epidemic startin' up."

For a long while, neither of them spoke. Glass seemed to push them faster instinctively, as if the bad news from the south were driving him quickly in the other direction.

Shadows stretched across the land as Glass rode ahead of her into the deserted camp. He held the Sharps rifle across his chest, letting his eyes take in the clearing.

"White men, our Arikara friends, and those goddamn wagons again," he said irritably. "Same thing we saw up north, only these fellers pulled out this morning." He swung to the ground, kicked up dirt, and loosed the smell of smoke. Finally he walked off into the trees and disappeared. A few moments later Jessie heard a yelp and jerked up her rifle. Glass came bounding into the clearing, a broad grin creasing his features.

"Christ A'mighty," he laughed, "there's a dead Injun rolled down in the gully back there. The other two were with him, and all three of 'em met up with Ki. His tracks and Yellow Wing's are all over the place. They got horses and took off east. The two Indians lit out after 'em. No wonder this meetin' broke up fast!"

"Thank God they made it!" Jessie ran a hand through her hair in relief. "Do you think we can catch them? They must be *hours* ahead!"

"You're right. Sixteen or so, I'd guess. From the looks of it, none of the whites joined the chase. Just took off fast and headed out."

Jessie gripped her saddlehorn and stepped to the ground. "Those wagons, Joseph. Can you tell if they're the same ones that made tracks up north?"

"Hard to say if they're part of that bunch. But if I was to make a guess, I'd say yeah."

"Where did they go when they left here? After Ki and Yellow Wing escaped?"

Glass picked up a stick and cleared space in the dirt with his foot. "The wagons and the white men ridin' with 'em went back south. Ki and Yellow Wing went east. If they kept on going, that'd take 'em into the Lewis Range and the Divide. Up in glacier country."

Jessie shook her head. "Ki won't run any farther than he has to. He'll either lose those two Arikaras or stop and fight. He'll get back to me as soon as he can."

"Think he'd head back to the old camp? He'll know we followed his tracks up here."

"Right. He'll come here first." Jessie took a stub of pencil

90

from her pocket and found a scrap of paper. "I'll write him a note and tell him where we're going."

"And where is it you're tellin' him we'll be?"

"Ki can take care of himself, Joseph. There's no use following if he's headed back here. If it's all right with you, I want to go after those wagons. I *don't* think Cavanaugh's hauling salt all over the territory."

"I don't either." Glass grinned and pulled at his beard. "We'll do 'er, then. Kinda curious about that myself."

Jessie left him and scribbled a hasty message. The words would make sense to no one else, but Ki would understand at once. She tore a strip of grass and wedged it in the bark of a tree a foot above her head. Ki would know to look for a message nearby, at a forty-five degree angle to the tree. She found a rock and stuck the note beneath it, then rejoined Glass in the clearing.

When they were back on the trail a few moments, Glass hefted a small object in his hand. "Found this over in the brush. Thought you might like to see it." He laid the object in Jessie's palm. It was a small, flat tin that had once held cigars. Jessie didn't bother reading the name of the maker. The word HAM-BURG jumped up and struck her like a blow.

"It's them," she said tightly, squeezing the box in her hand. "I knew they were here—I knew it!"

"Knew what?" Glass asked curiously. "That seegar tin tell you something?"

Jessie didn't answer. She tossed the tin to the ground and angrily spurred her horse ahead.

Some twenty miles to the south, the wagon tracks veered abruptly southeast. Glass said they were headed past the Flathead reservation, over toward the Mission Range. Jessie wanted to keep going, but Glass brought them to a halt and made camp.

"Can't follow 'em in the dark," he said firmly. "Besides, wherever they are, they got to stop too."

"They're a long way ahead of us," Jessie protested. "They could be anywhere now!"

"Wagons are going a hell of a lot slower than we are," said Glass. "We've been hitting it pretty hard, and we've cut down considerable on their lead. We'll cut it down some more in the morning."

Jessie knew he was right and didn't argue. Still, her thoughts raced beyond the small fire they'd build in the hollow, out past the darkness toward the east. Anyone could smoke German cigars, even in the wilds of Montana Territory. She knew, though, that whoever had dropped the tin was more than a man with a taste for exotic smokes. He was the cartel's man, an agent of the Prussians. Jebediah Baker had been right—the men who'd murdered her father were right here, and whatever they were after, Pierce Cavanaugh was part of it.

Jessie glanced at the fire again, at Joseph Glass hunched over the flames, warming his hands. With the coming of night, the temperature had dropped quickly, drawing all the heat out of the ground. Jessie stood, walked toward Glass, and sat beside him.

"I've got something to say," she said evenly. "You haven't asked a lot of questions and I haven't exactly handed out answers. I'm sorry. You're risking your neck on this, and you've a right to know what it's all about."

"Got a reason of my own, you'll recall. You want to tell me something, fine."

"I do, Joseph. I know you want to find Jeb's killer, but there's more to it than that. You're here, and I thought you ought to know what it is."

She told him all of it, right from the beginning. Who the cartel was, how her father had fought against them half his life. She told him that she and Ki had faced the ruthless organization more than once, and what she'd learned from these encounters.

"They'd like me dead and the Starbuck holdings under their thumb," she said flatly. "But that's just a little piece of the picture. They want the whole country, Joseph. All of it. And they'll take it any way they can get it—bribery, murder, extortion, it doesn't really matter, as long as they get what they want. The shame of it is, they don't *have* to do much besides spread their money around. There are only too many men like Pierce Cavanaugh ready and willing to lend a hand."

For a long moment, Glass said nothing. "I appreciate you telling me," he said finally. "Seems like you and Ki have taken on a peck of trouble."

"Lot of times it seems that way to me," Jessie sighed. She drew her jacket around her shoulders and huddled closer to the fire. The wind found its way down her neck and she shivered and pulled up her collar. Joseph settled his arm around her shoulder; it was an easy, natural gesture and Jessie nestled comfortably against him.

"Goin' to get colder," said Glass. "Even down here in the holler."

"You think so, huh?"

"Know it is for sure. *Real* cold."

Jessie read the tone of his voice and knew exactly what he was thinking. She looked up and grinned, and caught him grinning back.

"I was, uh...kinda scared to say anything," he told her. "Wasn't sure what you'd say."

Jessie gave him her best little-girl look. "Now why would you be scared of a thing like that? If I'm reading you right, Mr. Glass, you're saying we're both going to freeze unless we, uh...do everything we can to keep warm."

"Right." Glass nodded solemnly and cleared his throat. "It's the truth, you know. Two folks under their own blankets ain't goin' to keep near as warm as two sharin'."

"You don't have to convince me," Jessie said absently. "I sure don't want to freeze."

"Well then, by God, we...we just won't." Glass stood, walked to his pack, and came back with a short hand ax. Jessie watched while he chopped the soft earth by the fire, then scooped the dirt out with his hands to make a depression six inches deep. Next he took the ax up into the trees and brought back an armload of pine boughs. While Jessie spread them around, he went back and filled two blankets full of fallen pine needles, dropped them on the boughs, and returned for another load. Finally they laid all the blankets they had on their bed, and Glass added a cut-down buffalo robe to the top.

Jessie watched the proceedings silently. "Think that'll do it?"

"Oh yeah. Ought to do it just fine."

"Then I guess we might as well get in there, huh? Isn't getting any warmer out here."

"Yep." Glass nodded absently. "That's the thing to do, all right."

Neither of them looked at the other as they sat down and pulled off their boots. Jessie waited until she was under the

93

buffalo robe before she peeled off her jacket and folded it up for a pillow. Glass placed their rifles on the ground, close at hand, and then slid in the other side. They lay there in silence a long moment, staring at the star-filled sky, then both started laughing at once. Jessie turned to meet him, and Joseph took her in his arms.

"I'm glad we let this happen," he whispered. "I sure wanted it to."

"So did I. Just wasn't much time to think on it. I guess there is, now."

"We got nothin' to do till mornin'."

"And we *do* have to keep warm," she reminded him. "It's the sensible thing to do."

Glass laughed, and Jessie relaxed in his arms. He covered her face with kisses, then found her mouth and pressed his lips hungrily to hers. Jessie sighed and opened to his touch. He explored each moist and secret hollow, drinking in the sweet taste of her mouth. She felt his kisses race through the length of her body; they warmed her belly and tightened the tips of her breasts. She snaked her hands about his neck and caught his hair between her fingers. The man-smell of his body aroused her senses. She freed herself from his kisses and rubbed her face against the thick mat of his beard. Her lips found his throat, the hollow of his neck. She let her tongue sample the exciting taste of his flesh.

Joseph felt a need within her that matched his own. His arms slid down her back to her waist. His hands found the plush curve of her bottom, gripped the firm mounds of flesh, and pressed her loins against him. Jessie moaned with pleasure and boldly answered his thrust. He pushed against her harder, letting her feel the swell of his member between her thighs. Jessie gasped at his touch, sucked in a breath, and pushed him away.

"Lord, Joseph—I don't know about you, but I think we got it a little *too* hot in here!"

"I agree," he said. "Either the covers or the clothes have to go."

"Don't guess we need to vote on that, huh?"

"Not 'less we're both plumb crazy." Joseph pulled himself up on his arms and found the buttons of her shirt. Jessie lay still and watched his face. The dying fire turned his flesh to ruddy leather, tightened the lines about his mouth. His eyes turned from blue to agate-black. She could feel them on her skin, just as surely as the pressure of his hands. He freed the tail of her shirt from the top of her jeans and undid the last button, then let his hands slide under the fabric and pull it gently from her breasts. Her nipples stiffened instantly under his touch. His erection was iron-hard on her belly. She ground herself joyously against him, molding the hollow of her mound to fit his shaft. Joseph groaned within his chest and bent to take the swollen nipples into his mouth. Jessie arched her back against the pressure of his lips; her fingers tore at his hair, forcing the taut mounds into his mouth. His tongue teased the pert little buds, drawing first one and then the other past his lips. Jessie cried out and tossed her hair from side to side. Bright amber coils lashed at his face.

"Joseph," Jessie moaned, "pull my pants off and get in me . . . please! I want you inside me *now!*"

"Oh, is that so?" Joseph raised himself up from her breasts and gave her a lopsided grin. "I'd of never knowed that."

"This is no time to be funny," she scolded. "I mean it, Joseph. You'd better just—*aaaaaah!*"

Without taking his eyes from hers, he took her nipple lightly between his teeth, drew it into his mouth, and let it go. Jessie stared, her breath coming in short little gasps. Joseph drew the rosy peak into his mouth once more, flipping it rapidly with his tongue. Jessie sucked in a breath. She was so sensitive, now, that every touch sent a shudder through her body. She thrust her pelvis frantically against him, again and again and again. She pleaded with his body, begging him to take her. Joseph's mouth left her breasts and trailed to the gentle swell of her belly. His fingers found her belt, unbuckled it quickly, and went to work on the buttons of her jeans. Jessie dug her heels into the blanket and raised her bottom eagerly off the ground. He stripped her denims off her legs and threw them aside.

"My God, you are a fine-lookin' woman," Joseph told her. "You truly are, Jessie."

Jessie laughed and twitched her hips. "Now how do *you* know, mister? You're down there in the dark."

"Don't you worry about me. I can see just fine in the dark. Besides, I got a real good sense of feel."

"Yes, you . . . oh, *Lord*, Joseph!"

His hands pressed firmly against the hollows of her thighs, spreading her ivory legs wide. His tongue brushed lightly over the moist silken mound, moving in a slow, lazy circle that set her legs trembling. Joseph's mouth parted the delicate petals of flesh, baring the crown of her pleasure. His kiss caressed each coral fold; his tongue found the hard little pearl and teased it lightly.

Jessie's fingers tightened in his hair. Her head snapped back and the cords in her throat went rigid. Joseph's tongue plunged deeper and deeper inside her. The honeyed moisture of her flesh assailed his senses and heightened his pleasure. Jessie jerked against him in uncontrollable spasms of delight. Her body screamed for release; the white-hot fire between her legs raced through her veins and tingled in her breasts. She felt the warm, syrupy wave gathering strength deep within her, thundering past her belly and into her loins . . .

Jessie cried out, caught in a timeless moment of joy and pain. In the crest of that pleasure, Joseph spread her wide and drew the throbbing little bud into his mouth.

Jessie screamed as her orgasm swept her up and carried her away. It surged through her slender frame again and again, each new thrust of Joseph's tongue unleashing fresh waves of delight. Now she begged him to stop as desperately as she'd pleaded with him to take her. She felt herself slipping away, falling dizzily through a honey-velvet darkness. She flailed out frantically for support, gave a deep sigh, and let herself sink through the warm and lovely depths . . .

"Jessie? Hey, you all right?"

She opened her eyes and looked up at his grinning face. "My God," she said shakily, "what—what did you *do* to me, friend? I think I passed out for a minute."

"You did," said Joseph, a smile still curling the corners of his mouth. "Four or five minutes, I reckon."

"Well, you don't have to look so damn smug. Think you're pretty smart, don't you?"

"Uh-huh. Guess maybe I do."

"Hah! Could've killed me for sure, and you're just grinning from ear to ear. Oh my, Joseph!" She sighed and ran her hands over her throat. Her flesh was still slick with moisture. Copper tendrils of hair clung to her cheeks and the swell of her breasts.

"If I'm going to die, I guess that's the way I want to do it."

"There's worse ways to go, I reckon."

"You're a lovely man, you know?" She clasped his shoulders with her hands and drew him to her. "Honest to God, you are a— Hey, what's this?" She gave him a mischievous grin, raised the covers, and peeked under. "Looks like you were busy restin' up while I was out, huh? My, my, you are as fine-looking a man naked as you are dressed up. Even finer, maybe."

Joseph tousled her hair. "Remember what you said, lady? You can't see a thing under that blanket."

Jessie laughed. "No, but I can *feel* as good as you!" Loosing her hands from his neck, she trailed her fingers quickly down the hard, matted flesh of his chest, past his belly, to grasp his erection.

"Oh yes . . ." She bit her lip and closed her eyes. "My God, Joseph Glass, there isn't a she-grizzly in Montana safe with this thing runnin' loose!"

"Huh?" Joseph blinked in alarm. "Damn, girl, I never heard of such a thing!"

Jessie kicked her legs in delight at his expression. "All right, maybe you *don't* chase bears—but you sure as hell could if you wanted."

"Well, I don't," Joseph growled. "It ain't *that* lonely in the mountains. 'Specially right now. Jessie, those hands of yours are driving me crazy."

"Are they? Really?"

"You know what you're doing. Don't blink those eyes at me. Ahhhh, *yes!*"

He rose up higher on his knees so she could reach him. Jessie's hands caressed his member, letting the tips of her fingers ride gently along its length. He swelled under her touch, the flesh so taut it seemed to throb. Joseph closed his eyes and let a soft whisper of pleasure hiss through his teeth. Jessie's touch seared his flesh like a brand.

"Like that, huh?"

"What do *you* think?"

"What *I* think is that I've got something you'll like even better than that."

Extricating herself from his arms, she slid quickly past his chest until her head rested under his belly. She kissed the tip of his shaft, then teased it with the point of her tongue. Joseph

97

shuddered and let out a sigh. The pink tip of her tongue flicked out again, slicking his flesh with moisture. She opened her mouth to let her hot breath surround him; Joseph thrust himself against her and she moved deftly out of his reach.

"Damn, who's tryin' to kill who?" Joseph groaned.

Jessie didn't answer. She kissed him lightly, coming ever closer to his flesh, but denying him what he wanted. Her hands came up to stroke him; she kneaded his length with her fingers, letting her nails trail gently from the tip to the base of his shaft.

"You want me to beg, girl, I sure as hell will!" Joseph said hoarsely.

"I don't care," Jessie said lightly. "Beg all you want."

She stroked him again and again, sharing the pleasure of his excitement. She knew he was near to bursting, that he'd explode the instant she took him into her mouth. She lapped him with her tongue, circling him round and round like a ribbon. Joseph's thighs trembled. She could hear the breath heaving through his lungs. She let the strokes grow faster, then faster and faster still.

Joseph gave a sudden strangled cry as she took him into her mouth, her lips working rapidly along his length. Her cheeks went hollow as she strained to take him in. Her arms circled his hips and she drew herself to him until her face pressed hard against his body.

Joseph roared out his pleasure and filled her with his warmth. Jessie held on tight, clinging to his loins until the storm within had passed...

She lay in the hollow of his arms, her head nestled warmly against his shoulder. Her arm encircled his chest, and one slender leg draped wantonly over his belly.

"Guess what?" she whispered lazily into his ear. "I'm not cold at all."

Joseph laughed deep in his chest. "Damn, I'm sure glad to hear it."

"You sleeping or anything?"

"Anything, mostly."

Jessie grinned. "You're bragging, mister. Isn't any way you're going to—oh dear, you're *not* bragging, are you?" The crook of her leg found his member, pressed hard and flat against his belly. "Joseph Glass," she said soberly, "I was right the first time, I swear. There isn't a she-bear safe in the Rockies!"

98

"Not if she's under this blanket, she ain't."

"Mmmmmm..." Jessie nuzzled her face into his throat. "I don't even *want* to be safe, and that's a fact."

"I wanted to make love to you," Joseph said evenly, "right from the start, Jessie. When I first saw you up on that rock. 'Fore that, I guess. When I was up there above Mule."

"Well, you sure did get me, now didn't you?"

"Tell the truth, I didn't figure it'd happen."

"Oh? Any particular reason why not?"

"You bein' what you are, mostly. Where you come from and all."

Jessie turned over and folded her arms on his chest. "And just what do you think I am, Joseph Glass?" Her green eyes bored into his. "I'm a woman, I know that much. What else? Something I haven't noticed?"

"Come on, now." Joseph gave her a look. "You ain't just *any* woman, Jessie. You're somethin' special. Hell, there ain't many like you anywhere. And not in any of the places I've been."

"Well now, that's *your* fault, isn't it?" she teased him. "You can't expect to find women under rocks and perching in trees."

Joseph chuckled, and tousled her hair. "You know damn well what I'm talkin' about. I'm a mountain man. And you put your finger right on it. Women like you just don't wander around in my world."

"And why are *you* wandering around out here, Joseph?" she asked curiously. "I've done a little wondering about that."

"Me?" Joseph shrugged. "Why I'm, uh... just here, is all."

Jessie shook her head. "You're a pretty rare bird, and you know it. You're an honest-to-God mountain man, friend, there's no denying that. But you're also about forty or fifty years *late* getting started. I don't see a whole lot of demand these days for beaver hats."

"Now that's the truth," Joseph said distantly. The buffalo robe had slipped off her shoulders and he reached up and tucked it under her chin. His eyes were as black as stone in the dim glow of the fire. "Ain't much of a story. I never wanted to be anything but what I am. Ran away from a farm in Ohio when I was fourteen, walked through Indiana and Illinois and Ioway till I got to Nebraska, got a job on a freightwagon, and went all up and down the Dakotas. Couple of years later I met

99

Jebediah Baker down on the Platte in Colorado. Couple of fellers had took what money I had and left me for dead. I was a dumb, skinny kid goin' on seventeen. Jeb took me and turned me into a man."

"Oh Lord, Joseph." Jessie held him tight. "I didn't know. I guess I had no idea you were with him that long."

"Yeah, well . . ." He gave her a sober look. "You were askin' back there somewhere 'bout me and Yellow Wing. Why there wasn't any, you know, man-and-woman feelin's between us. Reason is we sort of grew up together. She was younger, 'bout nine when Jeb found me. So I've always been kind of a big brother."

"I understand," Jessie said gently.

"Yeah, well, I wanted you to." Joseph sighed and put his hands behind his head. Jessie snuggled in close against his body, resting her hand on his member. His erection had subsided, but now her gentle strokes brought him quickly back to life. Joseph stirred and gripped her shoulders. Jessie shook her head and pushed him back. Sliding her body over his, she knelt above his thighs, reached between her legs, and thrust his rigid member inside her. Joseph sighed and cupped her swollen breasts in his hands. Jessie lowered herself slowly on his shaft until she'd taken all his length. She ground herself against him, pressing every curve and hollow into the hard places of his body. She worked him gently, moving in lazy circles, using all her wiles to make their pleasure last. She stroked him with her body, caressing him with sweet and silken walls. Joseph groaned and thrust his loins against her. Jessie held him off, drawing one agonizing minute into another, and then another. Joseph's body trembled. Jessie pressed her hard nipples against his chest and thrust her tongue deeply into his mouth. Joseph gripped her firm little bottom with his hands, and pulled her savagely against him. Jessie screamed and bit her lip. The power of her orgasm wrenched every fiber of her being. Joseph emptied himself inside her, each surge of his pleasure triggering new explosions between her thighs . . .

When it was over, she lay back in his arms. Neither of them spoke. In a moment, Joseph's slow and easy breathing told her he was asleep. Jessie snuggled in close and stared at the dying fire. Her heart went out to the man beside her. She liked Joseph Glass a great deal; he was a good man, as proud and honest and open as the mountains he called his home. She wondered if he knew, or if he'd set it aside so long he really believed that was how it was. Jessie had seen it in his eyes and guessed the truth, even as he denied it. Yellow Wing might see Joseph as her brother, but Joseph didn't think of her as a sister. He was in love with the Indian girl, whether or not he'd let himself believe it...

Chapter 11

Ki lay on the flat shelf of stone above the valley. The rock was split by the roots of a twisted pine that had grown to accommodate the winds of a hundred years. Below the stony shelf, the slope curved steeply to a swiftly rushing river. Beyond the river, the foothills climbed to the faraway snow-capped peaks of the Lewis Range and the Divide. Ki guessed the peaks were some thirty miles away. The girl said the stream was the Flathead River.

"They're down there," he told her. "Not too far behind us, either."

"How do you know they are?" she asked. "You can't *see* them."

"No. I can't see them. But that's where they are. They'd follow our trail north along the valley floor."

"Unless they climbed up here like we did," she said absently.

Ki closed his eyes and let out a breath. "Yellow Wing, why would they do that? We didn't leave the valley until we passed it. They won't *know* we circled back until it's too late. And they're not going to follow our sign over solid rock. They won't know where we've gone."

"They'll know."

"What?"

"I said they'll know. They're not white men," she told him patiently. "They'll expect you to do something like this. They're not Sioux, but they're Indians, and any Indian—"

"I know," Ki said wearily. "Any Indian can out-track a white with his eyes closed. I don't believe that, and neither do you. Besides, I'm only half white. That means I'm only half as bad as a white man, and maybe half as good as an Indian."

Yellow Wing gave him a chilling laugh. "That doesn't make any sense at all!"

Ki sat up and faced her. The sun had been up less than an

102

hour, and the rock was still cold from the night. Each time he looked at the girl he was startled by her beauty—the proud curve of her cheeks, the pouty, sensuous mouth, and the striking contrast of dark flesh and ice-blue eyes. She leaned against the tree just above him, her arms folded below the gentle swell of her breasts. One foot was planted on the rock, the other at an angle against the tree. Standing that way shot one hip boldly forward and tightened the leather skirt over the lean curve of her thigh. How can she look like that, Ki wondered, and be such an irritating woman?

"All right," he told her, "what I said doesn't make any sense, Yellow Wing. It wasn't supposed to. I was trying to make a point."

"Oh. You're making a joke, is that it?" Her blue eyes narrowed and her chin shot out in defiance. "You're making fun of me?"

"No, I'm not making fun of you," he said evenly. "I have no reason to do that. All I want to do is get those two off our trail."

"They won't give up," she said. "You beat them back there, and killed one of their own. They have to make up for that."

"I won't give up either. If they won't leave us alone, I'll have to stop them. If that means we—" Ki stopped as motion in the valley caught his eye. He went flat at once and motioned her down. She crawled up beside him, so close her dark hair brushed his cheek.

"Down there," he said quietly. "At the far bend of the river."

"I see them." He caught the slight touch of disappointment in her voice. "You were right. But that doesn't mean they'll be fooled when they come to the place we started climbing. They're Arikaras, but they're not stupid. They'll know we didn't vanish into thin air."

"No. That's true. But by the time they figure out we circled back, we won't be here anymore."

"Maybe. We'll see."

Ki glared, backed off the shelf in a crouch, and made his way over to the horses.

"You're always getting mad," she said behind him.

"I'm not mad."

"Yes. I think I know when someone's mad and when he isn't."

Ki turned on the girl. "Would it make you any happier if they caught us? Then you'd be right and I'd be wrong!"

Yellow Wing looked pained. "Of course I don't want us to get caught. What a silly thing to say." She turned away and swung gracefully onto the bare back of the horse, showing him a flash of shapely thigh.

He led them down the far side of the hill, moving quickly now and not worrying about leaving sign. The girl was right; eventually the two Arikaras would discover what they'd done, that they were doubling back on the trail and heading south. He never imagined he'd be lucky enough to lose them. Climbing the shelf and watching for them to pass was only a way of buying time, keeping the Indians busy while he hightailed it back to find Jessie.

He knew very well what she'd do. As soon as she and Glass found them gone and read his message, they'd follow the Arikaras to Cavanaugh's camp. And would Cavanaugh and his people be gone? Ki had a good idea that they would be. Cavanaugh knew who he was, and knew from the Indians that Jessie was free. But he wouldn't know where she was now. That would worry him a bit—that and the fact that Ki had found their camp. He couldn't know what Ki had seen, or whether he'd guessed the significance of the Prussian's presence.

What the hell are they up to? Ki wondered. The heavy Prussian accent of Cavanaugh's friend and the fact that the man was clearly in charge told him a lot. But what were the two of them doing? What was the man's business with Cavanaugh?

They rode through the bottom of a hollow, dry stream bed that snaked its way down through a heavily forested slope.

"Are you sure you didn't see anything at all, hear anything in the camp?" he asked the girl.

"Nothing. I told you that before. I hardly even saw the white men in camp. Just the man who came to look at me once." She paused, and shot him a sober look. "Are you certain that was him? The one who had my grandfather killed?"

"Yes, Yellow Wing. I'm certain."

"Then you should have killed him," she said harshly. "You were right there. You had the chance and you let him go."

"What?" Ki reined up hard and stared. "If I had, I'd probably be dead right now. There were only ten or twelve men in that

104

camp, you know. And that fine Prussian doctor would have loved to get his hands on you."

"You don't know it would happen like that. You could have tried."

Ki looked at her. "What is it you don't like about me? Will you tell me that? Please? I mean, I got you out of there in one piece. I'm not asking for any thanks, but you don't have to *glare* at me all the time."

"Ha!" Yellow Wing tossed her hair in disdain. "That's it, isn't it? You expect me to look silly and stupid. Like a white girl."

"I don't expect anything of the kind."

"Yes, you do. I saw your woman Jessie. She smiles all the time. I expect she does everything you say."

Ki had to laugh. "She's not my woman, Yellow Wing. And Jessie Starbuck never did anything she didn't want to do. Sometimes she's just as stubborn as you."

"Well, then." She shot him a nasty grin. "You should be very pleased with me."

"It's not the same thing. Jessie's stubborn, but she'll listen to reason. She has respect for other peoples' opinions. She's not pigheaded."

"P-pig-headed!" The girl's face clouded. "Bastard! *Half-breed bastard!*" She spat in his direction and drove a small fist at his face. Ki grabbed her arm and held it, nearly wrenching her off her horse. The girl bared her teeth in anger and contempt.

"I'll kill you," she blurted. "I'll carve out your heart in your sleep!"

"Fine," Ki said calmly, "I'll try to remember that. But for now I think it might be a good idea if we rode on south. Then you can carve me up at your leisure."

Ki eased his grip and she jerked her wrist free, brought it to her mouth, and sucked the flesh. "You can ride anywhere you like. You're *not* riding with me!"

"Oh, now look—"

Yellow Wing spun her mount savagely about, forcing Ki to back off. She kicked the horse in the sides and set it climbing the steep slope into the trees.

Ki cursed under his breath, whipping his mount up the hill. He heard her horse protest, saw its hind legs paw frantically for footing. Dirt and loose stone clattered in Ki's direction. She forced the frightened animal through the trees, too angry to care what she was doing. Ki followed as best he could, using all the skill he could muster to keep his own horse from falling. He lost her for a moment, then spotted her again. She was pressed to the horse, so close she seemed a part of the animal herself. Her skirt was caught up about her thighs, her bare legs gripping the horse's flanks.

"She's going to break her neck, and mine too," Ki muttered darkly. He paused, searched the slope, and decided the left-hand route was better. Urging the mount forward, he guided it past a rotting log and up a reasonably gentle ridge. The shot clipped leaves a yard ahead and hit his horse below the eye. The animal folded, all four legs collapsing at once. Ki leaped free, hit the ground, and rolled against a tree to stop his fall. Somewhere above, the girl screamed. The Arikara came bounding down the hill on foot, levering another shell into his rifle.

The Indian fired wildly from the hip, loosing one rapid shot after another as his feet dug for support on the slope. Lead chewed bark near Ki's head. He gripped the trunk of the tree and slid behind it, slammed his feet against the base, and pushed off hard to the right. The Indian went to his knees and fired again. Ki pumped his legs and clawed dirt, fighting to gain height and better cover. The Arikara cursed and came at him, tearing through a tangle of brush and low branches. Ki grasped a *shuriken* throwing star from his shirt pocket and turned to face his foe. The cover was too thick, the weapon next to useless. His eyes swept the hillside up ahead. Yellow Wing's mount had snapped branches seconds before and gone silent. She'd escaped, then, back among the trees. Either that, or the other Indian had silenced her quickly.

He pulled himself forward another yard, then stopped and stepped back. The cover vanished abruptly, giving way to open ground. The first Arikara was clambering up behind him— where was the other? Ki gritted his teeth, took a deep breath, and sprinted into the clearing. The Indian stepped from cover just ahead. He grinned with delight at finding Ki unarmed, brought the rifle casually to his shoulder, and squeezed the trigger. Ki bent his knees and whipped the *shuriken* free. Razored steel struck the Indian under his chin and disappeared. The Arikara threw up his arms and gave a quick, strangled cry. Blood fountained from the wound; the Indian stepped backward and folded. Ki heard branches whip behind him, threw himself aside, and rolled. A bullet splintered stone at his heels. He sprang to his feet, saw the man behind him, and knew he'd moved a split second too late. The black bore of the muzzle found his heart. The Indian's features stretched in pleasure as the shot rang flat across the clearing. Ki's body tightened to meet pain, but a small black hole appeared an inch above the Arikara's eye. The Winchester went off, but it was already sagging toward the ground and the shot plowed uselessly into dirt as the Indian crumpled.

Ki jerked around and saw the warriors standing to his right. They both wore buckskin leggings and leather shirts. The one with the rifle wore a bright beaded vest. Ki knew at once they were Sioux.

"Thank you," he said calmly. "If you understand English, I'd like you to know I'm grateful."

The warrior didn't answer. He gestured uphill with the rifle and Ki complied. The other Sioux squatted and studied Ki's kill. Pulling the *shuriken* from the Arikara's throat, he wiped it on a leaf, turned it over in his hand, and looked curiously at Ki. Then he spoke rapidly to the man in the vest. The other Sioux answered. The man on the ground held up the *shuriken* and grinned at Ki. Ki grinned back and gave a silent sigh of relief. Clearly, they were impressed by the strange weapon and what it could do. He decided that was as good a sign as any.

A few yards up the hill he saw Yellow Wing waiting, standing by her pony and two others.

"I'm glad you're all right," he told her. "When I heard you cry out, I wasn't sure."

The girl nodded. "I'm all right. And I'm—I'm glad you're not hurt." Her eyes showed no expression, but Ki didn't complain. The fact that she'd showed concern was a pleasant surprise. She turned to the Indian in the vest and nodded at Ki.

"This is Red Elk. He and Little Hawk are Oglala Sioux. The Oglala are my people and Red Elk is a cousin of Crazy Horse." Her blue eyes shone with pride. "I am also related to the great chief."

"Please tell him I'm glad he happened along," said Ki. "Tell him I—"

"Tell him yourself," said Yellow Wing. "He speaks English as well as you do."

Ki was genuinely surprised. The Indian had ignored him

when he'd spoken before. "Thank you, Red Elk," he said evenly. "I appreciate what you did."

Red Elk shrugged. "The Arikaras are white men's dogs. It is good to stop their barking." He turned and spoke over his shoulder to his companion. Little Hawk handed the *shuriken* to Red Elk, and Red Elk gave it to Ki. "Throw the round knife again," he said. "That tree. The place where the bark is scarred."

Ki understood. It was the polite way of saying he'd have to prove that hitting the Arikara tracker wasn't luck. There were times when boasting could do some good; Ki figured this was one of those times. Without looking at the Indians, he pulled three more *shuriken* from his pocket and weighted them in the palm of his left hand. Turning, he walked casually away as if taking a leisurely stroll. Four more steps, then five, each one taking him farther from the tree. Suddenly he turned in a crouch, his right hand moving in a blur. The second throwing star was on its way when the first struck wood. The third and fourth followed, so quickly it almost seemed that all four weapons arrived at once. The *shuriken* were lined neatly on the target, one above the other, less than an inch between them.

The Indians pretended they weren't impressed. Ki read their eyes and knew better. Even the girl stared at the sight in wonder.

Red Elk didn't move. Little Hawk walked to the blades and touched them gingerly with his finger, as if they still might carry some magic. Then he drew his knife and pried the *shuriken* free and returned them solemnly to Ki.

Red Elk turned and faced him. "The Arikaras' horses are over the ridge," he said evenly. "You may have them both. We will take the rifles." Without waiting for an answer, he turned and mounted up and started through the trees. Yellow Wing and the other Sioux followed. Ki repressed a grin. A white man would have pounded him on the back and said his feat was a real wonder. The Indians showed their respect by ignoring the deed completely.

Ki found the horses, chose a pinto he liked, and led the other up the hill to find the Sioux. It was close to noon now, and from the height of the ridge, the snow-capped peaks blazed in the sun. Below and to the right was the ledge where he and the girl had watched the Arikaras ride up the valley. She'd been right and he'd been wrong. He'd thought he could fool the Indian trackers. Instead they'd followed his backtrail with no trouble at all. Ki made a mental note to tell her. She'd likely spit in his eye, but he had to do it. And damn it all, she *had* been concerned about his safety. He hadn't forgotten that. Maybe she didn't despise him after all. Another couple of years together, and she might even smile.

He knew what was bothering him, and didn't like to own up to the truth. Being so close to those startling blue eyes and luscious curves was getting to him. Every time her leather skirt bared a patch of thigh, something stirred in the pit of his stomach.

Ki needed to talk to Yellow Wing, but the girl wouldn't leave the Indian's side. For a good quarter-hour, the rapid music of the Sioux language passed between them. Ki wasn't surprised that the girl did most of the talking. Now and then, Red Elk nodded and answered back. Finally, when they were down the side of the mountain by the river, Red Elk raised his hand and called a halt. Little Hawk took the horses to the water. Red Elk leaned against a tree and chewed a piece of jerked meat.

"I need to see you," Ki told the girl, "before I talk to him. I want to get started back south after Jessie. It would be all right, wouldn't it, if I gave him the other horse as a present?"

Yellow Wing held his glance a long moment. "I talked to him. He's seen Jessie and Joseph."

"He has?" Ki showed his surprise. "Where? When was this?"

Yellow Wing told him about the meeting, and approximately where it had happened.

"That means they were following my trail and the Arikaras'. If you're right about the place Red Elk saw them, Jessie and Glass weren't all that far from Cavanaugh's camp." His dark eyes narrowed in thought. "They found it, and followed Cavanaugh's trail. Jessie would stick close, see what they were up to and where they went." He looked intently at the girl. "If we get started now, we can make good time before dark. Now that there's no one on our tail, we don't have to be careful. If you'll just—" Ki stopped, suddenly aware of the girl's expression. "What is it? What's wrong? Look, if you want to ride on with them, it's all right. You can get back together with Glass and his friends when it suits you."

"No, that's not it, Ki." She bit her lip and let out a breath.

109

"Just stop *talking* a minute and listen." She nodded over her shoulder, and he saw Red Elk watching from the tree. "Red Elk and Little Hawk are Oglala Sioux. I'm not sure you know what that means. The white men would like to see all the Sioux dead—especially the Oglala. These two are on their way north, past the mountains into Canada and Milk River country. They're going there to join Sitting Bull. Before that, they're meeting another party not far from here. They'll all cross over together."

The girl paused and Ki waited. "All right," he said finally. "What Red Elk does is his business. I just want to thank him and be on my way."

"You don't understand, do you?" Yellow Wing looked to the heavens. "These two are on the run. And the party they're meeting has jumped the reservation. Red Elk and Little Hawk are here to help them get north. If the bluecoats ever find them . . ."

"I understand," said Ki. "I know about the Sioux."

"That's just it," she said. "The Sioux don't know about *you*. They respect you, and both Red Elk and Little Hawk think you're a brave warrior. But they can't take the chance. Not now. When they get the others into Canada, you can go wherever you like. Until then, they won't let you leave."

"What?" Ki stared at the girl. "What do you mean, I can't leave? Who does he think I'm going to tell?"

"Ki . . ."

"He trusts Joseph Glass, but not me, is that it?" Ki blurted.

"I know what you're thinking. Joseph is a mountain man—but he's not like the old-timers. He respects the Indians and they know it. He hasn't been killing them for forty or fifty years."

"Neither have I," Ki said bluntly.

"They know that."

"I'm going to talk to him. I can't stay here with Jessie down south somewhere."

"Go ahead. Won't do you any good."

"And what about you?" he asked flatly. "The people I'm going after murdered your grandfather, Yellow Wing. Have you forgotten that? Are you not interested any more in seeing them pay?"

The girl went rigid. "You have no right to say that. It's not true!"

110

"Fine. Explain that to him."

"I—I can't."

"Why not? He's family, isn't he? You're both Oglala Sioux."

Yellow Wing turned away. "He's doing what's right for our people. I have to respect his wishes."

"I respect them too. He's got to believe me, that's all."

"He won't."

"He'd better."

"Ki!" For an instant he saw a flash of concern in her blue eyes. "He means what he says. Try to ride out of here and he'll kill you. He—he's got good reason, you know. Anyone who sees him will try to stop him. And with this cholera, every miner and settler in Montana is itchy enough to shoot an Indian on sight."

"Wait a minute." Ki turned her around. "What cholera? You didn't tell me about that."

Yellow Wing shrugged. "He met some Nez Percé. The sickness is showing up all over. That's why it's so dangerous right now. The whites and their families are scared and angry. A lot of them are running, leaving everything behind."

Ki frowned in thought. "Jessie saw some cholera victims being brought into Mule. I didn't know it was an epidemic."

"It is now," she assured him. "If it wasn't for that, maybe he'd listen to you, Ki."

Ki glared. "I don't have the time to wait till everything's just right in Montana, Yellow Wing. He's going to have to listen to me, now." He moved her aside and walked across the clearing to Red Elk. Clearly, the Indian knew what they'd been discussing. He was waiting for Ki to come. Ki wasted no time on greetings.

"Yellow Wing told me," he said plainly. "I can't stay here, Red Elk. The woman you saw with Glass is under my protection. I've taken an oath to see that she comes to no harm. It is a matter of honor with me."

Red Elk nodded. "If you have taken an oath, you must do what you can to carry it out."

The Indian's statement wasn't as simple as all that, and Ki knew it. "You won't stand aside? You won't trust me?"

Red Elk's dark eyes bored into Ki's. "At another time I might trust you. I think you are a man who has honor. I do not know you, but I believe this is so. You are not all white.

111

Your face tells me that blood like my own runs in your veins."

"Red Elk, if I had your trust, I wouldn't betray it."

"Yes. I believe this is true."

"Then why another time?" Ki persisted. "If I have honor tomorrow or next year, I have it today as well."

Red Elk shook his head. "In this day and the days to come, I am responsible for the lives of many others. I could call you friend and trust you. I cannot do that for another. It is the same as choosing a horse or a knife for a friend because it is the one you would choose for yourself. This is not a good idea."

Ki understood the man's logic. It was as sound as it could be, and hard to fault. "I won't lie to you," he said plainly. "I've got to go south. I'm going to leave here if I can."

Red Elk nodded. "Yes. That is what a man should do." He looked straight at Ki, never glancing at Little Hawk. That would have been a threat, an insult to a man he respected. Nevertheless, Little Hawk was there. Ki didn't have to look to know that the Sioux stood by the horses with a rifle cradled in his arms.

"All right," Ki said darkly, "at least we understand each other. I don't like it, but there it is. Now what? Are you headed northwest, up to glacier country?"

"Soon," Red Elk told him. "First, we go farther up this valley. There are twenty, maybe thirty people in the party we will meet. They will keep to cover and so will we." The Indian licked his lips in distaste. "Once, you could ride for days in this country and never see a bluecoat or a settler. Now they are everywhere. With the sickness about, they'll be as thick as lice in a blanket. Come, it's time to leave this place."

An hour later, they found the Sioux party.

There were seven men, an old woman, and two children. One of the men was badly hurt and wouldn't last out the day. The men led Red Elk and the others upriver and then west to a small creek that ran out of the hills. Ki counted eighteen dead, many of them women and children. The men who'd killed them had waited on a high sandy bank until the Indians bunched at the stream. From the way the bodies lay, it was clear to Ki that the killers had fired all at once and kept firing till it was over. The grass on the bank was littered with brass shell casings.

112

Red Elk walked among the dead, his face as hard as stone. Ki stayed out of his way. He could have ridden off and vanished, but the thought never entered his mind. Instead he wandered into the brush, following the riflemen's tracks to flat ground. When he turned and stopped, Yellow Wing was behind him.

"It wasn't the bluecoats," she said. "I talked to one of the men. He was in the rear and he saw them. They were just white men with guns."

"The hell they were," Ki said darkly. "It was *them*, Yellow Wing!"

"Who? What are you talking about?"

"Cavanaugh's people."

"You can't know that."

Ki kicked at the matted grass. "Wagon tracks," he said harshly. "What were those men doing with *wagons* up here? They weren't hunting Indians—the Sioux came along, and the men killed them just because they were there."

Yellow Wing shook her head. "Red Elk won't believe that, Ki."

Ki didn't answer. He knotted his fists at his sides and stalked angrily back to the creek.

Chapter 12

Jessie turned around in her saddle and looked back. Behind her, the snow-laden peaks of the Divide were etched against a pale blue sky. Ragged wisps of cloud tore at the lower heights, slicing the range neatly in half. Earlier in the day, she'd reined in her horse beside Joseph and squinted into the east, past the point where they stood now. It was a breathtaking view, all the more startling because the mountains gave way abruptly to the nearly endless stretch of the Great Plains. Now grassland and gently rolling prairie surrounded them on every side. Fort Shaw and the Sun River lay to the south, Fort Benton to the east.

"We'll camp in a couple of hours and head out in the morning," Glass muttered. "Might as well get to Fort Benton. Can't waste any more time than we have already."

"Joseph..." Jessie moved her mount up beside him and laid a hand on his arm. "Joseph, don't keep beating yourself, all right? You did the best you could. No one could've done any better."

"That so?" His mouth curled in a frown. "*I* could've done better, Jessie. Should have, too, goddammit. Should have followed my head 'stead of my nose and kept goin' south!"

"You don't know that for sure."

"Yeah, I do know it, too. They ain't up here anywhere. They're down *there,* down toward Goldcreek and Helena. We never saw wagon tracks movin' any way but south. Right from the start, that's the way they've been heading. Out of Canada, down through Kootenay country. Then, later on, from the camp where they had Yellow Wing. *South*—down between the Missions and the Flathead River."

"All right, Joseph."

"All right, what? It *ain't* all right! I lost the bastards, Jessie!"

114

He heeled his horse savagely and moved off. Jessie let him be, watching his broad back until he was far across the prairie. He'd ride out his anger alone, then slow down and let her catch up. It had happened the morning before, after he'd taken them far to the south, following the wagons west of the Divide. He was certain he was on them, even when the sign disappeared and there wasn't a hint of where they'd been. She'd heard him whoop with delight when he picked up the trail, the bare hint of tracks on rocky terrain, turning suddenly eastward. They'd followed the trail through high and treacherous country for a full day and all the next morning before he'd discovered he was wrong. They'd caught up with the wagons on the plains below the mountains, and found two old teamsters hauling freight.

Glass had exploded in a fury, cursing himself for leading them over the Divide on a false trail. Jessie wasn't surprised. A man as calm and easygoing as Joseph Glass had to vent his feelings one way or the other. More than once, their lovemaking had hinted at this powerful, savage side of his nature. He was a good and gentle man, but in the end he was a mountain man as well. Storms surged within him that other men seldom knew. Some of those storms brought intense, agonizing pleasure to every part of Jessie's body. It was excitement tinged with a fear that sometimes threatened to overwhelm her. He'd never hurt her, she knew, but the fury was always there; she didn't want to tame it and wouldn't try.

That night he surprised her by taking her gently. Jessie was the aggressor, and she delighted in the task. She brought him to climax again and again, each orgasm greater than the last, and each leaving her own body hungry for more. Toward morning, they sank into sleep in each other's arms. Jessie was glad no one bothered them during the night. She was certain they'd never have stirred in time to know it . . .

"Benton's not far," he told her. "We'll get there easy this afternoon." He shook his head and gave her a sheepish grin. "I'm sorry 'bout actin' such a fool. I made a mistake and there's no takin' it back."

"I'm not worried about that, and you now it. And Benton's not that bad an idea. I thought we agreed on that. We're going to need help, Joseph. Montana's big country, and two of us aren't going to cut it. Whatever Cavanaugh and his Prussian friends are up to, they're spread out more than we are."

"Now that's a fact," he said darkly.

"You've got friends in Fort Benton, and so do I. We run sternwheelers on the Missouri, and there's a Starbuck office there. And there's the telegraph, don't forget. I've got a few good questions, and I know the people who can give me the answers."

"Sure, if the Blackfoot haven't cut the wires for the hell of it this week."

Jessie's green eyes flashed with mischief. "After last night, mister, I'm ready to fight the whole damn Blackfoot nation."

Joseph frowned in alarm. "After last night, lady, you're going to have to handle 'em alone. I ain't got any fight left."

"We'll see about that." Jessie smiled. "I expect they've got a hotel and a bed in Fort Benton."

Fort Benton was a drab and colorless town in a flat and featureless land. The broad waters of the Missouri seemed wasted, for they added little life to the arid plains.

"Isn't the prettiest place I've ever seen," said Jessie. "Doesn't even come close."

Glass reined in his mount at the edge of the river. "Take a good look," he said flatly. "Whole place is likely to dry up and blow away 'fore Tuesday."

Jessie knew what he was saying. Fort Benton had had its day, but that day was fading fast. A small, sleepy community in the 1840s and 1850s, Fort Benton had suddenly become a gateway to the northern Rocky Mountains and points west. Overland routes were long and perilous. A sternwheeler could reach Fort Benton from St. Louis in thirty-five days—if the boiler didn't blow, and snags didn't rip out the bottom. From Benton, settlers, prospectors, and freight haulers blazed trails north into Canada, and south and west to the mining towns. For more than twenty years, forty riverboats a day had plied the Missouri when the water allowed, carrying goods west and hauling back beaver pelts and buffalo hides. Now, with the railroads closing in from the south and east, Fort Benton was on its way out—nothing more than the long way around to Montana.

"Place has got memories for old-timers like Henry and Roos-

116

ter-John and Philadelphy," said Glass. "Jeb used to talk about it all the time. For a trapper, I guess it was sorta like a big night in Chicago or St. Louis." His crooked smile faded, and he gave Jessie a long and sober look. "We'll head back south no later than tomorrow. I'm goin' to find those bastards, I promise you that."

"I know you will," she told him gently. Glass leaned over and gave her a kiss that nearly lifted her out of the saddle.

After leaving their horses at the livery, Jessie and Glass checked into the Great Falls Hotel and walked two doors down to the Buffalo Cafe. The steaks weren't tender but they were thick, and neither of the pair complained. Halfway through supper they had all the latest news; as far as Jessie could tell, it was all bad. A traveler had arrived that afternoon from the south, bringing a day-old paper from Helena. There were more reports of cholera, deaths as far east as the Judith Mountains, and southwest from Fort Missoula to Goldcreek, Butte, and Virginia City. No one knew how many had died, but it was said the toll was already three hundred or more. The territorial governor, local officials, and doctors had warned the public not to panic. Still, people being people, they were doing just that. Miners, settlers, and merchants were leaving the stricken areas in droves, abandoning their property and claims, or selling out for whatever they could get.

"Those two Sioux I met got it right," Glass said soberly. "Don't look real good, does it?"

"Not good at all," Jessie agreed. "Joseph, you know what this means, don't you? Whatever Cavanaugh and his friends are up to, a cholera epidemic is the best break they could get. Everyone's running scared—they're not even *thinking* about anything else, and I don't blame 'em. Whatever the cartel's after, they'll likely carry it off without even batting an eye!"

Glass frowned and nodded. He stared at his steak and tossed his napkin on the table. "Let's get out of here," he growled. "I'm not real hungry anymore."

Jessie hurried to the Western Union office, and Joseph went the other way to see if any of his friends were in town. Night was closing in, and Jessie pulled the collar of her sheepskin jacket tightly about her neck. Canada was less than a hundred miles away, and there was nothing between here and there to stop the cold autumn wind.

She wrote four messages, each slightly different, concerning nonexistent shipments of timber and nails. Her Starbuck managers in Helena, Salt Lake City, Denver, and Cheyenne would read her words another way and understand that Pierce Cavanaugh was involved in some criminal activity. She couldn't say what, but her people were instructed to learn what they could. It wasn't much of a start, but the men in those cities knew their business, and they'd start asking questions and turning over rocks.

Finally, Jessie encoded a longer, more involved message to U.S. Marshal Billy Vail in Denver. Vail and Deputy Marshal Custis Long were among the handful of people who really believed the cartel existed, and knew what that organization could do. She told Vail everything she knew, and asked him to alert federal officers in Montana Territory.

Alert them to what? she thought dismally. *Billy Vail will do what he can, but I didn't give him anything at all!*

Back outside, darkness blanketed the town, dropping the temperature a good ten degrees. The Western Union operator had given her directions. The Starbuck office would be empty, but someone nearby could tell her where the man lived. For Jessie, he could put his hands on money fast, and that was something she could use. Besides, John Hamilton had chosen his men well. Jessie would be very much surprised if her local manager didn't know a thing or two about Cavanaugh's affairs—legal or otherwise.

Crossing the street, she left the shelter of the buildings. A cold blast of wind hit her hard, and she quickened her pace. The streets were nearly empty; anyone who didn't have business outside was searching out a fire and a hot meal. A few windows cast dim rectangles of yellow light into the street.

Jessie sensed the two men a moment before she saw them. They were walking along the far side of the street, keeping to shadow, hands dug in the pockets of their coats. There was no reason to think they even knew she was alive. Jessie, though, knew they weren't thinking of anyone else. Ki had taught her to develop this sense that he called *kime*, to respect the warnings it gave and act upon them at once.

Taking a deep and calming breath, she walked straight ahead without glancing to either side. At the end of the block she turned and started east. The instant she was completely out of

118

sight, she jerked her hands out of her pockets and broke into a run. Ducking into an alley on her right, she flattened herself against the brick wall and caught her breath. Her left hand inched along the wall while her right brought the ivory-handled derringer out of her jacket pocket. There was no use running, she knew. The men were too close, and they'd outpace her quickly. The alley was full of broken glass and boxes; they'd hear her if she tried to go through. She'd stop and face them, damn it—they wouldn't expect a woman to do that.

Holding her breath, she listened again, letting her back slide down the wall until a narrow stack of crates hid her. She yearned for her .38 Colt, the weapon she'd lost when McCabe's cabin went up in flames. There were two shots in the derringer, two men on her tail—not the kind of odds she liked at all.

Footsteps outside the alley brought all her senses alert. She straightened her right arm, the small pistol steady in her hand.

"—spotted us and took off running," the man growled. "Shit, we gotta chase her now."

"She ain't real far," said the other. "Down the block to the left or right. You take one an' I'll take the other. Hey, check that alley. She ain't that dumb, but—*Christ Jesus!*"

A man's face appeared, then jerked around abruptly to see what had happened to his companion. Jessie caught the dark silhouette of a shotgun against the night; silver flashed in the half-light and the man vanished. Jessie shrank back. There was no sound at all in the street. She waited, her heart pounding frantically against her breast.

"Jessie, it's me," the voice said calmly. "Come on out of there."

"*Joseph?*" She lowered a trembling hand and stepped warily out of the alley. He stood there, tall and dark, with no features at all. The only thing she saw was the Bowie knife catching quicksilver light.

"Don't look too close," he said sharply. "It ain't real pretty."

Jessie swallowed and stood back, waiting while he dragged the two men far into the alley. When he was through, he tossed one of the shotguns into the alley and handed the other to Jessie.

"Use it," he said firmly. "You see a goddamn *fly* move out here, you shoot it and keep going."

"Joseph, how—how did you know? Who *were* they?"

"Cavanaugh's men," he said sharply, spitting out the words

with distaste. "'Fraid I flushed 'em out by asking questions, and they come lookin' for you. We can't stay here, Jessie, we got to get out of town fast. These ain't the only two."

Jessie stared in alarm. "The—the horses, Joseph. All our things at the hotel..."

"Got a friend takin' care of that." His big hand circled her waist and urged her on. "'Bout the only friend I got *left* in Fort Benton," he said darkly. "That cartel of yours is spendin' double eagles like it was Christmas."

Chapter 13

Jessie never saw the face of the man who brought their horses and gear out of town. Like Joseph, he had a talent for appearing out of shadow and vanishing just as quickly. She guessed he was a mountain man; Glass didn't say, and she didn't ask.

For more than an hour, Joseph said nothing at all. He led them through the dark, bearing southwest toward the Little Belt Mountains. The flat sagebrush prairie gave little cover and they rode hard and fast, finally stopping the lathered horses on the banks of one of the rivers that fed the Missouri. Motioning Jessie off her mount, he guided them over a narrow gravel bank to the cover of stunted trees. Jessie started to speak, but Joseph silenced her with a finger to his lips.

He stood unmoving at her side, the Winchester clutched in his fists, the big Sharps rifle close by. Jessie gave a start as a long line of shadows suddenly appeared across the river. She knew they were being pursued, but she'd never guessed the men were no more than minutes behind!

There were eight men on horseback, riding single file. They rode upstream and disappeared, Joseph's eyes following them all the way. Jessie's legs were growing numb when Glass touched her lightly and pointed across the water. He waited until clouds covered the moon, then led her across the shallows to cover that matched the brush they'd left behind.

A quarter-hour later the men circled back, passing directly through the spot where Jessie and Glass had stood before. Joseph made sure they were all there, then continued his path southwest. Finally he reined in and called a halt, scanned the dark horizon, and spat on the ground.

"Those boys been worth their salt, they'd of had us," he said contemptuously. "We coulda crossed that river back an' forth all night. Never occurred to those fellers to hit both sides at once."

Jessie pulled off her Stetson and ran a hand through her hair. "Joseph, can we talk now? I still don't know what happened back there. Are you certain Cavanaugh hired those men?"

"Certain as winter," he said solemnly. "Whatever this Cavanaugh's up to, it's somethin' big. Been hirin' guns for 'bout a month. Some of them come upriver from Bismarck. A few from as far south as St. Louis. Feller that brought our horses is a trapper. Says word's been out on you and me a couple of days. And Ki too. Offering good money for our scalps, no questions asked."

"My God," Jessie breathed.

"Uh-huh. And that ain't all. My friend says he *seen* a bunch of those wagons come through. Six or seven, as he recalls. He was out on the flats to the north and had sense enough to keep movin' and not ask questions. They come down past Three Buttes and the Bear Paw Mountains, crossed the Marias and the Tetons, and headed southwest of here. Maybe north of Great Falls."

"More wagons!" Jessie exclaimed. She shut her eyes briefly and pictured a map of the border country. "Down through the Kootenay lands west of the mountains. And now these others northeast. Whatever they're bringing in, it all seems to move out of Canada, doesn't it?"

Joseph nodded. "And that's just the ones we know about, Jessie. Maybe they brought some more past the Sweet Grass Hills. Be a good place. Hell, it could happen 'bout anywhere they liked."

Jessie pounded her saddle in frustration. "What's in those wagons, Joseph? Damn it all, what are they *doing!*"

Glass shook his head. "We got to quit talkin' and keep movin'. Those boys'll stop somewheres and come after us at first light. I don't know where Western Union runs from Benton, but someone'll likely send word we're movin' south. Which means it'd be a good idea if we cut back west—"

"Oh Lord," Jessie moaned abruptly, "I completely forgot about that. Joseph, those messages I sent—I'll bet a dollar to a dime they never *left* Fort Benton. Those men who were following me likely saw me go into Western Union. Even if they didn't, someone else will think about it."

"Reckon you're right." He pulled his mount around. "Looks like you and me are on our own again, Jessie."

At dawn, they were riding south and west, past the foothills of the Little Belt Mountains. Grassland and prairie gave way to rough country, and Glass urged their mounts through a network of arroyos and stony ground. Jessie reined in at the rumble of distant thunder, searched the morning sky, and found it clear. Joseph caught her glance and grinned. "Ain't goin' to rain, lady. Look there—off to the east."

Jessie stood in the saddle and shaded her eyes. At first she thought a dust storm was hugging the far horizon. Then a dark, wavering line appeared out of the cloud and swept steadily north and west. Suddenly she knew what she was watching, and a quick surge of excitement coursed through her body.

"Buffalo!" she cried. "That's what they are, aren't they?"

"Yeah, that's what they are." Glass narrowed his eyes at the rapidly moving herd. "Comin' up past Big Snowy, I reckon. Over the Judith River." He shook his head and Jessie saw the hurt in his eyes. "You know how many there was up here right after the war? Fourteen, maybe fifteen million. Northern herd stretched from Powder River country clear up into Canada. An' twice that many all across the Great Plains, till ten or fifteen years ago. Old Jeb said once that him and Philadelphy sat nearly a week on the Milk River, waitin' for 'em to pass. Watched 'em myself three days a couple of years back, on the Yellowstone. Take a good look, Jessie. Ain't more than a few thousand out there, and they ain't goin' to be there long."

Jessie knew he was right. Hunters were swarming into the territory to kill the great beasts. Word had it that what was happening now was just the beginning, that the next few years would see the herds completely destroyed. A .50-caliber Sharps would bring a buffalo to its knees at a thousand yards. A dozen men at a quarter of that distance could pick a herd to pieces.

An eastern organizer of one of the hunts had boasted that a hundred thousand hides would ride down the Missouri from Fort Benton. Jessie was well aware that Washington openly encouraged this slaughter. When their food supply vanished, the Blackfoot, Sioux, Assiniboines, Piegans, and the rest would cease to be a "problem." Whoever was left would be driven back to dirt-poor reservations that got smaller every year—leaving more land free for cattle, mining, and farming. Jessie, and a few others who shared her feelings, had continually

123

fought for the Indians' rights. She wouldn't give up, but she knew her efforts were like spitting into a gale.

Glass pulled his horse savagely about, rage clouding his features. "Come on," he said tightly, "I seen enough of this."

She huddled by the late-evening fire, listening to the wind whistling and moaning past the high butte overhead. Joseph brooded to her left, his hooded eyes scanning the land to the north and east. He'd sat in the same spot for hours, bent over the Sharps in his lap. Jessie knew he was angry, as restless as a cat in a cage, frustrated at being bottled up all day. Twice now, riders had come down from the north, two separate parties looking for sign. The great herd had trampled any tracks into dust, but the riders kept looking.

"They know we're around," Glass told her. "Ain't anyplace else to hide."

"You think they'll come in? After dark, maybe?"

"*I* wouldn't," Joseph said soberly. "Waste of time. Can't search every rock in the Little Belts." He sat back and showed her a crooked grin. "They ain't all that smart, so they likely will." He moved toward her and touched her cheek gently. "We can stay here, Jessie. Wait 'em out forever. They ain't goin' to find us up here."

"That won't get us any closer to those wagons."

"No. Not any closer a-tall."

She caught his eyes and held them. "When you think it's dark enough, I'm ready. I'm about as itchy as you are, friend."

Joseph smiled. "Don't guess I expected any other answer than that."

"Fine. 'Cause that's the one you've got."

Joseph nodded, slung his saddlebags over his shoulder, and picked up his weapons. Jessie checked her shotgun and followed him down the dark path. For a long while they walked, leading the mounts through a sandy ravine that cut through the badlands and opened onto the prairie. The ground muffled their boots and the horses' hooves. One party of riders was to the east; Jessie and Glass had watched them circle off just at dark. The others were likely closer, but that couldn't be helped. There wasn't going to be a perfect time.

"All right," he said finally, "mount up and keep it to a walk. This gully's going to end in a spell. I want to come out nice and easy, just like a turtle bobbin' up for air."

"I won't even breathe," Jessie promised.

"Good idea. Stay in my tracks and keep your eyes open. I make any sign, you move just as—Oh Christ, *get off your horse—now!*"

Jessie swung out of the saddle, keeping the horse between herself and the dark. Glass passed his reins back and went to his knees, the Sharps halfway to his shoulder. Jessie heard a horse blow air, the leather squeak of a saddle. Glass waved her back. She turned and led the mounts down the gully. Joseph retreated, his eyes searching the darkness, the heavy weapon swinging from side to side. He caught up, and his lips touched her ear.

"Six or eight of 'em. They don't know we're here. Take the horses and keep going. Once you get around the bend—"

"Huh-uh. I've got a weapon and I can use it, Joseph Glass. I'm not going anywhere you don't go."

Glass cursed under his breath but didn't argue. "Take the right. Don't try to aim that scattergun, just keep shootin'. When it starts, let the horses run, and go to your belly."

Jessie nodded and backed off. Seconds later, ghostly shapes emerged from the darkness. The shapes loomed closer, flowing together and then apart.

"Jim—there's somethin' down there," a voice said nervously. "Herb, Lewis—"

Joseph's Sharps exploded with a roar like a cannon to Jessie's left. A man screamed in agony as the fifty-caliber slug all but tore off his arm, kept going, and slammed the man behind him off his horse. Jessie went to ground, fired the shotgun twice, turned on her side and broke the breech and reloaded. White light blossomed from the end of the gully. A bullet snapped past her and dug into the sandy soil. Glass was using the Winchester now, sending a deadly volley into the night. A Colt answered once and went silent. A horse without a rider came straight at Jessie, veering off at the last instant. Suddenly the ravine was deadly silent.

Joseph cursed and came to his feet. "Couple of 'em are gettin' away. If I don't stop 'em, they'll go for help." He quickly thumbed shells into the rifle, turned to speak to Jessie, and froze. Jessie heard it too—the soft call of a bird up on the prairie.

125

"Well, I'll be a son of a bitch!" Joseph's face stretched into a grin. He cupped his hand and answered the call, then reached out and eased Jessie's shotgun aside. "Stand quiet," he told her. "Don't shoot at nothin', 'less I do first. All right?"

"All right, but—"

"Just hold on. You'll see."

No sound came from the gully. Jessie held her breath. In a moment two more riderless horses appeared, and then another. Joseph laid a hand on her arm and stepped out of shadow, deliberately pointing the rifle at the ground.

"Who is it I be talkin' to?" a deep voice said out of the dark. "Got a friend up on the flats lookin' right down your gullet."

"It's Glass," Joseph said clearly. "There's just me and the woman. Everybody else is gettin' cold."

"Damned if they ain't," the voice chuckled. "Come on in, Del. Reckon this chile's all right."

A figure suddenly appeared at the end of the gully. Clouds drifted past the moon and Jessie stared. The man on the horse was enormous, a broad-shouldered giant with a full and flowing beard. When he slid out of the saddle she saw he was a good six-four or maybe more. He wore a plain cotton shirt, a dark leather vest, and black trousers. A broad-brimmed hat with a rounded crown topped his head.

"Real glad you come around," Glass said plainly. He extended his hand to the big man and nodded in Jessie's direction. "This here's Jessie Starbuck, John. Jessie, this is John Johnson."

"I'm pleased," Jessie muttered, still in awe of the man's looming presence. "We thank you for your help."

"Glad to oblige," said Johnston. "That ugly chile there's Del Gue." He gestured over his shoulder and Glass stepped forward to greet a shorter, leaner version of Johnston, dressed in buckskins like his own.

"You got any coffee?" asked Johnston. "Me an' Del run out 'bout three fires back."

"Sure enough do," said Joseph. He walked back to his horse and got his pack. In a moment he was kneeling on the ground, rummaging through his sack of provisions.

Jessie stared in disbelief. Was Joseph out of his mind? Ten yards away, the gully was full of dead men; farther up lay more riders that Johnston and his friend had somehow silenced without a sound. And somewhere out there, another party was wandering around in the dark. Did these three really intend to squat down right here and drink *coffee*?

Del Gue brought in dry sticks and started a fire. Now Jessie could see that both Johnston and his friend were crowding sixty, grizzled mountain men with eyes that reminded her of Joseph's.

Glass briefly explained their situation, that they were looking for armed men traveling with wagons; that the riders they'd just met had followed them down from Fort Benton. He added no more than that, and Johnston didn't ask.

"Heard 'bout Jebediah," he said gruffly. "Damn shame. That was one fine ol' coon. Where them other bastards at?"

"Hard to say," Joseph told him. "Might be up on the Sun or further south."

Johnston grunted and sipped his coffee. In the flickering light, Jessie caught strands of red in his beard, dark shadows under his eyes. A Walker Colt and a Bowie knife were struck in his belt. The knife and the revolver had matching rosewood handles.

"Me and Del was over east last week, in the Judiths. Got more trouble over there than they can handle. Injuns is hungry and butcherin' cattle. 'Course, them Sioux is stealin' horses like always down on the Yellowstone. Cap'n Park's got two companies of the Third Infantry at Fort Maginnis. But that ain't goin' to stop them Injuns from eatin' if their bellies is empty."

"Did you hear anything about cholera?" Jessie asked. "Over in the east?"

Johnston looked up and met her eyes. "There was talk when we left, yes'm." His glance turned to Joseph. "Whole damn country's turnin' sour, that's the damn truth. Me and Del seen White-Eye Anderson and ol' Texas Jack Omohundro down in Leadville. Them two and Colorado Charley's give up trappin' altogether. Ain't nothin' but tenderfoots now."

"Reckon you're right," Glass agreed. "Where you two headed now?"

"Might go up to Milk River, I dunno." He stretched bearlike arms and grinned at Joseph. "Still some beaver and Assiniboines up there. Might skin us a few of both. On t'other hand, might stick around down here. Sheriff Tom Irvine over to Custer County wants to hire me on as deputy in Coulson. Be right nice to rest up fer a spell."

Del Gue laughed behind him. "You ain't goin' to be no deputy, John."

"You don't know what the hell I'm likely to be," Johnston growled. He stood abruptly and nodded at Joseph and Jessie. "I'm obliged fer the coffee and comp'ny. That other bunch of fellers that wants yer hides is 'bout ten miles up north, last we seen 'em. You stay west, you ain't goin' to cross their trail."

"Thank you," said Joseph. "We'll keep an eye open."

Johnston looked at Jessie. "Them wagons you was askin' about, ma'am—I don't know if I'm steerin' you right or wrong, but we seen a prospector yesterday morning. Said wagons was passin' west of the Missouri. 'Bout sixty miles from here, I guess." He turned soberly to Glass. "Watch yer backside, hoss."

Without another word, the two mountain men climbed onto their horses and disappeared up the gully. Joseph kicked out the fire and poured coffee on the embers.

"That's got to be them," Jessie exclaimed. "It can't be anyone else!"

"Wouldn't be surprised. Won't hurt us to go an' find out." He finished his work and stood. "Well, now you can say you saw him. Ain't many that has."

"What?" Jessie gave him a curious look. "You mean Johnston?"

A crooked grin creased his features. "Hell, you don't know, do you? That was the ol' Crow-killer hisself. *Dah-pih-ehk Absaroka . . .*"

"The—" Jessie's jaw fell. "Oh my God—*that* Johnston!"

Joseph laughed. "No need to worry. Never knew him to eat a liver 'cept a Crow's. Don't believe he ever tried a green-eyed gal . . ."

Chapter 14

Ki would have helped with the dead, but Yellow Wing shook her head and warned him off. This was not a thing for outsiders. He must walk to the creek and wait. She would come and find him when it was over.

Ki did as she asked. He was sorry for what had happened, angry at the ruthless slaughter. Still, there was no way he could bring the dead to life. Squatting on a log by the creek wasn't getting him closer to Jessie and the men with the wagons. What were they up to? he wondered. What were Cavanaugh and his cartel masters hauling south that was worth the lives of any who stood in their way? He had no idea where Jessie and Glass might be—but he knew Jessie Starbuck well. She wouldn't rest until she found the answer. Or got in more trouble than she could handle.

Damn it, he thought darkly, clenching his fists at his sides, *what am I doing here? I need to be with her!*

Yellow Wing didn't come to get him. Instead, it was Red Elk himself who appeared through the trees. Ki found it hard to meet his gaze. There was nothing there at all—no anger, no sorrow, nothing. His eyes were as empty as the dead he had buried.

"You may do as you wish," Red Elk told him at once. "I will not try to stop you."

Ki wasn't surprised at the Indian's change of heart. "I guess Yellow Wing told you about the wagon tracks I found. The men who killed your people are the ones I'm after. The girl didn't think you'd accept that."

"Women's hearts are often stronger than men's," Red Elk said solemnly. "But they do not understand about honor. This is not their fault. It is the way they are made. I believe you

129

about the wagons. If you say this is so, then it is. I wish I could follow them with you. There is blood to account for, this day." Red Elk lowered his head and scowled at the ground. "I am ashamed to tell you this, but you are a friend. The men who were left alive still wish me to take them to the north. They say there will be time to fight the whites when their numbers are greater. They say they will avenge the others when Sitting Bull leads them into battle." Red Elk spat on the ground and looked woodenly at Ki. "I would like to believe this will happen. I know in my heart it will never be. The men back there have been long on the reservation. They are content to fight battles in their heads. They look like Oglala, but I think their spirits are Crow."

Red Elk's words told Ki the depth of his contempt. Calling his brothers Crow was nearly as bad as calling them white.

"I would ask you to share food with me," said the Sioux. "I know you wish to ride to the south."

"Yes. Thank you."

"When I have taken these *children* to the Milk River, I will have done what I promised. Then I will come back. If you have not killed all the men who did this today, I will kill the rest. When we talk again, you will tell me of the land where you were born, where men have the eyes and bones of the Sioux."

Red Elk gripped Ki's shoulders, and Ki returned the gesture. He reached into his pocket, took out one of the razor-edged *shuriken,* and solemnly handed it to the Indian. Red Elk's eyes sparkled with pleasure, then he shook his head in dismay. "How can I take such a gift? I have nothing to give you as fine as the round knife!"

Ki realized what he'd done. A gift called for a gift of equal measure. The Seventh Cavalry stripes were the Sioux's most precious possession, Ki knew. It wasn't something he wanted, and wouldn't ask if he did.

"I don't need anything in return," he said solemnly, "but if you don't mind, I'd like to *look* at that bone-handled knife you been using. It's one of the finest blades I've ever seen."

"This?" Red Elk drew the knife, flipped it in a blur, and offered the handle to Ki. "You are right. It is a very fine knife. Not as fine as your gift, of course. Here. You must have it."

"It's a thing I would surely treasure," said Ki. He accepted

130

the blade and saw the relief in Red Elk's eyes.

"You know where to use it," the Sioux said darkly. "Let it strike many times. Come—we must find you the best horses to take you south."

Yellow Wing, Little Hawk, and the survivors of the raid were in the clearing downstream. Ki saw the girl's eyes flicker to his belt. They widened slightly in surprise at the sight of Red Elk's knife. She didn't have to ask what had happened between the two.

"We're leaving," he told her. "You're still coming along, I suppose?"

"Of course I am," she snapped. "What did you think?" She glanced past him at Red Elk and the horses. "He's giving you the best mounts he has. And an extra one as well."

"He's a good man, Yellow Wing. I like him."

She gave him a curious look, as if she saw something she hadn't seen before. "He's not happy with these men. He doesn't think they're worthy because they won't go back and fight the whites who slaughtered the others. He told them to their faces that the old woman, Snow Bird's Sister, is more of a warrior than they are. This is a terrible thing to say, yet none of them stood to face him."

"I know. He told me he was disappointed."

"He did?" she said in wonder. "He told you that?"

"Why shouldn't he?"

"You—you're not a Sioux. And you're half white."

"He gave me his blade," Ki said. "I thought you noticed."

"I know, but—"

"But I'm still half white." He gave her a sober grin. "So are you, Yellow Wing. Maybe you forgot."

The girl's eyes blazed in fury. "It's not the same thing. I'm half Sioux, too!" Yellow Wing lifted her chin in defiance and stalked off. Red Elk was proudly showing off his *shuriken* to an admiring Little Hawk. Ki stood aside and waited. He guessed it was nearly four in the afternoon. The air was already chilled, and that meant they could get bad weather later on. If something blew in, they wouldn't make much time. They'd hardly get back down the valley before dark. If they were lucky, they'd make it back to where they'd fought the Arikaras. All he seemed to be doing was getting farther and farther from Jessie.

He saw the Indian approach out of the corner of his eye,

but paid him no attention. Then the Sioux stopped directly in his path, showed his strong teeth, and began shouting furiously in Ki's face.

Ki frowned, backed off, and shook his head. "Sorry, I don't understand what you're saying, friend, but you're saying it a little too close."

Ki's answer seemed to anger the brave even more. Not all the rage was real, Ki knew; the man was puffing himself up like a toad, making his body shake and bringing beads of sweat to his face.

"Look," Ki said soberly, "I don't know what's bothering you, but whatever it is—"

Without warning, the Sioux stuck his arm out straight and hit Ki's chest with the flat of his palm. Ki went back on his heels, caught himself, and brought up his hands, fingers stiff and slightly bent. The Indian put his hands on his hips and laughed, pointing derisively at Ki's peculiar stance. Red Elk left the horses and stalked up quickly to face the other Sioux. His features were dark with anger, and he let the brave know he wasn't pleased. The man wasn't intimidated at all. He was shorter than Red Elk, built like a bull, low to the ground. His face was nearly flat, the brick-colored flesh stretched so tightly over his skull that his cheeks seemed ready to burst through the skin.

Across the clearing, Ki saw Yellow Wing's eyes go wide. She bit her lip and stepped back. A moment later, Red Elk turned to Ki.

"He wants the woman," the Sioux said flatly, his expression filled with disgust. "He wants to fight you for her. I told him you would not be a good man to fight. I also told him you were my friend, and that his action did me no honor. He does not greatly care about my honor." Red Elk shook his head. "His name is Bear Claw. I think Bear Tit is better. He has been a reservation farmer two years. He thinks fighting you will give him back his pride. He thinks it makes up for not going after the whites."

Ki let out a breath. Behind Red Elk, the stout Indian glared. "What do you want me to do? Did you tell him the woman wasn't mine?"

Red Elk shrugged. "He wouldn't believe that. She is with you, so she is yours."

Little Hawk shouted from a few yards away. Bear Claw made a threatening noise in his throat and shook his fist.

"Little Hawk says he'll be honored to fight him for you, even though he knows you could kill him with no trouble. He says he doesn't wish to bother you with this."

Ki grinned and waved at Little Hawk. The Sioux laughed heartily and waved back. "It's all right," Ki said. "I'll fight him if that's what he wants, but let's get to it. I don't have much time."

Red Elk nodded and stepped aside. Like Ki, he knew there was nothing else to do. Ki took two steps to the left and raised his hands. Bear Claw showed all his teeth and whipped a metal hatchet from his belt. It was an old trade weapon, made for sale to the Indians.

Ki ignored the man's weapon, leaving his new knife in his belt. The other Indians muttered their approval at this bravado. Bear Claw took it the only way he could, as an insult to his prowess. With a deep-throated bellow, he came at Ki with his head between his shoulders, the hatchet trailing at an angle behind his body. Ki held his ground and let the man come. At the last instant he leaped deftly aside, hands spread straight from his shoulders. The weapon cut air where he'd been, and Ki lashed out with his right foot. Bear Claw grunted as Ki's iron-hard heel struck him squarely in the chest. He staggered back, staring in disbelief at the smaller man who'd hurt him simply by jumping off the ground. He coughed and rubbed his chest, circling Ki with new respect.

Ki knew the man wouldn't make the same mistake twice. He'd hoped the first blow would keep him down, hurt him enough to dampen his anger. A lesser man would be flat on his back. Bear Claw was clearly going to take more convincing. Killing him would be hard enough; leaving him alive and out of action would be even harder. He had no intention of leaving the man permanently damaged—unless the Indian's strength forced him to do it.

Bear Claw circled him through the clearing, closing the gap between them each time. For all his bluster and false rage, Ki respected this opponent. For a man his size, he was remarkably quick on his feet. And if he ever made contact with that hatchet, the force behind his arm would cut bone.

Ki didn't intend to let that happen. As Bear Claw advanced,

133

Ki retreated. To the Indian, it looked as if he'd had second thoughts. The Sioux worked closer, shifting the weapon from his left hand to his right. That was a mistake, and Ki was grateful for it. If you could use both hands, it was stupid to tell your opponent.

Ki ignored the fancy action and watched the man's eyes, the hard muscle bunched at his neck and shoulders. Suddenly, tendons about his mouth went rigid, tightening cords in his throat. Ki went to his knees a split second before the hatchet sliced air above his head. Bear Claw slammed his feet to the earth and reared back for another blow. Ki braced his feet and hit the Indian's belly with his head. Bear Claw grunted and went sprawling. Ki stayed on him, clawing for his throat and riding him down. The Indian bellowed and tried to squeeze Ki with his legs. Ki slithered out of the grip and sprang to his feet. The last thing he needed were those strong limbs crushing him in a vise. Bear Claw rolled and came ponderously to his knees. Ki slammed him in the head with his foot. Bear Claw's face twisted in pain, blood spurting from his nose. Ki kicked him relentlessly, hitting the hard skull again and again. Bear Claw took it, blinking back sweat and spitting blood. He brought himself to his feet, hefted the weapon in his fist, and came at Ki like a bull. Ki stepped quickly aside. The Indian slashed again and again. Ki's foot slipped on the bank of the creek, and the blade carved a sharp red line down his arm. It felt as if the hatchet had been heated white hot.

The Indians roared and shook their fists. Bear Claw grinned and came on with a vengeance. Ki stepped in dangerously close, chopping the Sioux's face and throat with the sides of his palms. Bear Claw growled and knocked him away. Ki flailed for balance, knew he wouldn't make it, and rolled into a fall. Bear Claw pounded in to finish him off. His flat features twisted in fury and his dark eyes flashed. Ki hit the ground, brought his knees up under his chin, and snapped his body into a lance. His back came off the ground and his feet hit Bear Claw in the belly. The Indian staggered back, gasping for air like a fish. The hatchet fell from his hand. Ki rolled to his feet and kicked the weapon in the creek. Snapping his elbow back to the shoulder, he thrust his bent fingers like springs at the Indian's throat. He pulled the blow at the last instant, knowing the full force would crush the man's windpipe and kill him.

Bear Claw swayed, blinked drunkenly at Ki, and went down like a felled tree.

The Sioux braves muttered in anger. As long as their man was on his feet, they could safely applaud Ki's courage. Now that Bear Claw was down, they wanted the winner's blood.

Ki stepped back to get his breath, looked across the clearing, and caught Yellow Wing looking right at him. She held his glance a moment and turned away. Ki knew what he had to do. If he left Bear Claw alive, the man would almost certainly try to track him down and kill him. Ki couldn't let that happen. Not now. There was only one other way—shame his foe so badly there was no way he could ever face Ki again.

Blood coursed down his arm, and he prayed he wouldn't pass out in the clearing. Drawing Red Elk's blade, he walked to Bear Claw's still form and straddled his chest. Tearing the man's leather vest aside, he pricked a circle around the left nipple—deep enough to scar, but no deeper. He stood then, feeling lightheaded.

Red Elk roared with laughter. "Ha! It is as I said it should be!" he cried in English. "Bear Claw is truly Bear Tit now!" Then, turning to the others, he repeated his words in the Sioux tongue. Some of the warriors grinned at Ki's act, but most glared murderously in his direction.

Ki kept his eyes straight ahead, taking one step at a time toward the horses. Yellow Wing was waiting with the reins. He tore at his shirt with his good hand and wrapped it about his bloody arm as best he could.

Chapter 15

For a long time Yellow Wing rode behind, saying nothing and simply watching the trail on either side. Finally she kicked her pony lightly and matched his pace. Ki felt her eyes upon him, going over him critically an inch at a time.

"Do you see anything interesting?" he said shortly. "Anything I ought to know about?"

"Yes I do," she said soberly. "I see a man who is going to fall off his horse and die if he doesn't stop!"

"Yellow Wing, I know I have to stop. I just want to put some miles behind us first."

The girl shook her head. "You don't have to worry. Red Elk won't let Bear Claw's friends come after us."

"You know that, do you?"

"Yes, Ki, I know that. Get off that animal right now."

Ki knew she was right. His head felt funny, and there were brightly colored spots before his eyes. He nodded and let her lead him off the trail and down to the creek. When he slipped one leg over the pony, he dropped limply to the ground.

"Your bandage is soaked through, and you're bleeding badly. You lost a lot of blood."

"I've lost some before."

"Shut up and keep still, all right?" She took the knife from his belt and cut a long strip from her leather skirt. Ki studied the honey color of her legs and decided he wasn't dead yet. She left him, went to the stream for fresh water, returned, and washed the wound thoroughly before wrapping the leather strip about his arm.

"That'll help," she said, "but you need rest and food. Fresh meat. That's the best thing when you've lost a lot of blood."

"Good idea," he said wearily, "but I don't feel a lot like hunting."

"You're not going to," she said coolly. "I am. I am not some helpless white woman, you know."

"Yellow Wing—"

"Just ride ahead. Keep on the trail south and try not to fall off your horse." Digging her heels in hard, she guided the pony through the trees and disappeared. When she was gone, it occurred to him that it wasn't a good idea to fire a gun unless it was absolutely necessary. He wasn't worried about Bear Claw's friends; there were plenty of other people he didn't want to meet. More of Cavanaugh's men, and the miners, settlers, and ranchers who'd very likely shoot whatever they saw and worry about it later.

The trail was getting hazy, nightfall only half an hour away, when he heard her coming back. Turning, he saw her riding up the ravine, the Winchester cradled in her arm. Tied behind her was a young elk, a small doe.

"I see you got meat," he said.

"Of course I got meat," she said. "That's why I went *hunting*, Ki. . . ."

The high dirt bank of the stream made a break against the wind, curving into a hollow that hid their fire and sheltered them from the light drizzling rain that came with the night. Ki lay comfortably on his blanket, shamefully full of good roast meat. Yellow Wing had meal left in her pack, and made flat circles of cornbread in the skillet. Ki had to admit he felt better. He didn't know if meat made blood, as the girl said, but he was already getting back his strength.

After she'd cut up the elk for roasting, Yellow Wing brought a bloody organ to him and bound it lightly to his wound. Ki thought it was a liver, but wasn't sure. It seemed to ease the pain and draw out the angry red color. Before the elk was done, she took the organ back, washed it in the stream, and skewered it on a stick over the flames. Ki politely declined the offer of a slice. Yellow Wing ate a large portion, rolling her eyes with obvious pleasure.

"That was a good idea," she said abruptly. "I've been thinking about it and you were right."

"Right about what?"

137

"Bear Claw." She sucked on a rib, examined it carefully, and licked her fingers. "Leaving him alive. At first I thought it was stupid. I know why you did it. Because Red Elk made you his brother."

"Partly, yes. Mostly it was because I didn't want to kill him."

"Why not?"

"I don't like to kill. Bear Claw or anyone else."

She laughed as if she appreciated his joke. Ki sat up and frowned. "Why do you think that's funny?"

"I saw you fight when you took me from the white man's camp. I saw you kill the Arikara with the round knife. I saw you fight Bear Claw."

"And?"

"You are a warrior," she said simply. "Anyone can see that. How can you be a warrior and not want to kill? You only killed the Arikara, but I think you could have killed all the others if you wanted."

"I *had* to kill him," Ki said darkly. "I didn't have a choice."

"Joseph said the woman Jessie told him you come from an island across the Western Sea."

"Yes. The islands of the Japans. My mother was Japanese and my father was an American. I think I told you that before."

Yellow Wing bit her lip in thought. "I have seen men like you. Kind of like you, anyway."

"You probably saw the Chinese. China is a land very close to the Japans."

"Oh. Yes, I know."

Ki knew she didn't know at all, that she had no idea how far the Orient was across the Pacific, or what was really there. She was too stubborn to admit there might be something she didn't know everything about.

"This Japans. Is that where you learned to be a warrior? Where you learned to fight in such a peculiar way?"

"Yes," he told her. "That's the kind of fighting that's learned by a samurai."

"Sah-moo-rye . . ." She tasted the words on her tongue. "And these sah-moo-rye. They all move faster than the eye—but they do not like to kill?"

"Some of them do and some of them don't," Ki said plainly. "Men of the East are not all that different from men of the

West. There are Japanese like the Arikaras who took you away, and like Joseph Glass and Red Elk and Bear Claw. Like your grandfather must have been. All kinds of men."

Blue eyes flashed a challenge across the fire. "My grandfather was the best man who ever lived!"

"I'm sure he was, Yellow Wing."

"I don't like you saying his name with the Arikaras. Or Bear Claw, either."

"I'm going to sleep now," he told her, knowing an argument was starting that he didn't want to finish. "I've got to ride tomorrow. And you never can tell, I might want to kill someone."

"You're making fun of me," she said between her teeth. "I don't like that."

Ki grinned and held up his hand in peace. "All right, I'm sorry. And, Yellow Wing, thank you for taking care of my arm. And for killing the elk and making a very fine supper."

"You didn't think I could shoot an elk, did you?"

He studied her a long moment. "I think you could do most anything you put your mind to."

"You do?"

"Yes. I certainly do."

"Well . . ." She pulled the blankets about her shoulders and turned away. "I guess you're right. I probably could."

He opened his eyes the moment she touched him. She was sitting above him, the blanket forming a hood over her head.

"What is it?" he asked. "Is something wrong?" The fire had burned to embers and he knew the night was half gone.

"You cried out. I thought your arm was hurting."

"Thank you. I think it's all right."

"You'd better let me see. I may have to rub some elk fat on it."

"Yellow Wing—"

Before he could protest, she pulled his blanket aside and edged in beside him. Her hand found his arm, and her fingers worked carefully under the bandage. "It's a little hot," she reported, "but that's to be expected. The blade went very deep."

"Thank you. I appreciate your checking."

"Ki . . ."

"Yes?"

"I would like to stay here if it won't bother you. It's getting cold. I think it might rain before morning."

Ki looked surprised. "That's fine," he said dryly. "You won't bother me at all." It was a lie, of course. Her presence bothered him a lot. He could feel one leg pressed firmly against his own. Her head lay just below his shoulder; with every breath he inhaled the sweet scent of her flesh.

"Good night, Ki," she said softly. "Thank you for letting me stay." With a sigh, she turned away and snuggled her back into the hollow of his chest. Ki welcomed her in and dropped his hand across her waist. With a start, he pulled his fingers away as if he'd touched a hot stove.

"What's wrong?" she asked sleepily.

"Uh, nothing. Nothing at all."

"You're jumpy. Guess that's the white man in you."

Ki took a breath and held it, and laid his hand gently against her again. He knew she'd had a blanket when she joined him. It sure as hell wasn't there now. There was nothing except the sleek, warm texture of her flesh. He wasn't sure what to do next. For all his experience with women, right now he felt like a fool—a kid behind the barn with his first girl. He'd thought more than once about feeling that lovely skin next to his. He'd never imagined he'd get a chance to touch her, that she'd come crawling naked under his blanket. Any one of a hundred girls, maybe—but not Yellow Wing!

What is wrong with you? he chided himself. *She's here, isn't she? What more do you want to know?*

Easing his hand past her waist, he trailed his fingers gently along her ribs to the firm swell of her breasts. Yellow Wing reached up irritably and pushed his hand away. "Ki, if you're going to do things like that," she scolded, "I'm not going to stay."

"What?" Ki raised up on his arms. *"You* crawled under my blanket. I didn't crawl under yours."

"I know." She turned and held the covers demurely under her chin. "I want you to make love to me, Ki," she said frankly. "I've never done that before and I'd like to try. I just don't want to *hurry,* is all."

Ki blinked. "You mean you've never—"

"No. Of course not." Her blue eyes narrowed. "Who would I do it *with?*"

140

"Well, that isn't any of my business. Uh, Joseph, I guess."

"*Joseph!*" Yellow Wing looked appalled. "Ki, Joseph is my *brother!* Well, almost. We grew up together. What a terrible thing to say!"

"All right, I'm sorry." Ki shook his head, not certain how to begin. "Look, I'm flattered. I can't think of anything I'd rather do than make love to you right now."

"Oh, well, fine." She gave him a pleasant smile. "Why don't we, then?"

"I don't know how much you know about it," he said dryly, "but it's hard to do without touching. I don't think I ever heard of anyone doing it that way."

"You're mad again, aren't you?" She showed him her lower lip. "I didn't mean you can't touch. I'm not stupid, you know. I just meant I want you to go real slow, so I'll be sure to see what's happening."

Ki exploded with laughter. "I can't really believe this. I didn't think you even *liked* me very much. Now here we are, all ready to—"

"I don't. Not a whole lot."

"Then why—?"

"I said I *don't* like you much. But I do like you better than I did."

"Well, thanks..."

Yellow Wing frowned. "What's that got to do with anything? We can still do it, can't we?"

Ki lay back and stared at the dark cliff, listening to light rain rattle dead leaves on the ground. "You have a lot to learn about... getting a man interested."

"I told you I haven't done this before."

"I believe it."

"Ki..." She reached over and took his hand. "Why don't we... start where we were? Would that help any?" She cupped his hand firmly under her breast. "Now, how's that?"

"That's—that's just fine. As good a start as any."

Yellow Wing giggled. "I don't know much. But I thought maybe it was."

Ki turned and took her breasts in both hands. The touch of her flesh sent a quick wave of pleasure through his loins. He marveled at the lovely little mounds. They were a young girl's breasts, firm and apple-hard, yet soft and fully fleshed. He let his fingers come together until they gently squeezed her nipples. The dimpled flesh went hard, the rosy tips swelling to rigid nubs.

"Oh! Oh my!" Yellow Wing's eyes went wide with surprise. "I never felt *any*thing like that before!"

"You told me," said Ki. "It gets even better."

"It does? I don't know if I can—Oooooh, *Ki!*"

He pulled the blanket down to her waist and drew her nipples into his mouth. Yellow Wing arched her neck and gave a strangled little cry. Her breasts began to rise, slowly at first, then faster, as a heat she'd never known pulsed through her body. Her nipples swelled to ripe peaks, each touch of his tongue bringing her to greater heights of pleasure. Her body stirred beneath him; her belly began to squirm in a lazy circle, moving in an easy, natural motion to the rhythm of his mouth. Unconsciously she reached up and stroked the hard mounds herself, kneading the moist nipples with her fingers, letting him suck her fingers into his mouth along with softer flesh. The sweet, musky taste of her body heightened Ki's excitement. He reached up to strip his shirt over his shoulders and found her there to help him. When the garment was tossed aside, he bent to his knees and quickly shed his trousers.

The touch of his naked flesh set her whole body trembling. Ki found her mouth and gently touched the corner of her lips. Yellow Wing gave a joyous cry at this new sensation, and buried her fingers in his hair. She answered his kisses with a quick and desperate need. Her moist lips opened like a flower, and Ki let the tip of his tongue flick into her mouth.

Yellow Wing jerked beneath him and ground her pelvis into his loins. Ki thrust past her lips to taste each sweet and secret hollow. His kisses seemed to loose some fire within her. Her slender young form writhed against him, lashing out wildly with a fury all its own. Her face was slick with moisture, her flesh stretched tautly over her cheeks. In the dying embers of the fire, her body turned to cinnamon and honey. Light danced on the smooth flanks of her thighs, the lovely length of her legs. Again, Ki gently cupped the firm breasts in his hands, kissing the dusky nipples until they sprang into hard little points.

She glanced up, her eyes wide with wonder and fascination. "Ki, I didn't know," she whispered. "I didn't dream how it'd be!" Her soft lips opened until all their color was gone. Her nails dug into his shoulders. "You—you do it *all* to me, you hear?" she demanded. "I want to know everything there is. And you better not leave anything out!"

Ki laughed and took her in his arms. "If you put it that way, I guess there's no way I can say no . . ."

Once more he explored the warmth of her mouth, letting the spicy woman-taste assail his senses. Yellow Wing answered with a hunger of her own; she guided his tongue where she wanted, showing him the way with gasps of pleasure.

Ki let his mouth trail down the column of her throat. A vein throbbed wildly in her neck. He slid his hands down her body. The startling blue eyes never left him; she watched him with open wonder, waiting for each new sensation. Ki's hands moved lightly over her belly, circled the feathery nest between her legs, and rested on her thighs. At his touch, her eyes went wide. She drew in a breath and held it.

"Ki . . . Ki, I'm scared," she whispered softly.

"It's all right," he promised. "It's all right."

He stroked her body gently, letting his fingers brush her tender thighs, stroking her as he would to calm some small wild creature. He moved his hands carefully across the hollow of her belly, past the tight ringlets that guarded her treasure. Gently he touched the plush mound with the tips of his fingers. Yellow Wing twitched her bottom and thrust herself up to meet him. Slowly he parted the downy nest no man had touched before. Yellow Wing held her breath. He kneaded the tender mound, letting the tips of his fingers draw closer and closer to the moist and delicate flesh. Her coltish legs spread wide and her hips arched off the ground. Ki touched the soft petals and let his fingers slide between them. Her young loins released a surge of moist warmth; her thighs were fragrant with the scent of fresh desire.

Ki entered her with his fingers, probing gently along the incredibly silken walls. He hesitated, unwilling to hurt her; he knew a careless thrust would carry a young girl into womanhood. When it came, he wanted that moment to bring her joy. He teased her softly, slipping his fingers in and out, each time brushing the little pearl at the center of her pleasure. He tried to be gentle, but Yellow Wing's hunger overpowered his caution. Digging the soles of her feet into the blanket, she thrust herself wantonly against him, pounding savagely against his hand.

143

When it happened, whatever pain there might have been was buried in her desire to take him in, to force his fingers deeper and deeper inside her. Ki came to his knees and her small hand grasped his erection. A cry of wonder stuck in her throat; she pumped his member joyously back and forth, as if she'd performed that act a hundred times before.

Ki tried to enter her gently. Yellow Wing cried out fiercely, grasped his erection, and thrust his length inside her. Her trim legs snaked about his waist and held him tight. Ki gave her everything he had. The girl scorned easy loving; she wanted him to take her, and take her hard. He pounded her relentlessly, slamming himself against her again and again. Her naked flesh was hot with moisture; the cords of her throat were rigid, wrenching her mouth open wide.

Ki felt the thunder beginning to build within his loins. It smoldered, swelled, then surged through his shaft and rushed inside her. Yellow Wing cried out with joy and raked her nails along his spine. Her breasts flattened against his chest. The tight little nest spasmed about his member, stroking him to release once more. The fierce, churning wave exploded between his legs and burst within her. His mouth found her breast and drew a pointy nipple into his mouth. Yellow Wing screamed, gave a final cry of pleasure, and went limp. Her hands fell away and her legs slid from his back.

Ki wrapped blankets about them both, and Yellow Wing snuggled against his shoulder with a sigh.

"I was right," she said smugly. "I am very glad, Ki."

"Right about what?"

"That this was a thing I wanted to do. I guess you can't know how much you want it until it happens." She lay her cheek against his chest. "And I am glad that it was you. You have brought me great joy."

"It was my pleasure," he murmured.

Yellow Wing touched his lips with her fingers. "Yes. That is a thing I noticed too." The tight braids of hair had come loose during their loving. He saw her now as he'd never seen her before: high cheeks and blue eyes framed by a tousled veil of raven tresses.

"You're a very beautiful woman," he said gently.

Yellow Wing grinned. "Not a girl? A beautiful *woman?*"

"Yes. It is easy to call you a woman."

"I feel like a woman. I don't feel like a girl. I am someone else now," she said proudly. She ran long fingers through her hair and shook her head. "I am *not* what I was. I am a woman and I have given my body to a man. And I have shown him good loving." She touched his chin and turned him to face her, an anxious look in her eyes. "That's true, isn't it? I *did* show you good loving?"

"Yellow Wing." Ki took her face between his hands. "Once, just before the Arikaras found us, you spat in my face and called me half-breed."

"Ki . . ."

"No." She tried to move out of his grasp. "I know why you did that. I think I knew then. You do not *become* someone by making love. It is a marvelous thing between a man and a woman, but it does not make you a *person*. You were that before."

Her eyes flashed and her lips curled in anger. "You are a man. You can fight back if someone calls you half-breed!"

"Yes, and I've done it a couple of times," Ki admitted. "Damn it, Yellow Wing, you've got plenty to be proud of. Jebediah Baker was a fine man, and I'm sure your grandmother was a good woman, and your mother too."

"And my father?" The girl's eyes narrowed in defiance. "You haven't asked me about *him*."

"No, I don't think that's my business, unless you want to tell me."

"I can't," she said bitterly. "I don't know. He was . . . A bunch of trappers came into camp while Jeb and my grandmother were gone. My mother was there with two other Sioux women. The trappers were drunk. They raped all three girls, and one of them died."

"I'm sorry," Ki said solemnly.

"Jeb found all four of the men and killed them. It took him five years, but he did it. My mother and my grandmother died of smallpox when I was two years old." Angry tears welled in her eyes, but her gaze didn't falter. "You see? I'm more of a half-breed than you think. But I do not have shame anymore." She took him in her arms and held him tightly. *"I chose the man I wanted. I gave my body to him, and I took as much pleasure as I gave. This is so, isn't it?"*

"Yes," he said gently, "it's so, Yellow Wing."

145

She rested in his arms once more, and in a moment she was asleep. Ki watched her a long time, holding the lovely young girl who'd become a woman close against him. She had it all worked out in her head, everything the way it was supposed to be. And if it made her happy to think loving had somehow changed her, turned her into something she hadn't been, he wasn't about to tell her differently.

By morning, the clouds and rain disappeared and the autumn day promised to slide back into summer. Ki woke to find the girl stalking unashamedly naked about the camp, humming to herself and slicing thin elk steaks into a pan. He'd never seen her bare body in daylight before. The sight sent a surge of heat through his veins. Her form was long and sleek, a sensuous mix of soft hollows and lanky planes. She walked tall and proud, with the easy, natural grace of an animal on the prowl. She caught him watching and grinned, turned on her heels, and sucked in a breath. The motion tilted her breasts at a saucy angle and narrowed her waist. Sunlight danced down her legs and turned her bottom golden. Ki kicked the blankets aside and sprang to his feet. Yellow Wing shrieked and ran toward the creek, then exploded into laughter as he caught her and swept her up in his arms. Neither smelled their breakfast burning to cinders in the skillet.

Just after noon they crossed the shallow river and paused for a cold meal. Ki was uneasy, for the cover they'd known before had disappeared. Now, high peaks rose to the south and west; the east was open prairie, grasslands, and rolling hills against a nearly flat horizon.

"The Missouri is over there somewhere," Yellow Wing told him. "I've been close to this place before."

"Looks like you could see for a hundred miles," he said soberly. "Which means anyone else out there can do the same." He wondered, not for the first time, if they'd done the right thing, and decided there'd been little choice. He'd found the killers' wagon tracks again an hour before, hugging the foothills of the mountains. They'd followed the trail south, then veered to the east. Suddenly they were out in the open with no cover; Ki felt naked and vulnerable, as if a rifle were sighting in on him that moment. Maybe they weren't the right tracks at all.

There were wagons all over Montana, tracks covering thousands of square miles. And as far as Jessie was concerned—well, she and Glass could be anywhere by now.

"Ki, are we just going to stand out here?" Yellow Wing asked. "We might as well keep going."

"I guess so," he said, and urged his pony south.

A quarter-hour later, he looked over his shoulder and caught a hint of motion on the horizon. He guided the girl quickly into a gully between the hills, then climbed back to the rise on foot. Whoever was there, they were several miles away, moving in a column from west to east. Sun winked on metal, and dust rose to show him they were moving fairly fast. When he was certain they weren't veering south, he turned and climbed back down the hill. For an instant his heart nearly stopped. Two riders were coming toward him through the grass, heading right for Yellow Wing. While he'd been watching for trouble, they'd ridden right down his neck!

The riders stopped. One of them raised his hand, and Ki grinned in relief. He waved back and ran down the hill toward the girl.

Red Elk sat his pony and gave them both a sober look. "Sometimes a man needs four eyes. I think maybe this is so." The edge of a grin touched his mouth. "You are better than a white dirt farmer. You are not yet a Sioux."

"I've only had a couple of days' practice," said Ki. He reached up and grasped the man's wrist, then greeted Little Hawk. "I'm glad it was you two. I'd have been dead two or three times."

"I saw them," Yellow Wing said softly. "*I* knew they were there."

"I will tell you why I am here," Red Elk announced. "Those children who pretend to be Sioux decided there was danger to the north. They wished to go west for awhile. They said there would be less chance of the bluecoats finding them there. Later they would go north again and find Sitting Bull." Red Elk made a face. "I told them to go wherever they wished. I had promised to take them north. Nothing was said about other directions. I told them I owed them nothing." The Indian clasped a fist over his chest. "Now I am here. And Little Hawk as well. We go with you to find the men who killed our people."

"I'm glad you came," Ki said. "We picked up some tracks

147

a ways back, but I'm not sure they belong to the right wagons."

"They are the right sign," Red Elk said firmly. "And they are not far ahead. Half a day, maybe less. Twenty men on horses. Eight wagons. Maybe more."

Ki stood up straight. "Red Elk, there weren't nearly that many riders—or wagons, either, back where they ambushed your people!"

"No. Others have joined them now. From the west and from the north."

Ki cursed under his breath and looked at Yellow Wing. "That's got to mean something. I don't know what, but something. It could be Cavanaugh's bringing together whatever it is he's got, for some reason."

"Yes, it might be," she said.

Little Hawk began talking and gesturing north. Red Elk nodded and turned to Ki. "Little Hawk wishes me to tell you it was he who found the tracks his friend Round-Knife-Fast-as-the-Wind follows. He says we will kill many enemies together."

"Tell him I'm grateful," said Ki, trying not to grin at the fancy name.

"He also says it is good that Bear-Tit stayed behind. He and the other women who walk like men would be frightened."

Now Ki laughed aloud. Yellow Wing grinned proudly and lowered her eyes.

"We should be riding," Red Elk said abruptly. "The men to the north may circle back. It would not be wise to stay here."

Ki nodded, then glanced sharply at the Sioux. "You mean *those* riders? The ones I was watching? Hell, Red Elk, are they part of this, too?"

"Yes, of course," Red Elk said without expression. "You didn't know this?"

"No, I didn't know it."

"They are riding hard, but I cannot say why. They did not see Little Elk and myself." He spat on the ground and grinned. "Maybe they are just riding hard to kill horses. I have seen white men do this before."

Ki didn't answer. He mounted up again and followed Red Elk south. Twenty men in Cavanaugh's party, he thought. And ten, fifteen maybe, in the column to the north. Which meant there could be thirty or more in the whole bunch, and every one of them armed and looking for trouble. He glanced at the two Sioux braves and Yellow Wing. Any way he counted, it came out to four.

Late in the afternoon, Red Elk called a halt while Little Hawk scouted the land ahead. Moving south, the Missouri curved in somewhere to the left, around the northern edge of the Big Belt Mountains. Their path lay between the Big Belt range and the Divide, looming down upon them from the west.

"It doesn't make sense," said Ki. "We're getting close to civilization, Yellow Wing. Unless I'm wrong, Helena's not too far south. Why would Cavanaugh and his friends be heading there?"

Yellow Wing shrugged but didn't answer. Ki shifted on his pony, worked his sore arm, and squinted at the bald rocky point just ahead. Red Elk stopped and touched the stock of his rifle. Little Hawk appeared and the Sioux relaxed. The two spoke quickly, the urgency in the other Indian's voice plain to Ki.

Red Elk's face clouded. "This is not good," he said flatly. "Little Hawk went only a mile before he came upon men in a clearing. There are miners and wooden buildings. And past that, a well-made road running north and south. There are many people about. There is even a small store and white women. The road is much traveled. There are telegraph wires on poles by the road."

"Did anyone see him?" asked Yellow Wing.

"No. But the cover is not good." He looked grimly at Ki. "There is no sign of the men we are seeking. There are too many tracks, too many people. We will have to hunt them out. Soon, someone will see us. It disturbs white men to see a Sioux with a rifle instead of a hoe."

Ki grinned at that. "I could go in and look around. I might even get a chance to use that Western Union."

"We will not stay out of a fight," Red Elk said darkly.

"I know that." Ki looked at the Indian and smiled. "There's so many of them, don't you think I'd save a couple for you?"

Red Elk threw back his head and laughed. "Round Knife is generous with his friends."

Ki turned his pony around and started off to the south. "Ask Little Hawk to get us as near to that road as he can without taking us past the mining shacks. We'll find a better place to

149

ride on the other side, don't you think? And I'll take a look at things from there."

Red Elk nodded and spoke to Little Hawk. The Sioux led them along the draw and up a narrow ridge. Ten minutes later, Little Hawk pointed. Ki urged his pony forward. The country was rough, but the road was in good condition. Red Elk moved from cover, saw no one about and waved the others on. Yellow Wing dug her heels in the pony's side and slapped the animal's neck with her reins. Ki followed, then Red Elk and Little Hawk.

The shot sounded flat and hollow in the rocky terrain. Little Hawk's pony folded and fell forward on its neck. The Sioux clawed air, hit the ground hard and came to his feet running. The second shot clipped his heels. The third sent him diving for cover.

Red Elk reined in quickly, his mount pawing air. He emptied his rifle at the gunman's position until Little Hawk leaped up behind Yellow Wing. Red Elk and the girl kicked their mounts to cover as a volley of fire echoed through the rocks. Ki saw them spill out of the brush, five riders firing as they rode.

Chapter 16

Red Elk waved the others on, shaking his rifle angrily in the air. When the horses moved past, he kicked his mount into a run.

"Up there," he shouted, "hurry!"

Ki glanced ahead and saw that Red Elk was driving them to higher ground. It was the same badlands terrain they'd left across the road—boulder-strewn heights and treacherous draws. A shot whined off to Ki's left. He kicked his pony close to Yellow Wing. She tossed the Winchester to him on the run. Ki levered a shell in the chamber and came up behind Red Elk. There was only one plan that made sense, and the Indian was playing it out—Yellow Wing and Little Hawk wouldn't make it riding double. Ki and Red Elk had to buy them time.

The Sioux waved Ki to the left, and Ki nodded. The five riders came up the draw, bunched together and raising dust. Red Elk grinned in pleasure. If the men spread out, they could easily keep their quarry on the run. Instead they were coming on like a county horse race.

Ki and Red Elk fired at once. Two riders went down and a third clutched his arm. The survivors turned and bent over their saddles, flailing their mounts into a run.

Red Elk laughed and struck his chest. "There are some men who have not fought the Sioux before!"

"Look." Ki pointed. "They aren't headed back to the road. They're going southwest. Hell, it could be them. Part of the bunch we're after. Putting roving guards around the area makes sense."

Red Elk frowned. "Maybe. They could be anyone else just as well, Round Knife. Everyone shoots at Indians. They do not need a reason."

Ki was almost certain he was right. "Little Hawk and the girl will be all right. We can find them again easily. I want to go after those bastards."

151

Red Elk's dark features split in a grin. "I think my friend has a taste for trouble. I think maybe he likes it more than meat."

"I don't like it." Ki muttered. "I get a lot more of it than I need."

Trailing the men was easy. One was hurt and the others were scared, convinced they'd flushed a savage war party. Red Elk and Ki rode above them, paralleling their path from the ridge. Ki had guessed right about their course. They were heading southwest, well away from the traveled road. That convinced him they were Cavanaugh's men. Riders who happened on Indians would go for help at once—back to the mining settlement, to other men with guns.

"Round Knife, wait!" Red Elk came suddenly alert. He reined in, sat up straight and sniffed the air. "You smell it?"

"No. What is it?"

"Smoke. A fire, over there somewhere." He pointed to a rock-strewn hillside ahead. "Hah, you see? You were right. The rabbits have led us to their hole." Red Elk slid quickly off his pony and led it past a high rock wall. Ki followed, then joined the Indian on foot. The Sioux climbed back to where the riders had disappeared, went to his belly, and inched over a sandy ledge. Ki peered over the ridge. The riders had reined in below. From out of a narrow ravine to their right, six more men on horseback suddenly appeared. The man who'd been wounded rode past them and vanished. The others pointed excitedly down the trail where they'd come. The leader of the riders cursed the pair soundly, then led his men down the trail, rifles at the ready.

"Guess they're going after us," said Ki. "You think we need to warn Yellow Wing?"

Red Elk laughed scornfully. "Little Hawk and the woman are safe. Now let us see where these riders come from, friend."

Moving back off the ledge, they led their ponies along the ridge, making their way quietly up the hill where the riders had emerged. Moments later, Red Elk brought them to a halt. Touching Ki lightly, he pointed ahead. Ki squinted, then saw him—a man with a rifle, sitting cross-legged in the shadow of a boulder.

"If it's what we're after, they'll have sentries all around," Ki whispered. Red Elk made a knifelike motion across his

152

throat. "No," Ki told him. "If we can, let's leave everything like it is for the moment. I want to get a good look."

Red Elk shrugged and motioned him forward. He studied the terrain a long moment, then left the ponies again. They climbed in silence, the sentry just above them to the left. Now Ki could smell smoke and hear voices. Cautiously he bellied up the slope behind a patch of dry scrub, parted it, and looked down into the draw.

Blood pumped rapidly through his veins. This was it! He'd found it! Whatever Pierce Cavanaugh and the Prussian were up to, it was all down there in the hollow. Quickly he let his eyes take in the scene, trying to make sense of what he saw. Right off, he knew they'd underestimated the camp's strength. Not counting the men doing sentry duty or the bunch who'd ridden out, there were forty or more men down below.

The wagons were bunched together at the far end of the draw, big freightwagons like the ones he'd seen before, covered tightly in heavy-grade canvas. Ki counted twenty-eight, and guessed there might be more around the bend. What were they for? he wondered. What was the cartel hauling that was worth whatever lives it might cost?

Closer, nearly directly below their perch, was a makeshift rope corral for the team horses and mounts. Across the camp was a scattering of bedrolls and packs and several fires. Farther away, some twenty yards up the far slope, were two tents.

Ki let his eyes mark every man he could see. In a moment he spotted two of Cavanaugh's men—one in a bowler hat, the other in riding breeches. Cavanaugh, though, was nowhere in sight.

Suddenly, movement near one of the tents caught his eye. A girl in a pale blue dress walked into the open. Bright yellow hair in tight ringlets framed her face. At first Ki thought she was a child. Then the girl paused and stretched, brought both hands to her head and ran her fingers through her hair. Ki's mouth went dry. It was an easy hundred yards across the draw, but there was no mistaking the sensuous movement of her body, the way one hip thrust wantonly ahead of the other. He remembered Jessie had told him about a girl who was with Cavanaugh in Mule. This one certainly fit the description.

At that moment he saw a familiar figure appear. His fists clenched tightly at his sides. The Prussian, that was him for certain—the fat little bastard who'd been so anxious to "question" Yellow Wing! He waddled down the hill from somewhere up in the rocks. The girl saw him, turned, and disappeared back inside her tent. The Prussian quickened his pace and marched in behind her. Almost at once the girl burst into the open, the fat man on her heels. The girl's face twisted in anger; she backed off, clutching the torn bodice of her gown over her breasts. The Prussian walked toward her, gesturing wildly. The girl stamped her foot and kicked at his shins, then stalked back into the tent. The Prussian fumed a moment then shrugged and walked down the draw.

Ki turned and saw that Red Elk had watched the pair with interest. "You know them?" he asked Ki. "The man and the girl with gold hair?"

"I know who they are. The man was in the camp where the Arikaras had Yellow Wing. The girl belongs to Cavanaugh." He looked Red Elk in the eye. "Cavanaugh and the fat man are the leaders. They run the men who killed Yellow Wing's grandfather. The same ones who ambushed your people."

Red Elk closed his eyes and looked at the sky. "My prayers have been answered. They will not live long. I promise that now."

Ki knew he meant it, but at the moment he wasn't sure how he'd bring that promise to pass. Their war party wasn't all that impressive just now.

"Let's get back," Ki suggested. "These people aren't going anywhere for a while."

Red Elk nodded and they backed off slowly down the ledge. Halfway to the ponies, both men froze as three shots sounded off to their left.

Ki looked anxiously at the Sioux. "Wouldn't be Yellow Wing and Little Hawk, would it?"

"No." Red Elk shook his head. "Not over there." He led his pony the way they'd come and Ki followed. They stopped where they'd first seen the riders come out of the camp. In a moment, two men on horseback appeared. After them came the rest of the party, riding single file.

Ki stared and pulled up straight. He felt as if someone had hit him in the gut with a club. "No!" he said. "They've got Jessie and Glass!"

* * *

After Johnston and Del Gue rode off, Jessie and Joseph moved west the rest of the night, crossing the Smith River in the dark. Stopping to rest their horses, they reached the east bank of the Missouri just before dawn. They slept in a shallow arroyo and ate a cold breakfast. After scouting in every direction, Glass could find no sign of the riders Johnston had seen to the north. With great good luck, he told Jessie, they'd turned and gone back to Fort Benton. There was a better chance, though, that they'd send someone to check when the other riders failed to return.

"We don't know that the wagons that feller told Johnston about was the right ones," said Joseph. "Could be, though. Eight of 'em, he said."

"That's a lot of wagons," she said hopefully. "And they're headed *south*, Joseph. It all adds up. We've got to have a look."

Joseph took off his hat and ran a hand through his thick black hair. "Christ, lady—you're goin' to get to see all of Montana 'fore this is over."

"I want to see what's in those wagons," she said tightly. "I'll settle for that."

They found the road west of the river. Joseph said it was the old Mullan Wagon Road, and that it went all over hell and gone in Montana.

"Couldn't tell if they'd passed five minutes before us," Joseph scowled. "Too much of everything else messin' it up. If they used this road, though, someone saw them. That's our best bet. Of course they didn't *have* to use it at all," he added. "Might be sticking to the foothills west."

"What's farther south? I can't remember my maps." She squinted at the Big Belt range to the south, the high peaks of the Divide to the west.

"Helena's fifty or sixty miles. Nothin' west except mountains and rough country. Where we come from before." He read her thoughts and nodded. "South'd make sense. Don't know why they'd come this far just to take whatever they got back up the Rockies. 'Course, we don't know what the hell they're doin', anyhow. So anything we figure's just guessing."

"They're here," Jessie said grimly. "They're here, Joseph."

By noon, Glass began moving past the low hills to the west. There were people about now, lone wagons and riders and

155

occasional settlers' shacks. Once, they stopped to talk to an old couple moving south. They rode a flatbed wagon led by two bony mules. The bed of the wagon was piled high with their worldly goods—boxes, chests, an iron bedstead, and a pen full of squawking chickens. A milk cow with all her ribs showing was tied on back. They told Jessie and Glass they'd had a store east of Lewis and Clark's Pass. Three cholera victims had been found in the settlement, and some others up north on the Teton River. More than a dozen families had left the town, leaving whatever they had behind.

Jessie and Glass rode on, and it was clear the couple were glad to see them go. They weren't all that interested in getting close to strangers.

"I've seen people die from cholera, Joseph," Jessie said evenly. "It's not a pretty thing to see."

"Yeah, so have I," he told her. "Whole village full of Blackfoot once." He whipped his horse and moved off. They went on south, rocky foothills to their right, keeping a ridge and a screen of brush between their path and the road.

"I don't care if we haven't found their tracks," Jessie said fiercely. "They're here. We're close, Joseph."

Joseph scratched his head. "Goin' toward Helena? I don't know, Jessie . . ."

"Why not? Who's after them, Joseph? You and me? Those telegrams I tried to send died right in Fort Benton, and Cavanaugh's people know it. It's not as if the cavalry or a posse is on their trail. Hell, we don't even know what they're doing wrong!" She sighed and looked at Joseph. "I wish Ki and Yellow Wing knew where we were. I'd feel a lot better if they were here."

"They're all right. That feller can take care of himself."

"I know, that's not the point. I jus—" Jessie stopped as the shots rang out flat and clear, the sound rolling for seconds through the rocks.

"Close," snapped Glass. He pulled his horse around and looked narrowly to the south. "That way. Stay here, Jessie."

"To hell with that."

Glass scowled and pulled his rifle out of its soft leather case. Jessie stayed with him as he cut through scrub and rode west, urging his mount through narrow channels of red stone. He stopped finally, gave her a warning glance, and disappeared.

156

After a quarter-hour he was back, his face covered with fine white dust.

"Saw tracks. Lots of 'em. Might be a few Indians stealing horses, I don't know."

"What do you want to do?"

"What I'd *like* to do is cut 'round this place for a couple of hundred miles," he said darkly. "Don't guess we got time for that. Hell, I can't figure if it's safer out here or on the road. 'Bout six of one and half a dozen of the other." He hefted his rifle and climbed out of the gully. Whatever they did, it seemed a good idea to get back to high ground, someplace where they could see what was coming.

Jessie followed as he led her up a winding path to a spot that was sheltered by the water-smoothed walls of a narrow canyon. Centuries before, a river had carved its way through, leaving a sandy defile a bit wider at the bottom than at the top. No sound at all reached the floor; directly above, Jessie could see a strip of blue sky. The ground at the end of the canyon sloped upward, and Glass urged his horse up the path. They were nearly at the top when a man stepped out from behind a rock and leveled his rifle at Joseph's head.

Glass thought about trying, and knew it was too late. The man grinned in agreement. "Good thinking, mister. Now what you folks doin' out here?"

"Tryin' not to get shot, looks like." Glass showed him an easy grin. "First a bunch of goddamn Injuns pop up out of nowhere, and now you."

"Yeah? You run into 'em too, did you?" The man lowered his weapon an inch. "Just riding through or what?"

"Me and my missus are goin' down to Helena to buy a little furniture for our place up north. Thought maybe we'd—"

Two riders came around the bend, jerked their horses to a stop, and took in the scene. The heavyset man looked at his friend on the ground, then turned to Jessie and stared. "Jesus Christ," he blurted, "you gone and made yourself some money, Slim." He levered a shell in his rifle and fired three shots in the air. "That's *her*—the goddamn Starbuck woman!"

Chapter 17

Jessie's heart sank as they rode through the narrow defile into camp. Men glanced up from cookfires as she passed. They grinned and made rude jokes she didn't hear. Her eyes were locked on the far end of the camp, where canvas-covered wagons stood in the shadow of rocky walls. She wasn't surprised to see them, but she was startled by their number.

"Well, we found 'em," Joseph said dryly. "We sure as hell did."

"Oh, Joseph," she moaned, "I'm sorry I got you into all this!"

"You didn't get me into nothin'," he said flatly. His pale eyes flashed in defiance. "I don't want to hear you say that again."

"Joseph—"

"You! Shut your goddamn mouth!" The rider next to Glass raised his rifle in a warning.

"And you go straight to hell," said Joseph.

The man grinned, turned his weapon around, and slammed the butt in Joseph's stomach. Joseph went double, gasped, and fell from his horse. His hands were bound, so he hit the ground hard.

"You son of a bitch!" Jessie shouted.

The rider and his friends laughed. Glass lay in the dirt, his face twisted in pain. The man dismounted and kicked him in the ribs.

"Get up, feller," he said darkly, "you don't like ridin' quiet, you can walk. Come on, damn you!" He jerked a revolver from his belt, thumbed back the hammer, and pressed the muzzle to Joseph's head. Joseph struggled to his knees, braced himself, and stood. The man kicked him and sent him sprawling. Joseph set his teeth and stood again. The man jammed the pistol in his belly.

"Now—you got anything else to say, Kit Carson?" He stuck his Colt in his belt. "If you don't, let's jus' walk easy-like over to tha—"

Joseph's knees came up hard in the man's groin. He screamed and rolled to the ground, clutching himself between his legs. A gunman cursed, drew his pistol, and leveled it at Glass.

"No, *don't!*" Jessie begged.

"Hold it, Pete. Leave him be."

Jessie turned. Cavanaugh's man, the one who liked English riding clothes, stood just behind her.

"He's askin' for it," Pete growled. "Christ, look what he did to Mack!"

"I said leave him be. Take them both to one of the tents. Put a guard outside but don't bother them. Do you understand that?"

"Yeah, I got it," Pete muttered. The man in riding clothes turned and walked away. Pete followed him with his eyes. "Fancy goddamn bastard," he said under his breath. "Come on, you heard the man. Get 'em out of here. And someone do somethin' for Mack." He looked at Glass and grinned crookedly at Jessie. "I hope to hell I'm there when Mr. Cavanaugh finishes that one off." He licked his lips meaningfully at Jessie. "And you too, darlin'..."

"Joseph, are you all right?" she asked anxiously. She could see the guard's shadow on the tent, but he was plainly out of hearing.

"Guess I'm some better'n that other feller," said Glass. He grinned but his heart wasn't in it.

"That was a dumb thing to do, you know? You don't tell a man like that to go to hell, Joseph—not with your hands tied behind you."

"Uh-huh. Seemed like a good idea at the time." He turned on his side and groaned. "I don't suppose you got anything on you I don't know about, do you?"

"Like what?"

"Oh, a little ol' blade in your boot'd be good. Somethin' sewed in the band of your hat."

Jessie flushed. "Are your serious? If I'd had a—a *freckle* hidden away, that bastard would have found it. There's only one place he didn't look, and I figured he was getting to that!"

"Used to carry this little pigsticker in my belt," said Joseph. "Figured if something like this ever happened, I'd have me some help. My horse throwed me once, and that goddamn blade near run through my belly."

Jessie gave him a narrow look. "That's a wonderful story, Joseph."

"Kinda thought you'd like it."

"Cavanaugh's going to roast us on a spit if we don't figure some way out of this, friend. You got any ideas at all?"

"I'm workin' on these ropes," he told her. "That's 'bout the only idea I've got at the moment. And that's not all that promising."

She'd already tried her own ropes and knew the task was hopeless. And even if they managed to get free—then what? Everyone in camp was armed; they wouldn't get ten feet from the tent.

It seemed like a good half hour before the tent flap opened and the sandy-haired man in riding breeches walked in. A guard came with him, bent to cut their ropes, and motioned them to their feet with a .44.

"Mr. Cavanaugh's back," the man said. "He's very pleased that you're here. Johnny Dee," he spoke without turning. "If either of these two even look like they're stepping out of line, shoot 'em in the knees. Mr. Cavanaugh wants them alive, but he doesn't much care if they're standing."

"Yes sir. I'll do just that, Mr. Harris," the guard said eagerly. It was the first time she'd heard the fancy dresser's name. Harris walked out and Johnny Dee motioned Jessie and Glass to follow.

They walked down the hill and started across the ravine. Jessie drew in a breath and exchanged a quick glance with Joseph. The wagons! Harris was taking them right to the wagons! Closer, she could see there were even more than she'd first imagined. A bend in the granite walls had masked a dozen more. There had to be twenty-five or thirty, at least!

Harris motioned them to stop. In a moment, two figures emerged from the shadowed wall to Jessie's left. She recognized the taller man at once—Pierce Cavanaugh, dressed in an elegant tailored suit in a small checked pattern, with a gold vest and a cream-colored Stetson. He was clad for a business dinner in Chicago or Denver—certainly not for tromping about outdoors. She'd never seen the short, chubby, sallow man with thick spectacles that rode on his nose. Yet she knew instinctively who he was. Even without the oddly cut suit and close-cropped hair, she knew him for the cartel's man. He looked right at her and something turned over in her stomach.

Cavanaugh stepped forward, his hands behind his back, glanced curiously at Glass, and nodded at Jessie. "Well, Miss Starbuck," he said gently, "I see you didn't take my advice. Somehow I didn't think you would."

"Now what advice was that?" Jessie forced a smile. "You mean getting out of Mule so your boys could bury me in the mountains? Sorry—that didn't seem like a good idea."

Cavanaugh pretended not to hear. "And this gentleman with you would be . . . ?"

"George Armstrong Custer," Joseph said blandly. "You likely read about me."

"There was an old receipt for supplies in his pack," Harris put in. "His name's Joseph Glass, Mr. Cavanaugh."

"Oh, is it now?" Cavanaugh raised a brow. "I *have* heard of you, Mr. Glass. Apparently you've taken up with crude company, Miss Starbuck."

"Not until just now," Jessie said dryly.

The Prussian's face colored. Cavanaugh's expression didn't change. "And where's your other friend?" he asked. "The Jappo, Ki?"

"Goddamn you!" Jessie's green eyes flashed in pretended anger. "You tell *me*, mister! Your tame Indians took him and the girl!"

For an instant, Cavanaugh seemed to buy it. Then he shook his head slowly, a pained expression in his eyes. "Please. It's a little late for games, isn't it? I think you know I don't have them. I think you— Ah, but no matter. It's not important now."

"I do not agree, Caff-anaugh," the Prussian blurted. "If they are alife somewhere, then they are trouble. We must haff her tell us where they are."

"The Arikaras handled them," Cavanaugh said evenly. "I told you that, Doctor."

"*Ja*, the saffages, yes?" He showed Cavanaugh a testy smile. "The saffages that do not appear."

"We've been moving kind of fast. They'll be here, my friend."

161

The Prussian made a noise in his throat. "I want to examine this woman," he said thickly. He shook a stubby finger in Jessie's face. "I will get the truth out of you. Haff no question about that!"

"Fine, you'll get your chance," Cavanaugh told him.

The Prussian looked narrowly at Jessie, his eyes as big as dollars behind the thick glasses. His glance touched her breasts and trailed openly down her body. Jessie's skin crawled. There was something in his eyes, something a lot more than a man looking over a woman. Whatever it was, she didn't want to see it any closer.

The Prussian turned away and walked angrily across the ravine to his tent.

"The good doctor likes you, I think." Cavanaugh grinned. "Maybe you two'll get to know each other better."

"You son of a bitch!" Glass bunched his shoulders and lunged straight for Cavanaugh.

"Joseph, *don't!*" Jessie grabbed his shoulders and held him. Harris and Johnny Dee leveled their pistols at his head.

Cavanaugh looked amused. "What did you expect would happen if we caught her, Mr. Glass? You can't be that naïve and unlettered. Come now, as long as you're here, you might as well see what it's all about. That's what you came for, isn't it?"

He led them a few steps farther, picked up a dry stick, and pointed. "It's all over there, in the wagons. The key to Montana Territory. And after that, the rest of the great Northwest." He showed Jessie an easy smile. "You're a woman with a good head for business. I don't have to tell you what's happening up here. Montana's bursting at the seams with natural wealth. Gold, silver, cattle, timber, rich grazing and farming land. Not to mention the biggest treasure of all—more copper than you can dig out of the earth in a hundred years!" He saw Jessie's expression and smiled. "Ah, you know about that, do you? I figured John Hamilton was nosing around. John was a real smart fellow, always respected the man."

"Don't you even mention his name!" Jessie said fiercely.

"That's over and done, now isn't it?" Cavanaugh shook his head and swept the stick in a wide circle. "All of it's right here, Miss Cavanaugh. Just waiting for capital to turn the land into double eagles." His deep brown eyes seemed to sparkle at the thought.

162

"And that's where your European friends come in, right?" Jessie said boldly. "The railroads are opening up the territory and folks are cryin' for foreign money. And the cartel's happy to oblige."

"A very astute group of men," Cavanaugh said with real respect. "Very astute indeed."

Jessie frowned in thought. "I've seen the cartel spend money before. They're damn good at it, I know. Bribery, extortion, a little cold-blooded murder thrown in . . ." She shook her head firmly. "But that won't do it, mister. They can't plain *steal* Montana overnight. They're going to have to put some *honest* money in, too. And I do know a little about business. Even the cartel hasn't enough money to take over Montana."

"Of course they haven't," Cavanaugh said impatiently. "They don't *have* to, you know that. As long as they have the *right* interests, the right timber and cattle lands. And especially the right copper veins, Miss Starbuck. You only have to hold the seat of power to win it all. Banking, politics, men in key positions . . ." He squeezed his hand into a fist. "It all falls easily into place."

"And what's in the wagons?" Jessie asked bluntly. "You going to get around to that? What is it—enough foreign gold to make it happen?"

Cavanaugh gave her a broad wink. "Better than gold, believe me. You hit a very important point, Miss Starbuck. It takes a lot of money to sit in a high-stakes game. And there are plenty of greedy hands trying to beat you out of the pot." He paused and smiled again. "The only way to win is to scare off the other players. Buy the pot cheap."

Jessie frowned, puzzled at his words. Then, all at once it struck her. "Oh my God!" She stared and drew a breath. Cavanaugh beamed and she knew she'd guessed right. "The—the *cholera* epidemic!" she exclaimed. "You—you're *using* the epidemic, aren't you? Taking advantage of peoples' fears, buying folks out for pennies on the dollar because they're scared!"

Cavanaugh stared, then exploded into laughter. He threw back his head and the sound echoed through the canyon. Tossing the stick aside, he stalked to the nearest wagon and threw the canvas cover aside. The wagon was filled with chunks of Milky River ice. Nestled in layers were bulky shapes wrapped in canvas. Cavanaugh climbed atop the wagon and kicked savagely at the ice with his boot. Beside her, Jessie saw Harris

163

and the gunman turn white. Cavanaugh kicked until one of the bulky shapes came loose. He gave it a final blow and the thing tumbled to the ground. A flap of canvas fell away, revealing the horror inside.

Jessie shrank back. The young man's face and naked chest were pale as wax. His eyes stared emptily at nothing, his mouth twisted forever in pain.

Cavanaugh folded his arms and laughed. "You almost had it, Miss Starbuck. We aren't *using* the cholera epidemic. By God, we *are* the epidemic!"

"Oh Lord—*no!*" Jessie shook her head in disbelief. "That's—monstrous! All those people!"

Cavanaugh jumped lightly off the wagon. "Please—I didn't kill them, Miss Starbuck. Cholera hit a settlement south of the Milk River in Canada and wiped out everyone in town. One of the doctor's men heard about it and figured it was something we could use."

"Something you could *use!*" Jessie recoiled from the man's words.

"It's business," Cavanaugh said coolly. "Didn't you hear me, woman? We didn't go in and slaughter a whole town. They were there, already dead."

"Yeah, I reckon that makes it all right," Glass said absently.

Cavanaugh shot him a look. "Maybe we'll just add you to the body count, mister. A cholera victim with a hole between the eyes."

"And you—packed all these people in ice," Jessie said shakily. "Brought the wagons down three or four routes into the territory and let the victims get...discovered."

Cavanaugh smiled. "Rather effective, wouldn't you say? Considering we didn't even know about the settlement six days ago."

"And no one's stopped to wonder why all the victims are strangers? People no one's ever seen before?"

"My God, lady." Cavanaugh looked at the sky. "No one asks questions about cholera. No one *cares* who they are, as long as it's not them. The damn doctors don't even want to look close. The Prussian said they wouldn't, and he was right. Of course, we make sure one of our own, ah, *physicians* is on hand to confirm any doubts. Give a man a black bag and he's a doctor, you know?"

"It isn't going to work," Jessie said sharply. "Someone'll wise up, and you know it. It's not as simple as that."

Cavanaugh looked pained. "It's already worked, Miss Starbuck. Use your head. You were in Fort Benton. Did you see the newspapers there? They're claiming three hundred deaths already. Hell, there weren't two hundred people in that settlement. We've only dumped twenty or thirty bodies so far. Fear and imagination have done the rest. Fear and imagination. They're reporting casualties in Goldcreek, Butte, Virginia City, Helena . . . we haven't even *been* there yet." He showed her a tolerant smile. "I don't have to tell you it's going to work. Anyone who dies of snakebite or pneumonia in Montana is going to have cholera."

"If I had a dyin' breath, mister, you know how I'd spend it?" said Glass. "I'd get my hands 'round your neck, is what I'd do. Jus' for a minute or so . . ."

Cavanaugh's mouth twisted in a scar, but Jessie saw that the mountain man's gaze had struck home. "Get them out of here," Cavanaugh spat harshly. "Get them out of my sight!"

"They did it right this time," groaned Joseph. "I mighta done something with those ropes before, but there's not a chance in hell now."

Jessie knew he was right. They'd bound them separately, then tied them back to back for good measure. She could hardly move a muscle, much less struggle to get loose.

"It's going to work, damn it," she said dully. "I know those people, Joseph, and they can do it. They've saved their big push for where it counts. People are already scared out of their wits. You know what's going to happen when those bodies start showing up in Helena? Cholera all over the streets in the territorial capital? And then there's Butte and Virginia City, which just happen to be in rich mining country. God, those towns'll be near empty in three days. The banks, businesses, every mining claim the cartel wants—everything! And the same thing's happening across the Divide. All the rich claims along Clark Fork and the Bitterroot River. And you can bet there'll be a couple of cases in the Judith Mountains and down on the Yellowstone. They won't have to worry about the eastern end of Montana—not with a stranglehold on the west!"

"Smart bunch of bastards, all right," Joseph muttered.

"Lord, is that all you've got to say?"

"What'd you like me to say, Jessie? I could tell you I got a Gatling gun in my pocket, but I'd be lyin'.'"

"I'm sorry. I didn't mean that. I just—"

"Yeah, I know." He was silent a long moment. "Goddamn salt," he mumbled. "Shoulda told me something."

"What?"

"The salt. Where the wagons was bunched up in that valley in Kootenay country. I worked in the Dakotas when I run away from home. Cut ice on the rivers one winter—stored it in sawdust and hay till summer and shipped it south. Sometimes you use salt to keep stuff cold."

"I knew that too," Jessie sighed. "I've been in an icehouse before. Who'd make the connection?"

"No one, I guess. Jessie, look—I'm going to put this as straight as I can. Don't waste your strength tryin' to get loose. You can't do it. We're goin' to get one chance. Maybe. They jus' might untie us 'fore they . . ."

"Before they shoot us, Joseph. Go ahead and say it."

"All right. I'm sorry, goddammit, but that's the way it winds down. If I can, I'm goin' to jump one of those bastards. When I do, you do whatever you can. Run, get a horse if one's handy—"

"Joseph!"

"Don't, Jessie," he said harshly. "I ain't bein' no hero, I'm just makin' sense. We got nothin' else goin', so we got to give it a try. And don't worry, lady—if I can, I'm goin' to be running right behind you."

Jessie didn't answer. She knew it was a lie, and that if the moment ever came, he wouldn't do any running. He'd stay and fight and die and give her every chance he could. *We'll see about that,* she thought. *We'll see about that when it happens, Joseph Glass . . .*

"Jessie," he said suddenly, "listen—you hear anything?"

"What? No, I—yes, yes I do." A chill touched her spine and she knew at once what it was. It was a sound she'd heard countless times before. The rattle of harness, the hollow rumble of iron wheels on rocky ground. "They're moving out, Joseph. They're getting ready to move the wagons!"

"Figures," Joseph cursed under his breath. "It's gettin' late afternoon; they start moving, they'll get in Helena during the night without causing any fuss. They'll leave the wagons they

166

want to and move the others on south."

"And there's nothing we can do to stop them," Jessie said angrily. "God, Joseph!"

"Jessie, I wish there was. Those folks down there got trouble on the way. But we got all we can handle up here."

"I know. You're right. It's just—" Jessie stopped as a sudden sharp scream of pain cut the night. "Oh Jesus, don't!" the voice begged. *"Don't, oh God, please!"*

A man laughed, a deep, choking sound like the cough of a dog.

"Christ, what's that?" Joseph breathed.

The cry faded to a low, hopeless wail, like the sound of a terrified child or some small wounded creature. "I know what it is," Jessie said shakily. "It's Marcie. Cavanaugh's got her here, and he's given her to the Prussian."

Ki watched in silence, anger and frustration cording the tendons at his throat. He saw the man hit Glass with the butt of his rifle, slamming him off his horse. Moments later, Glass kneed the man and doubled him over. Ki thought it was finished for sure, that they'd blow the mountain man's head off then and there. He watched as the sandy-haired man in riding breeches came on the scene, and waited until Jessie and Glass had been thrown into a tent under guard.

"I have to get them out of there, Red Elk," he said plainly. "I don't know how, but I have to do it."

"Huh!" Red Elk made a noise in his throat. "Nothing is easy. Everything a man does is trouble. That is a saying among the Sioux."

"It's a saying among the Japanese too," Ki said soberly. "There probably isn't anyone who hasn't got one like it."

Yellow Wing listened intently as Ki told her what they'd seen. "Ki," she said, "how are we going to do it? Forty men, you say? Maybe more?"

"Yes, but they are all white," Red Elk added.

Ki shot him a look. "We've got a while, I guess. Whatever we do, it's going to have to wait for night. Do you agree?" He looked at Red Elk, and the Indian shook his head, then turned and spoke to Little Hawk, and the Sioux picked up his rifle and vanished through the rocks.

"He will watch the camp," Red Elk said. "I have told him

to come back at once if anything happens."

Ki nodded agreement. Yellow Wing and Little Hawk had holed up in a narrow, blind canyon. It was hand to find, and the rocky trail leading in left no tracks.

"The way I see it," said Ki, "it won't take much time to work a plan. We haven't exactly got an army. All we can do is get in and get 'em out under cover of darkness. I'm going in. You and Little Hawk give me cover."

Red Elk shook his head. *"I* go in. I mean no disrespect, Round Knife. But I can do this better."

"I don't mean any disrespect, either," Ki said evenly. "But I've had some experience at this kind of thing, too. This one is mine, friend."

Red Elk started to protest, but Ki cut him off. "There's one thing I think you've forgotten. There are a lot of men down there, and I look more like them than you do. If they see an Indian strolling around camp, they're going to shoot and start yelling. Anyone who gets close enough to me to say hello isn't going to say much more."

"You are right," the Sioux admitted. "I will agree to this." He looked sourly at the ground and folded his arms. "If you get the man and the woman out safely, there is a chance there will be no killing at all."

Ki read the disappointment in the Indian's broad features, and said dryly, "We could line up on the hill at first light, and shoot them all when they wake up."

"Yes, that would be a good idea," Red Elk said soberly. If he guessed Ki was joking, his expression didn't show it.

"And what am I supposed to be doing?" Yellow Wing asked coolly. "Hauling water and sewing buffalo robes?"

Red Elk laughed aloud.

"You can if you like," said Ki. "What I'd hoped was that you'd take on something important."

"Like what?"

"Like having the horses ready when we need them. Making sure they don't bolt if any shooting starts."

"Yes, I can do that. I am very good with horses, you'll remember."

"I do remember. That's why I want you to do it."

"You want me to do it because there is no one else to ask," she said flatly. "And because I am a woman."

Red Elk snapped at the girl in the Sioux tongue. Yellow

Wing colored and lowered her eyes. Whatever he'd said, Ki noticed that it seemed to work.

"It'll be dark soon. Can you think of anything else we ought to do?"

"Yes," Red Elk told him. "Decide which way we're going to leave. We do not know this country in the dark. I think we should go north and then west. Into the mountains. No one is going to follow us there at night."

"May a woman speak?" Yellow Wing interrupted. "I would like to make a suggestion. I was just wondering—you haven't mentioned it yet, but I'm sure your plan calls for someone to steal three more horses. Two for Jessie and Joseph, and one for Little Hawk. It is a small matter, I know . . ."

Ki shot Red Elk a look.

"We were getting to that," the Sioux said darkly.

"I was sure that you were."

"Little Hawk will handle it. It will be no problem."

"That will leave the whole job of covering me to you," said Ki.

"We will manage with what we have. As you have said, Round Knife, this is not a very large war party. We must—" Red Elk came suddenly alert. Alarm spread over his features and he reached out desperately for his weapon.

"Hold 'er right there, Injun!" a voice said sharply from the brush. "Blink an' I'll put a hole in yer red belly!" The man stepped out of the rocks, his rifle leveled at Red Elk. Ki stared. He recognized the grizzled features at once.

"Philadelphy," he said tightly, "put down that weapon. You're pointing it at a friend!"

The old man's rheumy eyes narrowed. "Ain't any friend of mine. You all right, Yellow Wing?"

"Of course I'm all right," she said evenly. "Philadelphy, this is Red Elk. He is not your enemy."

"Ain't, huh?" The mountain man and the Sioux exchanged murderous glances. "How come he looks like he wants to borrow my hair?"

Ki turned abruptly as Little Hawk came up the path, his face clouded with shame and anger. Rooster-John and Henry Clark marched behind him, rifles at his back. Red Elk cursed and made a noise in his throat.

"Howdy, Ki—Yellow Wing." Rooster-John showed them a crooked grin. "Found this chile hightailin' it back up here.

Reckon he's a friend of that other Injun."

Yellow Wing stormed up to the pair and stamped her foot. "What is the matter with you!" she raged. "Red Elk is part of my family, and Little Hawk is a friend. You give them back their weapons right now!"

Rooster-John scratched his head and looked puzzled. "Now, I don't recall ever givin' a Injun no rifle. Don't seem like a good idea."

Little Hawk spoke rapidly to Red Elk. The Sioux frowned and looked at Ki. "He says he was coming back to tell us. They are getting ready to move out the wagons."

Ki cursed under his breath. "Lower your rifles," he said angrily. "Just do it, all right? We don't have time for this!"

The three looked narrowly at Ki, and reluctantly crooked their weapons in their arms. Henry Clark returned Little Hawk's rifle with a pained look on his face. Red Elk didn't move.

Ki quickly filled the mountain men in on what had happened. None of them seemed surprised to learn that Jessie and Joseph were being held in the ravine.

"We seen that when we spotted the Injun," said Henry. "Picked up your tracks and theirs, and sorta figured what had happened."

A sudden thought struck Ki. "How do you happen to be here in the first place? Was that just luck, or what?"

Rooster-John grinned. "Luck by the name o' John Johnston is what it was. Him and Del Gue picked up our sign up on the Sun River an' run us down. Said they happened on Joseph an' Miss Jessie and that they was likely sniffin' up trouble. We picked up their trail and then yours."

Red Elk went rigid. *"Dah-pih-ehk Absaroka?* The one who eats the livers of Crows?"

"Uh-huh." Rooster-John gave the Indian a wary eye. "Ain't got any argyment with a feller what kills Crows, do ye?"

"A Sioux has no love for Crows," he said darkly. "They are white men's dogs, like the Arikara. If you think this means I am a friend of men like *Dah-pih-ehk Absaroka* and yourself, you are wrong!"

Philadelphy shrugged. "Well, suit yourself."

"Now look," Ki said tightly. "I don't have time to make peace between Indians and mountain men. There's reason for bad feelings both ways. Right now we've got to get Jessie and

Joseph out of that camp. We're going to have to work together, whether any of you like it or not."

Henry Clark slapped the stock of his rifle. "You got our help, Ki, an' you know it. But, ah, with all due respect, Yellow Wing, we ain't real anxious to fight beside yer kin."

"Hah! We agree on something, then," Red Elk said fiercely. "Little Hawk and I will do our part. But alone—not with them!"

Ki let his gaze sweep the circle of angry faces. "All right," he said calmly. "If that's the way you want it." He turned and deliberately walked away.

"Hey, where you goin'?" Philadelphy called out.

Ki turned abruptly and glared fiercely at them all. "I'm going down there and try to get Jessie and Joseph out. And I don't want your help—any of you. Stay here and kill each other if you like. But don't make any noise while you're doing it!" He turned again and stalked down the path, leaving the others staring at his back.

Chapter 18

"I can't see a thing," said Jessie. "Just a lot of lanterns bobbing around—which means they'll be pulling out soon. If you could—push me a little farther, Joseph. Maybe I could peek under the bottom of the tent. It's sort of loose there."

"Forget it," Glass said shortly. "I can't, and there's nothin' we need to see. We know what's goin' on, and it ain't going to help us get loose."

He didn't come right out and say, in so many words, that whatever happened outside didn't matter. When the wagons pulled out, Cavanaugh would put a bullet through their heads and drop them in a hole. She wanted to tell him she was sorry, that she'd never meant to bring him to this. She knew, though, that was something he didn't want to hear.

It had been some time since Marcie's cries had faded. Jessie prayed the girl was dead, that her heart had cheated the Prussian before he could hurt her any more. *My God*, she thought, *what kind of man is Pierce Cavanaugh? Did he simply give the girl to that monster to amuse him? Keep him happy until the deal was over?* To Jessie's way of thinking, that made Cavanaugh worse than the Prussian. The cartel's man was obviously insane but Cavanaugh knew exactly what he was doing.

"Jessie!"

"What?" Jessie gave a start. "What, Joseph?"

"Someone's coming," he said tightly. "If I—if I get a chance, I'm going to take it."

"Oh Lord, Joseph!"

"Jessie!" His body went rigid at her back. "Goddammit, Jessie, do it. Do you understand? Don't let me down!"

"All right." The calm, steady sound of her own voice surprised her. "All right, Joseph. I won't let you down."

A lantern bobbed nearby; the tent flap opened and the harsh, unfamiliar light blinded the pair for a moment. The Prussian loomed above her, two guards at his side. His tiny eyes were enormous behind the thick glasses. In the glow of the lantern they were a sick, unnatural yellow. Jessie's skin crawled. She closed her eyes and looked away.

"Just the woman," the Prussian told the guard. "Leave the man here."

She felt one of the gunmen squatting above her, smelled the sweat and whiskey on his breath. A blade parted the ropes at her back. In a moment her legs were free. The man lifted her roughly and held her. Feeling rushed into her legs; she gritted her teeth against the pain. She looked down at Joseph and wanted to cry. He was helpless, a Winchester at his head. A heavy boot crushed his face against the ground while a second gunman carefully checked his ropes. He couldn't even see her as the Prussian shoved her roughly out of the tent, passing the lantern back to the guard. The two men stopped and watched them go. The Prussian jammed a pistol in her back and motioned her up the hill past the tents.

Jessie's mind raced, fighting off the fear that threatened to overwhelm her. *I've got to try,* she thought desperately. The memory of Marcie's terrible cries still echoed in her mind. *Even if he shoots me in the back, I've got to try. It's better than going up there!*

"Don't, Fräulein," the Prussian said thickly. He seemed to guess her thoughts. "I will not kill you if you run. I will stop you, but I will not kill you."

Jessie scarcely heard him. Her eyes darted frantically through the night. A dark stand of trees suddenly appeared out of the night, stunted pines surrounding a circle of shoulder-high rocks. Jessie stumbled. The Prussian caught her and muttered angrily under his breath. Grasping her shoulders, he pushed her roughly into the hollow and sent her sprawling.

"I am going to untie you," he whispered, his face close to hers. "You giff me trouble and I will hurt you badly, yes?"

Jessie forced a nervous laugh. "And if I don't, you'll take me to the dance, right?"

"Don't you *talk* to me like that!" he rasped. "I will not haff a woman *talk* to me like that!"

"Listen, you bastard—"

His open hand whipped out and caught the side of her face. Jessie gasped and tears filled her eyes. He hit her again, slamming her head to the ground. Darkness closed in, threatening to pull her under. He lifted her by her hair, his hand lashing out against her cheeks until she fell back limply to the earth.

She knew he was handling her, slashing at her ropes. She tried to move, to pull away from his touch. Her limbs were too heavy, the effort more than she could manage. She was dimly aware of the cold. Somehow the night wind was reaching her flesh.

Something that felt like a white-hot wire touched her flesh. The terrible pain brought her fully alert. She screamed, but no sound came from her throat. She choked, and realized a thick bandanna was stuffed in her mouth. Jessie strained her neck and stared. The stub of a candle glowed on a rock. The pale yellow flame shone off his glasses. She could see the swell of her breasts and knew she was naked, her arms and legs staked wide. The Prussian squatted on the ground between her thighs.

"You are comfortable, yes?" It was cold, but his chubby features glistened with droplets of sweat. "Now we examine you a little, I think, and I ask you a question or two."

His eyes gleamed and his full lips stretched in a grin. He reached for something beside him, and Jessie stretched to see. Her eyes went wide with horror and she strained against her bonds. He picked up the small black case and laid it on her belly. Inside, shiny metal instruments were neatly aligned in a row, each in its own proper place. He chose one carefully, and held its quicksilver brightness to the light. He hummed as he worked, examining the razored edge with a critical eye. Finally he replaced the instrument and chose another.

As he moved, something directly behind him caught Jessie's eye for just an instant. A pale blue fabric lay under the tree. The fabric was soaked with something dark. Jessie blinked, and the hazy image suddenly fell into place. There was a patch of milk-white flesh beneath the fabric. Bright yellow ringlets, a pale coral mouth, and a single china-blue eye . . .

Ki stopped as the shadow moved quietly down the hill behind him. Philadelphy squatted on the trail and scratched his beard.

"Reckon we wasn't thinkin' real straight," he muttered. "Hell, me and the boys'll do what you want."

"What does Red Elk say?"

"Says he—" Philadelphy clamped his jaws shut. "Goddammit, I ain't goin' to tell you what he said. It's too insultin'."

174

Him and that other'n is takin' their horses down to where the riders and the wagons'll go through. I'll give him an owl-hoot when you get the folks free. Him and his friend'll raise hell and draw some fire. That's if you need it," the mountain man added quickly. "I ain't goin' to call him if ever'thing goes off."

Ki nodded. "And Rooster-John and Henry will close the sack if the Indians pull Cavanaugh's people down the draw."

"Uh-huh." Philadelphy gave him a near-toothless grin. "Sounds excitin', don't it? Like we 'bout got 'em surrounded."

Ki didn't answer. The whole idea was insane, six men and a woman ambushing a canyon full of gunmen. "Come on," he told Philadelphy, "there's a lot of confusion out there with those wagons, and that will help. And try to stay away from the lanterns."

"This chile didn't fall outta his nest this mornin'," the mountain man growled.

They waited for their chance, then stepped out of cover behind a man carrying a box of supplies. Four wagons were pulling up in a line, teamsters adjusting harness and making sure the rigs were secure. A lantern hung from each wagon on the right side. Ki kept well to the left. Philadelphy touched his arm and pointed. Ki nodded and kept walking. A man was coming straight toward them, a rifle hanging loosely in his hand. There was no way now to move out of his path.

The man stopped, squinting at them in the dark. "Hey, you two," he called out, "if you haven't got anything to do, get on back and see Parker. There's plenty of—hey, what the hell!"

Ki's left hand covered the man's mouth while his right grabbed his shirt and jerked him forward. His knee came up hard in the man's belly and he folded like a sack. Ki chopped him with the side of his hand between the shoulder and the neck. Philadelphy stood guard while Ki dragged the limp form into the brush. The whole encounter was over in seconds. Ki retrieved the man's weapon and joined Philadelphy. They gave the wagons a wide berth and walked across the ravine toward the tents.

"They'll have her in there," he told Philadelphy. "That one—the one with the guard."

"When I stumble, you be sure an' catch me," said Philadelphy.

"What?"

"I'm goin' to have me a heart attack or something," the

175

man growled. "Goddamn, if you ain't full of questions. Oh *Gawd!*" Philadelphy went rigid and folded. Ki held him up, keeping his own head down.

The guard before the tent stood up straight, leveling his rifle at Ki. "What is it? What's wrong with him?"

"Old man just dropped on me," Ki muttered. "Here, give me a hand." The guard hesitated, then took a step forward. Philadelphy groaned and stuck out a hand for support. The guard caught him and Philadelphy hugged him like a lover. Ki never saw the bowie knife flash straight up through the sternum. The guard simply collapsed without a sound. Philadelphy walked him quickly past the flap and inside. Ki came in in a crouch, sweeping the rifle about the tent. Joseph stared up from the ground in surprise.

"Ki, Philadelphy! Well, I'm a son of a bitch!"

"Keep your eyes open," Ki snapped, tossing the rifle to Philadelphy. He went to his knees and quickly cut Joseph's bonds. "Where is she? Where's Jessie?"

"Damn little German took her," Glass said darkly. He rubbed his arms and came shakily to his feet. "Ki, we got to get to her fast. He done somethin' awful to that girl, and he's got Jessie. Feller's crazy as a bedbug!"

Ki's belly went tight, and Joseph nodded to the west. "He had the girl close by. One of the other tents. Then he dragged her off somewhere else. Shit, I ain't got any idea where. Yellow Wing—she with you?"

"She's all right. She's got the horses."

"How many men you got?"

Ki let out a breath. "Rooster-John and Henry. And Red Elk and Little Hawk."

"They're here? Damn, and that's all? Six of you?"

"Seven now," Philadelphy drawled. "Hell, that's better'n five." He peered outside past the flap and looked at Joseph and Ki. "Someone's goin' to notice this dead feller ain't standin' up straight outside. Just as soon be in the dark when they do."

Ki and Joseph nodded and stepped into shadow away from the tent.

Ki looked around helplessly. "We have to find Jessie. I don't even know where to start looking!"

"Got to be up there." Glass nodded at the hillside above. "Wouldn't take her down below. Henry and the Indians— where are they?"

Ki told him quickly. "Philadelphy's supposed to give Red Elk a hoot when we get you and Jessie. That's the last thing we need right now."

"Right. A war ain't going to do us any good. We—*shit, get down!*"

The three went flat on the ground as two men came out of the darkness toward the tents. Ki's eyes narrowed as he recognized Cavanaugh's man in the bowler hat. The other was his friend in riding breeches.

"They're comin' right here," Glass whispered. "They see that guard's missin' . . ."

Ki nodded and touched Joseph's shoulder. He bellied down the hill, came up in a crouch behind the men, and started walking, keeping his head low. "'Scuse me," he said, masking his voice behind his hand. "Listen, we got a problem down at the wagons."

The men stopped. "Who's that? Jake? What's wrong now?"

Ki's hand shot out in a blur. The flashing *shuriken* caught his target just below the bridge of his nose. The bowler hat went sailing and the man fell back into the rocks. The man with riding breeches clawed for his gun. Joseph came off the ground like a shadow, took the man's head between his hands, and pulled him to the ground.

"Now," he said gently, "if you was to have one guess— and one's exactly what you got—where you figure that fat little shit took Miss Starbuck?"

The man named Harris stared in horror at Joseph's face. He winced as Glass laid the cold blade of a Bowie knife flat across his cheek. "I—he's got a place up there. He—he hangs out up on the ridge sometimes."

"And that's where he's got her?"

"Shit, mister, I don't know! Cavanaugh talks to him, I don't. He's crazy as hell. Look—be careful with that thing, will you?"

"Oh yeah, I sure will," said Glass. "You remember an old man named Jebediah Baker?"

All the color drained from Harris's face. "I had nothing to do with that. I swear. Honest to God, I—" Joseph's knife flashed across his throat. Harris's mouth fell open, Glass dropped the limp body to the ground.

"You heard him," Joseph said tightly. "Up on the ridge."

"I'll get her," said Ki. "You and Philadelphy—"

"Hell with that," snapped Glass. "We'll *both* get her!"

Ki started to answer, but a shot echoed down the ravine. A man shouted, and a shrill Sioux war cry shattered the dark. In an instant, light from a dozen weapons flashed through the canyon. Ki bolted up the hill. Glass started after him, took one step, and dove for cover. Ki heard Philadelphy curse, then Joseph's Winchester went into action. He glanced back once to make certain the two were all right. They'd edged down the slope to decent cover, and Ki kept going. He wondered whether the Indian had jumped the gun or if one of Cavanaugh's men had forced his hand. It didn't much matter—the fat was sure as hell in the fire.

"Yell, Jessie," he muttered between his teeth. "Shout, damn it! *Let me know where you are!*"

At the first gunfire, the Prussian's owlish eyes blinked in surprise. He cocked his head to listen, concern crossing his features. He glanced quickly at Jessie, then bent to his collection of tiny knives. Jessie sucked in a breath as he laid the blades one by one on her belly

"Caff-anaugh is a fool," he muttered under his breath. "Do not worry about the saffages, *Herr Doktor, ja?* They are after the horses, always after the horses." He shook his head in disdain, then bent close to her breasts as if he meant to share his secret. "We will not let the Indians bother us, dear lady. We haff the time, yes? Let Caff-anaugh fight his *gott-*damn saffages." He laughed at his joke, his belly shaking beneath his vest. Jessie screamed into her gag as he picked up one of the instruments and gently pricked her skin. A small dark sphere of blood appeared below her navel. He set the knife down and found the stub of a pencil in his pocket, studied her belly a moment, then drew a careful line from her navel to the patch of amber hair directly below . . . .

Chapter 19

When the first shot echoed down the canyon, the men by the wagons grabbed their weapons and ran quickly in the direction of fire. The shrill Indian yell told them the Sioux they'd driven off earlier in the day were back in force. Men with horses handy reached the scene first, gunmen on foot at their heels. There were a few scattered shots, but not enough to cause concern. The riders plunged ahead, firing their rifles blindly into the night.

Rooster-John and Henry Clark waited, one on each side of the ravine at ground level—waited and watched the riders and the men on foot go by. The Indians kept them busy, drawing them on with short volleys from above. Finally twenty or more men were bunched together, searching the night for targets. Rooster-John and Henry didn't share this problem; they had all the targets they could handle. The fact that it was dark didn't matter. After forty years of practice, night and day made little difference. Both had learned to shoot when a man had to make his first shot count—an Indian or a grizzly didn't give you much time to reload. As far as they were concerned, a Winchester repeater was as good as a Gatling gun.

Fire blossomed at the end of the canyon, and Joseph Glass sprinted across the clearing to the cover of the now deserted wagons. Philadelphy laughed, grinning from ear to ear.

"Goddamn, boy, this chile's missin' all the fun. Them two ol' 'gators is givin' 'em what-for!"

"Ain't goin' to work more'n once," Glass said tightly. "Rooster and Henry will turn 'em—and we'll get 'em back in our laps."

"Suits the hell out of me," said Philadelphy. He leaned against a wagon, calmly levering shells into his weapon.

Joseph shot him a look. "This ain't the Alamo, you old bastard. Get on across and find Yellow Wing. Take the mounts down the far end of the ravine and up across the other side to the tents. I'll draw fire and try to keep 'em off your ass."

"Uh-huh." Philadelphy raised a shaggy brow. "An' who's playin' Jim Bowie now?"

"Go on," snapped Glass, "they're comin' back!" Philadelphy muttered under his breath and disappeared. Glass took a deep breath and wiped sweat off the stock of his rifle. Philadelphy was right. It didn't make sense, but that wasn't out of line in this crazy mess. To take on a whole herd of gunmen and try to ride out with your skin—it wasn't exactly the Alamo, but it didn't miss by much.

It shaped up in his mind, the way it ought to happen. Philadelphy and Yellow Wing would get the horses across. Philadelphy would find Ki and take Jessie and Yellow Wing on up the far ridge. Ki would join him down here and help cover the girls' escape, waiting for Rooster-John and Henry and the Sioux. They'd grab the extra mounts that Philadelphy would stake out, and lose themselves in the dark.

Joseph laughed and leveled his rifle. Shit, it wouldn't happen like that at all. Likely wouldn't even come close.

The riders were turning back, coming straight at him out of the heavy fire to their rear. He squeezed the trigger and lifted a man out of the saddle. His second shot missed. Lead came out of the dark, as thick as rain. He fired again, sending another rider tumbling. Heavy fire forced him back. He dove for the cover of the wagons, levered a shell into the chamber, and came up shooting. *Christ,* he thought, *looks like the whole northern buffalo herd thundering down past Big Snowy ...*

Philadelphy had his string some forty yards down the draw when he heard them off to his left. Joseph's rifle opened up, one sharp crack after another. Yellow Wing paused beside him and stared back up the ravine.

"Come on," Philadelphy said harshly, "just keep goin' straight over, girl."

"Joseph—we can't just *leave* him out there!"

"Can and will. Now *git!*" The old man drove his horse roughly into her mount, slapped the animal's rump, and sent it bolting. He jerked the lead in one hand and clutched his rifle in the other. A little luck was what they needed—about half a minute's worth. Keep to the shadow and ease up the hill. Joseph was as slick as a minnow, and they'd play hell pinning him down. Philadelphy grinned and shook his head. *Some goddamn army, for sure. Three ol' coons pushin' seventy, and two wild Injuns who'd been there to cut down Custer. What'd Jebediah have thought of that? Wouldn't have believed it, is what. Damndest bunch of—*

"Philadelphy, look out!"

He jerked around fast as the girl shouted, saw the men coming up behind him, and snapped off a shot. A rider cursed and fell out of his saddle. Philadelphy swept his rifle to cover the girl, saw her sitting her pony easily, her legs clutching the animal's sides as she squeezed off one shot after another.

A bunch of them had bolted right past the wagons and nearly run him down! Well, by God, he had somethin' to cure that! Turning his mount in a half-circle, he fired and cut a man down. A rider shouted, and Philadelphy shot him in the head. He kicked the mount savagely, trying to break through to the girl. Something hot seared his belly, and he gasped. Roaring in anger, he swung the barrel of his rifle around hard. Metal cracked bone, and the gunman stumbled back. Another clawed at his leg, and Philadelphy kicked out, cursing in Comanche and moving effortlessly into Pawnee. Christ, his belly hurt! Worse than that arrow he'd taken in '52 on the Snake. Or, hell, was it '53? He couldn't remember at all. Jebediah, now, he'd remember. Ought to, he was there and dug the thing out.

The night was getting darker, and he couldn't figure that. He gripped the barrel of his rifle and lashed out blindly at anyone who dared get close. The bastards were all over him, trying to pull him down. He had to get 'em off and see to Yellow Wing. If anything happened to that girl, Jebediah'd skin him Kiowa-style and have him for breakfast...

Glass heard the sudden scattering of fire at his back, but couldn't turn to look. He stood between the wagons, legs spread wide, firing the Winchester into the dark. The trigger clicked empty and he tossed the weapon aside. A horse reared up and pawed air; the rider swung a Colt toward Joseph's head. Joseph leaped as the flare of the explosion seared his face. He dragged the man off and cracked his skull against the ground. Something

181

pulled at his leg and he kicked free, jerked the knife from his belt, and slashed out wildly. A man shrieked and clawed at his eyes. Glass stepped over him and ran. The riders saw him, shouted, and circled around to cut him off. Glass threw himself aside as lead splintered wood over his head. He came to his feet, clutching the blade. A man stepped around the wagon, saw Glass, and jerked back, poking a shotgun in his face. Glass froze, brought up a hand to shield his eyes, and knew he'd never make it. A terrible cry split the air. The man with the shotgun paused half a second. A dark form leaped out of shadow, a long blade flashing in its fist. The man cried out as the blade disappeared into his chest, and the gun exploded. Joseph went to his knees, turned the limp form over, and saw that it was cut in half.

"Red Elk!" he bellowed in anger. "You dumb son of a bitch! Why the hell did you do that!"

A pistol exploded overhead. Glass cried out and dropped the lifeless body. The gunman fired again and jerked back as Glass slashed out at his leg. *Cavanaugh!* Joseph saw his face in the flash of the muzzle, and then he was gone.

He took a step forward, stumbled, and went to his knees. Pulling himself up the side of a wagon, he fell again. Goddamn, what was the matter with his legs? *That* had never happened before. He sat back on his heels and took a breath. His shoulder burned something awful. He touched his shirt and stared dumbly at his hand. The palm was dark and sticky. Damn it all, now that wouldn't do . . . no time for something like that. Now where the hell was his knife? He felt around on the ground, patting the earth with wet hands.

"Shit, boy, git yourself down!"

Something shoved him roughly aside. A rifle cracked in his ears. A gunman dropped his pistol and folded. Rooster-John knelt above him, frantically levering shells into his rifle.

"Where the hell you think you are, son?" the old man snapped. "Christ A'mighty, you was strollin' around like it was Denver!"

"Almost got runned over once in Denver," Glass said weakly. "Goddamn beer wagon come out of an alley . . ."

"Easy, hoss. You're hurt some, boy."

When Joseph looked up again, Henry Clark and Little Hawk were crouched above him. The firing seemed to have stopped.

The silence bothered him a lot. It didn't sound right. He looked into Little Hawk's sad dark eyes.

"Red Elk . . ." he tried to explain. "Jesus, Little Hawk, I'm sorry . . ."

"He don't understand English," Henry Clark muttered.

"Don't guess he has to," said Rooster-John . . .

In some far corner of her mind, Jessie was dimly aware of gunfire in the camp below. Her gaze was locked in horror on the Prussian. Her flesh recoiled from the cold touch of his blades. She wanted to shut her eyes, make him go away, wake up and find herself somewhere else. Still, she couldn't bring herself to turn away.

He looked at her and smiled, touched his finger to the tiny droplet of red on her belly, and brought it to the tip of his tongue.

Sour bile rose in her throat and she choked it back. The Prussian laughed. "That other one, Caff-anaugh's woman— she fainted, she was weak. You are not weak, are you? I think you haff more courage. I think you will stay awake and share this with me, *ja?*"

Jessie shuddered as he picked up one of the blades in his fingers and brought it down to her belly.

"If you are strong," he explained, "I will make it easier for you. There are places to cut, you see. Ways to do this. A doctor knows, yes? A doctor knows these things . . ."

The blade found her flesh. Jessie thrashed in terror and screamed into her gag. The Prussian paused. A drop of red glistened on his blade. "You haff to be still, you see? How can I work if you move?" he said patiently. "If you move, I could hurt you badly."

He touched her with the knife—then stopped, jerked back and opened his mouth in surprise. His eyes went wide and his jaws began to spasm open and shut. His fingers went stiff and the knife fell away. He clawed at something invisible in the air. Suddenly a high, piercing cry exploded from his throat. He thrashed about wildly, his body bobbing up and down. Jessie knew he was trying to stand, trying desperately to get to his feet. Something in his body wouldn't work. He waddled helplessly about, arms flailing the air.

The Prussian crowed in terrible pain. He stumbled over her outstretched legs and tried to crawl.

Jessie saw it then...

The small, frail body was neatly ribboned, the pale flesh razored in furrows of red. She'd dragged herself to him without a face. The china-blue eye was as slick as glass and couldn't see. Jessie knew she was dead; nothing that looked like that could be alive. Still, the fragile hand that grasped the silver scalpel moved up and down, up and down, like a broken machine that wouldn't stop...

The Prussian dragged himself over the dirt, his hands clutching frantically between his legs. His fingers tried desperately to keep his organs from spilling on the ground. Nothing seemed to work, but he wouldn't stop. He looked at Jessie and screamed. The thick glasses hung crookedly on his nose.

Jessie saw the shadow pass between her and the dim flicker of the candle. Ki stared at her in horror, glanced at the Prussian and the girl. He picked up the pistol the Prussian had laid on his neatly folded jacket. He aimed the pistol at the girl, then stopped. It was clear she no longer needed his help.

The Prussian's eyes pleaded. An awful sound came from his throat. *"Help me kill me help me kill me...please... pleeeeeease!"*

Ki had seen wounds in the groin and belly before. A man could last a long time. He could crawl away and drag his life behind him. He aimed the pistol at the Prussian's head, thumbed back the hammer...Then eased the hammer down, looked at the weapon, and tossed it into the trees. The Prussian didn't stop screaming. Ki bent down and covered Jessie with her jacket, pulled the gag gently out of her mouth, and sliced the ropes at her wrists and ankles to set her free...

Chapter 20

There was a faint smudge of pink against the sky. Jessie threw a stick on the fire and wrapped the blanket tightly about Joseph's chin. He opened his eyes and gave her a weary smile.

"Guess I . . . drifted off some, Jessie . . ."

"Yeah, I guess maybe you did," she said gently.

"Jessie, I—Christ, Jessie, we got to get movin'! We—" His features went taut with alarm. "The—the men with the—"

"They're gone, Joseph. You hurt 'em real bad, and they're gone. I guess they figured a whole army was on their tail. Getting shot up wasn't worth a day's pay."

Joseph's face clouded. "Red Elk—he's dead, Jessie. Christ, I didn't hardly know him, and he—"

"Yes, Joseph. I know."

"Yellow Wing? Rooster-John and the others?"

"Everyone's fine. Rooster-John rode hard back to the road. There's a settlement there, remember? And a Western Union line. I expect we'll have more soldiers and U.S. marshals than we can handle in a couple of hours."

"Good," Joseph said weakly. "That's fine." His eyes closed and he drifted back into sleep. Jessie touched his brow, stood, and walked away from the fire.

"Is he doing all right?" Ki asked.

"He'll make it," she sighed.

Ki looked at the ground. "You didn't tell him, did you?"

"About Yellow Wing and Philadelphy?" Jessie leaned in against him and rested her head on his shoulder. "He doesn't need that right now. He's got enough hurt to handle." She glanced in his eyes and saw the pain. "I guess we all do."

Ki didn't answer.

"Henry Clark says there's maybe twenty-five dead out there, Ki. God, if they'd ever guessed how few we were!"

Ki's face went dark. "Cavanaugh should be down there with

the others. All this is his doing!"

"He won't get far," said Jessie. "You think they won't turn over every rock in Montana? Especially after they see what's in those wagons?" Jessie shook her head. "I looked in his tent, Ki. Saw some of the papers he left behind. All I could stand to read. It's all there, the whole thing. The names of the miners he killed around Mule to get their claims—the murders they hanged Jebediah for. That and a lot more. Everything they planned to take over. Names and places, the works."

"That's not enough. The bastard's got to pay."

Jessie looked past him up the ridge, saw the grove of trees where the Prussian had taken her, and turned quickly away. In the pale light of first dawn she saw Henry Clark standing atop the ridge, his rifle in his arms.

"Little Hawk left while you were with Joseph," Ki told her. "He . . . took Red Elk up in the hills." Ki tried to smile. "You know what they named me? Round Knife. That's something, isn't it?"

Jessie kissed his cheek and edged in closer under his shoulder. He hadn't mentioned Yellow Wing or what had happened between them. She knew him well and didn't have to ask. The hurt in his eyes told him all she needed to know.

"Ki, after everybody gets here, there's going to be a lot of questions to answer. I expect the army and the U.S. marshal will want to talk to me in Helena. And I'd kind of like to stay there anyway, till Joseph gets better."

Her voice trailed off and he gave her a curious look.

"I thought maybe you could go down to Helena with me, then ride over the pass back west," she continued.

"Back west? What for?"

"I'd like you to take another look around Will McCabe's place. That Colt of mine with the peachwood grips—it *could* have escaped the fire, you know. I didn't have time to look real carefully. That gun means a lot to me, Ki."

Ki gave her a weary smile. "And should I say hello to Angel while looking for the gun?" Ki shook his head. "Thanks. I appreciate what you're trying to do. I don't think so."

"Angel's got troubles. She could use a little help."

"And so could I, right? Jessie . . ."

"No, whatever you think. Maybe you'll change your mind."

Ki nodded and moved off down the hill to check the horses.

186

Jessie decided she wouldn't ask him again—not for a day or so. And if he didn't respond then, she'd wait another day.

Little Hawk slouched on his pony, the autumn sun warm against his back. The white man rested by the creek below the hill. Little Hawk could tell that he was tired. He didn't know what to do outside of a town. For the last three hours he'd been walking in a circle. Little Hawk found it hard to tell one white man from another. He knew, though, that this was the right one. His friend Round Knife had pointed the man out to Red Elk, and Red Elk had told him who he was.

Little Hawk was in no hurry. In an hour, maybe, he'd let the man know he was there. Maybe he'd even let him make camp. He'd be tired and hungry and frightened in the morning. Then, when Little Hawk was ready, he'd go in and take him. They would go up into the mountains together. They would stay there a long time. Little Hawk had each day planned in his mind. How they would spend each moment. How he would keep the white man alive. How careful he would be to make certain he didn't die. Little Hawk vowed that he would never grow angry or impatient. He would remember his friend Red Elk, and do what needed to be done.

Watch for

LONE STAR AND THE STOCKYARD SHOWDOWN

twenty-sixth novel in the exciting
LONE STAR series from Jove

coming in October!